*Fragments of splintered
emotions littered the pavement
of their lives. Yellow, red, black,
and green colored their souls.
Cowardice, anger, despair, and
jealousy lay crushed like shards
of a broken kaleidoscope, each
holding a piece of the secret
binding them together.*

Kaleidoscope

BARBARA GALVIN

Kaleidoscope

ISBN: 979-8-630-99285-7

Editorial development and creative design support by Ascent:
www.spreadyourfire.net

Printed in the United States of America

To my husband, Jim

.

ACKNOWLEDGMENTS

I am deeply grateful for my wonderful husband of fifty years, for his loving support and encouragement of this endeavor, without which this novel may never have been written and published.

I owe a great debt of gratitude to my coach, David Hazard, who painstakingly guided and instructed me through the writing process and taught me the meaning of "growing out, then trimming the topiary."

Many thanks to my beta readers, Meredith, Barbara, Holly, and my husband, Jim, who generously offered to read and give feedback. Your comments were invaluable.

I would also like to thank the members of my AWA Writing group, who gave me the confidence I needed to launch this endeavor.

Prologue

RESCUE VEHICLES screamed down the highway, lights flashing, horns blaring, radios crackling: multi-vehicle collision—possible fatalities.

Twisted metal splayed out across the highway. The smell of gasoline hung in the air. Glass shards sprinkled the pavement, glittering in the glow of the streetlamps; flares eerily lit up the cloudy late afternoon sky. An overturned tractor-trailer lay mangled among the heap of vehicles sandwiched together. Injuries were catastrophic as rescue personnel used the Jaws of Life to extricate the victims.

With steely precision, rescue workers tended to the injured. Lauren Foster was among them. Her hair, tangled and stained with blood, hung limply across her face like a curtain, covering the terror in her eyes. They carefully unwrapped her fingers still tightly clutched around the steering wheel. She was alive but in critical condition.

She was so close to her destination before the accident occurred—only minutes from the exit for her campus. And now those same precious minutes were needed to stabilize her for transport.

"What do you think her chances are?" asked one of the paramedics.

"Too soon to tell."

A gloved hand pulled a white sheet over her passenger.

"Tragic."

HER BODY LAY MOTIONLESS on the kitchen floor, blood pooling around it. Fragments of a shattered wine goblet were clutched in her hand, slivers of bloodied glass flecking the white marble floor. A faint voice rose from a cell phone lying on the floor beside her.

Hearing the glass break, Danny yelled down to his mother.

"You okay?"

She didn't answer.

"Mom?"

Still no answer.

Worried, he charged down the stairs and ran to the kitchen, his body fueled with adrenaline. He stopped short in the doorway, shaken by what he saw. His mother lay curled in a fetal position, blood running down the length of her arm, spreading out from her hand across the floor, painting the tiles crimson.

Danny ran to her and crouched down, carefully avoiding the glass, to feel for a pulse. Relieved to find one, he reached for his phone to call 9-1-1, but she roused and shoved his hand away.

"No. No ambulance."

"But. . ."

"NO.

Please no, not my baby," she cried, attempting to sit up, smearing blood across the floor.

The words, 'my baby' tore through his gut as an image of his little sister lying injured somewhere terrified him. He shook his mother to keep her from passing out, shouting, "What happened to Jenny?"

"Jenny's fine. Lauren's. . . There's been. . . ." A torrent of tears halted her speech.

"Been—what?"

"An accident," she said, gasping for breath.

Then without warning, like Jekyll and Hyde, she exploded with anger. "Damn, damn, damn. Damn your father."

"What?"

"Your father—giving her that car when he knew I didn't want her driving that far back to school. This is all on him."

Everything suddenly made sense, and Danny unloaded.

"That was supposed to be my car. Why the hell did she

need it on campus anyway? She suckered you both. Now the car is probably totaled, and it's no use to either of us."

Rose's eyes turned deadly cold as she stared up at him.

"Your sister could be dead, and that's all you care about? The damn car?"

"Sorry. I just get so. . . Oh, forget it. So, Jenny's okay, right? I mean, you said your baby, so I thought. . . ."

"Call your father. Tell him to get home—now, or I'm leaving without him."

Relieved that his little sister was okay, Danny began wrapping his mother's arm in some gauze.

"Stay here. Don't move. I'll go over to Lisa's and get Jenny."

"No. Let her stay there. She doesn't need to know."

"We can't just dump her on the Franconi's without an explanation."

"I said, leave her. She doesn't need us. Lauren does."

Of course, she does. She always does. There may as well be only one kid in this family. . .and it sure as hell isn't me.

Put down as always and sick to death of the constant friction with his mother, Danny called his dad and waited for him to come home and take over.

Tom tore into the driveway and ran up the back steps

into the kitchen. The sight of broken glass and smeared blood glaring under the fluorescent kitchen lights baffled him.

"What the hell? What happened here? I thought you said Lauren was in an accident." Noticing the bloody gauze on Rose's arm, he said, "You gotta' get this looked at right now."

"Never mind me. It can wait. And yes, Lauren's been in an accident and is lying in a hospital, no thanks to you."

"Me?"

"Never mind. Pack a bag. Fast.

"You, too," she said, jabbing a finger toward Danny. "We're not leaving her down there alone."

Of course not. But I guess it's fine to leave Jenny here alone.

Ramming down the anger always percolating in his gut, he did as he was told, threw some clothes in a duffle bag, and followed his parents to the car.

❖ ❖ ❖ ❖

"Can't you go any faster?" Rose nagged.

"I'm already way over the speed limit. You want us to have an accident, too?"

"She never would have had an accident if you hadn't given her the car. You knew I didn't want her to have it."

"We've already had this conversation. I thought it was our decision. She needs her independence."

"And now my little girl is in the hospital because she needs her independence? What a bunch of bull."

"Oh, don't start that with me again."

Danny couldn't take the constant sniping anymore. He popped in his earbuds to block the sound just as he did as a little kid covering his ears so he wouldn't have to listen.

Why can't you just leave her alone? Let her do it for herself.

She needs my help, Tom.

Does she need it, or do you need to give it to her?

And on it went.

He'd heard about helicopter parents, but his mom's obsession with Lauren was over the top. Yeah, maybe she deserved the attention right now, but it had always been this way.

He was five.

Running across the hot, sand beach, his feet burning, he tried to make it to the water. He was in pain but trying to keep up with his mother as she carried Lauren to the blanket.

As he got to the cooling water, his mother shouted, "Get back here."

"But it hurts."

"Remember your sandals next time."

Re-burying the memory always hiding just under the surface, Danny asked, "Do you know how she is?"

"Do I look like I know?" his mother snapped.

"We know she's alive, or we would have had police showing up at our door," his father answered.

"Is that supposed to be some kind of consolation?"

"You know I'm missing play tryouts," Danny broke in randomly.

"What did you just say?" Rose barked, her face turning crimson.

"How can you think about that right now? I've had enough of this play crap."

She never did understand.

From an early age, Danny's artistic talent was evident—to everyone except his parents. By the time he was in the sixth grade, he was already involved in set design for his school plays. He watched and listened from backstage as the actors brought their roles to life. And it wasn't long before he started seeing himself on the stage instead of behind it. By the eighth grade, his passion for acting was born.

But it didn't go over well with his parents.

"Tom, tell him he has to stop with this silliness. What 13-year-old boy wants to act? It's not normal."

"I'll talk to him, Rose. It's just a phase."

"Why don't you spend some time with him throwing around a football or catching a baseball. That's what most boys do. Instead, he's upstairs playing Barbies with his sister."

"I said I'd talk to him. Just let him be."

They thought he didn't hear them—but he did. And it hurt. And it still did.

I guess this wasn't a good time to bring up play tryouts. I gotta' think about my sister now.

So, he filed the memory away, along with so many others, into a little drawer inside his head.

❖ ❖ ❖ ❖

"Oh, hell, I forgot about Jenny. Where is she?" his father blurted out halfway to the hospital.

"She's at Lisa's," Danny responded. *God. Even he forgot about her.*

"Does she know?"

"No," Rose snapped. "I don't want her to. We don't know what we're dealing with yet."

"You did call Lisa's mom to see if Jenny could stay for a few nights, didn't you?" she asked Danny.

"Was I supposed to?"

Words flew out of her mouth like shards of glass, piercing him.

"For God's sake, do I have to do all the thinking around here? Call Angela now. Don't tell her anything, just that we had to go out of town at the last minute."

Danny pulled the phone from his pocket and dialed the Franconi residence, wishing he was any place but where he was.

Two

"WHERE'S MY DAUGHTER?" Rose demanded, charging through the ER waiting room teeming with frantic relatives desperate for news of their loved ones.

"I'm sorry, Ma'am, you'll have to wait your turn," one of the nurses replied. "And you'll need that arm looked at. Just fill out these forms, and we'll get to you as soon as possible."

Shoving the papers across the counter, Rose looked down at the blood seeping through the bandages.

"Don't touch me. I want to see my daughter. *Now.*"

She barged past the front desk and into the patient area. It was a scene of controlled chaos. Gurneys lined the walls in the hall; IVs hung from cold steel poles; curtains shielded other patients from prying eyes. The most critical had already been taken to surgery.

She was stopped in her tracks by a security guard and escorted back to the waiting area.

"You can't do this. I have to be back there with her," she screamed, pummeling the guard's chest.

"Sorry about that," Tom said, catching up to Rose. "I'll take care of her." He reached out to comfort her and calm her down, but she flung her arms out, shoving him away.

"Be patient. They'll let us know when we can see her," Tom said, trying to mute his growing frustration. His wife's rudeness was infuriating—and embarrassing. His face, contorted with a mix of anxiety and exasperation, was enough to tell Danny he was close to his breaking point.

A wail of anguish rose from behind a curtain.

"Another one didn't make it," muttered a man shifting uncomfortably in one of the hard waiting room chairs.

Rose began to moan, struggling past Tom. "Do something," she cried.

All the while, Danny watched the ailing mass of humanity sunken in their chairs, waiting for news. He listened to their shaky voices.

"Please tell me he's going to be alright."

"Thank God it's just some broken bones. Look at what they're dealing with over there."

"There's so much blood."

Unreal. I'm gonna' wake up and find this is a bad dream.

Tears stung his eyes, but he forced himself not to cry.

Boys don't cry, Tom had told him years ago. *They man up.*

Why don't you man up to mom? She makes a doormat out of you. He was sick and tired of the platitudes.

Moments later, a nurse came around the corner into the waiting area.

"Mr. and Mrs. Foster? Come with me, please."

The nurse led them to one of the ER cubicles, Danny trailing behind, and drew back the curtain. The screech of the rings drowned out the moaning from the bed next door. Lauren was hooked up to IVs, a breathing tube inserted down her throat. Contusions and lacerations covered her body. Her matted blonde curls were pushed back from her face, exposing her shuttered eyes.

Rose's knees buckled, and Danny heard a whispered 'Oh, sweetheart' escape her lips as the silent drip of the IV bag thundered in their heads.

His sister looked so fragile and tiny under the crisp white sheets of the hospital bed, and Danny knew his mom feared the worst—what if she didn't make it?

"We're here, Lauren. You're going to be okay," he heard Rose utter just as the doctor entered, his stark white coat glaring under the overhead lights.

"Your daughter is in critical but stable condition. We're watching for signs of internal bleeding, particularly of the brain, after such severe trauma. We're also concerned about the possibility of paralysis. We'll be transferring her to Intensive Care as soon as there is a room available."

Danny glanced at his parents and saw the shock register on their faces. Fear had entered the room and surrounded them, cutting off their air supply. He had to remind himself to breathe. He pounded his fist into the wall, the pain numbed by what he had just heard.

From somewhere in the stupor they were all in, he heard his dad's trembling voice.

"When will you know—about the paralysis?" He was drawing on every ounce of strength he had to keep from breaking down in front of his wife and his son.

"It will take some time for the spinal cord swelling to decrease before we know. We have to be patient."

His parents' eyes were glazed over as if they hadn't heard—or wouldn't listen. Danny had heard but was at a loss to help them because he didn't even know how he felt. His deep-seated resentment of his sister was gone for now, leaving his feelings in limbo. There was just so much history between them.

He slipped out into the corridor and texted his best friend, Josh, telling him what happened and why he wasn't in school.

> let u know soon. its bad. sure wish i had a joint. couldn't sneak my flask out—too risky. I'm dyin' here.

Moments later, his dad came out of the cubicle.

"Let's go. We need to find a place to stay for the night."

"What about mom?"

"She won't leave Lauren's side until she wakes up. But

if we don't get some sleep, we won't be any use to either of them."

"Is she going to be alright?"

"I don't know."

✧ ✧ ✧ ✧

Fighting to stay awake against bone-deep fatigue, Tom pulled into the hotel parking lot. Twenty-four hours ago, he was wrapping up a massive deal at the company—a deal that had sucked up almost all his time for the entire month. And now he had a son he scarcely knew, a daughter fighting for her life, a wife he could barely communicate with and a child he almost forgot. He slipped back in time to avoid the present.

Twenty-five years ago, I fell in love with the most beautiful girl in town—blond hair and bewitching blue eyes sweeping me magically under her spell.

She wasn't just beautiful; she was strong, determined. Yet underneath lay a vulnerability she tried to mask. A hidden fragility that had appeared and disappeared without warning always making him uneasy.

For months, romantic dinners, lectures, and visits to museums consumed them. They thrived on each other, neatly filling in the voids in each other's lives.

She was the part of me that was always missing. And we were so happy then. Until....

Danny's voice shook him out of his nostalgia.

"Dad, we're here."

"Yeah. Come on, let's get a room before I collapse."

Grabbing their bags, Danny felt a moment of pity for his father—and his mother. And for himself.

The faint ring of Tom's cell phone woke him. Forcing one eye open, Danny looked at the hotel clock—4:27. He bolted up, his chest tightening.

From across the room, faintly lit by a sliver of light coming under the door from the hallway, he heard his father say, "When? What room? Okay, we'll be right there."

"What's happening?"

"Your sister's awake."

"How is she?"

"I don't know. Mom just said she's awake. She's in Intensive Care now. Throw on some clothes and meet me at the car."

The ride over to the hospital was silent, full of stifled, unspoken words filling the crevices of the car. Danny's eyes rested on the sinewy chords of his dad's throat, pulsing with every beat of his heart.

He's terrified.

The corridor to her room was endlessly long, the beeping of machines the only audible sound. The sterile, antiseptic air assaulted their senses. The scent of fear filled their nostrils.

When they reached the room, 139 steps from the elevator, Tom grabbed Danny by the shoulder and stopped him. "Wait in the hall. Let me see what's going on."

Danny leaned against the door of room 401, looking in. He could see his mother hovering over Lauren's bed and strained to see Lauren's face, but he couldn't. But, the steady, regular beep of the machines gave him hope that she was stable.

His back pocket vibrated.

> hey man, sorry about ur sister. hope she's gonna' be all right. let me know. k? wish I could get u some stuff

> gonna' slip over to the store and clip some booze as soon as i can. no use in standing around here

He felt a pang of wrenching guilt, ashamed that he hadn't given a shit whether Lauren was okay when he first heard about the accident. His first thoughts had been the car and then Jenny. Or was it Jenny and then the car? Whatever. It still made him a total jerk.

When it dawned on him that his father had forgotten about him, he snuck out. Three blocks from the hospital, he found the nearest convenience store. Pretending to look for some Coke, he snagged a small bottle of cheap whiskey and slipped it into the pocket of his ski jacket—just enough to tide him over.

For days, Lauren slipped in and out of consciousness. Tom and Danny went back and forth between the hospital and the hotel, but Rose refused to leave Lauren's side, instead sleeping in the recliner next to her bed. Danny still had not seen his sister, always being told 'later.' Slowly one morning, Lauren's eyelids began to flutter again, and her hand twitched. Rose flew to her side.

"Oh, Lauren, sweetheart, welcome back."

Hearing her mother's voice, Lauren fought to keep her eyes open. Rose's face, first a blurry haze, slowly came into focus, the edges merging. She struggled to make sense of her mother's appearance. The wrinkled clothes, unkempt hair, and lack of make-up were so unlike her. Lauren's eyes drifted to the bandage on her mother's arm.

"Where—where am I?" She was floating in a drug-induced haze pierced by wracking pain. An IV line was taped to her hand, and heavy, white bandages lay like patchwork on her body.

"What's going on?" she mumbled.

"You're in the hospital, honey. You were in an accident," Rose said, stroking her forehead.

Lauren winced. Then, slowly, piece by piece, images of the crash filtered in. . .flashing lights punctuating the darkness, sirens piercing the quiet, voices screaming orders. Then, a vision of Maddy, covered in blood, her vacant eyes wide open, was gaping at her, causing her body to shake uncontrollably. She began thrashing and pulling on her IV lines.

"Nurse, please help," Rose yelled into the corridor.

A nurse rushed in, the squeak of her rubber-soled shoes competing with the sudden irregular beeps of the machines. Raising a needle toward Lauren's arm, she injected a sedative into the IV.

"Maddy," was the last word Lauren murmured before mercifully sinking into the blackness.

The next time she opened her eyes, her father was sitting in the chair next to her bed. Several days' growth of beard shadowed his chin. He forced a smile, the corners of his mouth not quite managing to curve.

"Well, sunshine, good morning," he said, his voice a cheery lie.

"Dad," she said, her voice raspy. "What. . .?"

"Shhh. Don't try to talk. Save your energy."

"How long have I been here?" she whispered.

"Almost a week now, honey. It's so good to see you awake again. You had us a bit worried."

Still confused, she studied the expression on her father's face. His blue eyes, puffy from lack of sleep, were hiding something. Something he wasn't telling her.

Tom caught her questioning look and rapidly changed gears.

"I'll get your mom. She's out in the lounge resting. Danny's here, too."

Hazily she remembered faces hovering over her, mumbled voices talking about her while they poked and prodded her. What was wrong with her?

Maddy. The car. The truck. The jolt. . . .

Once again, bits and pieces tried to surface, pushing through her confusion. Before anything emerged, though, her mother charged into the room.

"Oh, thank heaven, you're awake. I was so worried. You've given us quite a scare."

"Where's Maddy?"

Rose looked away, busying herself with pouring Lauren a glass of water.

"You just worry about yourself, sweetheart," she finally replied, avoiding her daughter's eyes.

"Where *is* she? What room is she in? I want to see her."

Quick to distract her daughter, Rose announced, "Danny's been waiting to see you. He's very worried. I'll go get him."

"But. . . ."

Rushing out to find Danny, Rose knew she had to stall Lauren's questions.

"Lauren's awake. Do you want to go in to see her now?"

No way was in his head, but he said, "Sure."

His feet had memorized the long walk down the polished hallway from the waiting room: 203 steps. Not 202 or 204. Always 203.

He peered in before entering. It was painful to look at her. Her face was pale, her green eyes sunken and underlined with ashen circles. Strands of blood-streaked blonde hair lay clumped on the pillow. Stepping inside the room, Danny focused on the liquid dripping through her IV, one bead at a time, before speaking.

"Hey. How are you?"

"I feel like shit—it hurts."

"I guess that was a pretty stupid question. Listen, um, I'm really sorry about Maddy."

"What do you mean? What about Maddy?"

Shit, I thought she knew. I can't believe they didn't tell her.

Now all hell would break loose when they found out he had told her.

"Danny, where is she? I want to see her."

Watching him stammer, Lauren's sudden change of expression told him she knew.

"*No*," she screamed. "*Please, no.*"

Hearing the scream, Rose charged back into the room.

"What did you just tell her?" she said, glaring at Danny.

"I. . . ."

"What the hell is wrong with you?" she shouted, pointing her finger at him. "How could you hurt your sister like that? Now get out of here. You've done enough damage."

He was back at the beach again, sand burning his feet.

Rose turned back to her daughter and saw the hurt Danny's words had inflicted. Lauren was struggling to gulp air, gasping for breath.

"Don't think about it, Lauren. It will be okay."

"No. It will never. . ."

The bottom dropped out of Lauren's stomach like a giant sinkhole swallowing her up. Suddenly the pain in her heart surpassed the pain in her body as she fought against the words forming in her brain. If she didn't say them, they wouldn't be real.

Turning her face away, Lauren tried to block out Rose's

voice trying to make her feel better. NOTHING could make her feel better ever again. She couldn't listen anymore.

"Stop it, Mother. Just go away. Leave me alone."

Maddy, I'm so sorry.

Ignored, distraught, Rose stepped out of the room. Grief flooded in, engulfing Lauren, squeezing the air out of her lungs. Her mind sank beneath the pressure and pain.

Maddy sat on the bed beside her and tried to push the pain away—but she was not strong enough.

Lauren reached for her best friend. . . but she vanished.

Three

THIS IS POINTLESS, Danny muttered to himself as he paced in the lounge. *Why am I even here? I'm way behind in school, and I missed all the tryouts for the next play. I should have been home looking after Jenny. Good thing she's got Lisa's mom to take care of her. Poor kid's ignored at home. I should call her, but mom doesn't want her to know anything. Maybe she's right. I don't know. I don't know anything anymore.*

He was on his mom's shit list—again, and she wouldn't even talk to him. Nobody would, and all he did was wait. And he didn't even know what he was waiting for. How did he know they hadn't told her? How could they lie to her about something like that? Did they think she wouldn't find out? Why were they always protecting her? It made him sick. He didn't even enter their picture of a family. There might as well just be the three of them. He didn't even know where Jenny fit.

He let a memory slip out of one of the drawers.

He was buzzed after the high school's production of *It's a Wonderful Life*—and without the booze to boost him. As Clarence, the Angel, Second Class, trying desperately to get his wings, he'd gotten rave reviews in the local newspapers. But no one was there to see him—not his mother or father or Jenny. Nobody.

"We don't have any free time right now, Danny. And besides, what's with this "angel" thing. Couldn't you get a decent part?" This coming from his father who just wanted him to be a jock.

They didn't get it, or him. They never had. He thought about his most famous speech.

"Strange, isn't it? Each man's life touches so many other lives. When he isn't around, he leaves an awful hole, doesn't he?"

So much power in such a simple line. "Delivered with great poise and depth by such a young actor," one reviewer wrote.

It's just as well they didn't come. They wouldn't have understood it anyway.

He thought about the small bottle of whiskey he'd hidden outside in the hospital parking lot behind some bushes. It was more than half-empty now. He had to get home.

He corralled his dad as he came around the corner into the lounge.

Here goes.

"Hey, Dad. I know you want to be here for Lauren and Mom, but I gotta' get home. I'm missing a lot of school, and we need to get Jenny. She can't stay at Lisa's forever. I can go back and take care of her."

"Probably a good idea. There's no point in you hanging around anymore. I'll tell your mom. Wait here."

Sure, Dad. I'll just wait—again. He saw his dad lean into the room and motion to his mom.

When they were in the hallway, she hissed at him. "What is it now, Tom? What's so important? I need to be in there with my daughter."

Danny noticed his dad didn't even fight the word "my" anymore. Probably a losing battle.

Can you say doormat?

"I'm taking Danny home and getting Jenny from Lisa's."

"Fine, Tom. Do what you have to do, but I'm not leaving Lauren."

"I don't want to leave her either, but we do have two other children to take care of, in case you've forgotten."

"How dare you accuse me of that. I'm well aware they're my children, too. But they don't need me now. She does," she said, motioning her head toward the door.

"I'm sorry I said that. I understand what you're going through."

"Do you really? I don't think you ever really understood."

"I'm trying, Rose. I've always tried. Now how do you want me to handle things with Jenny?"

"Tell her whatever you want, Tom. I'm sure you'll think of something."

Trying to dispel the tension, his dad leaned in to hug his mother, but she turned away—not even a good-bye.

His face crumbled at her dismissal.

Why the hell does he take that crap from her?

"Let's go, Danny. It's a long ride home."

A hollow silence echoed inside the car. But Danny's embattled feelings surrounding his sister screamed into the void. He fought against his resentment of how she was always treated better than everyone else, especially him, and his sorrow for what was happening to her. Rose's obsessive hovering over her was hard to watch. Yes, Lauren was hurt very badly. Yes, she might be paralyzed. But his mom seemed to want to own the grief—not allow anyone else into its space. She wouldn't let anyone slip in between her and her daughter, even in tragedy.

His dad gripped the steering wheel firmly as he drove, his knuckles blanched. Danny tried to read his face, but all the words were blurred. Anger, confusion, grief, sadness. They were all there, just scrambled.

I know how he feels, and it sucks.

Questions pounded in his ears, competing with the road noise.

Jenny. What was he going to say to her? How do you tell a happy little seven-year-old girl that her older sister's been in a terrible accident? How do you explain why her mom won't be coming home for a while? How do you reassure her that everything will be okay?

He didn't have any answers.

The January darkness cast the trees by the house in shadows, rendering them almost invisible by the time Danny and Tom pulled into their driveway. The house looked cold, dark, and abandoned. Lifeless.

Remnants of reddish-brown dried blood greeted them when they entered the kitchen, a curious pattern staining the floor like a Jackson Pollock abstract painting. Danny's father averted the mess, ignoring it, but Danny went to the cabinet beneath the sink and took out the floor cleaner. He couldn't let Jenny see the blood.

His father called to him.

"Danny, go over to the Franconi's and get your sister."

"Do you want me to tell her anything? She'll ask me a lot of questions."

"No, I'll take care of it. I'm not sure how much I want her to know."

Danny walked the three blocks, counting his steps again. The repetitive counting always had a way of calming or, at least, distracting him.

He approached the door of a home just like his—from the outside. But he knew inside was love and acceptance—and peace. He wanted to move in.

"Jenny, your brother's here," Lisa yelled when she saw Danny at the door.

Jenny emerged from the kitchen, flew into his arms, and squeezed him around the neck. Then she started pummeling his chest with her fists.

"Where have you been?" Her last punch nailed him in the gut.

"*Ouch*. Hey, I'm sorry. We had to go down to see Lauren. They made me go, too. Dad will explain when we get home."

"Why couldn't I go?"

"We thought you'd have more fun here. Now grab your things, and let's go."

Angela Franconi walked in, a veiled look concealing her concern.

"I hope you don't mind, but I went over to the house to get a few changes of clothes for Jenny. I saw the—"

She stopped herself just before the word 'blood.'

"Is everything okay?"

Danny's eyes darted toward Jenny, ignoring the question, and Angela understood.

"Hey, sweetheart, come on over any time. You and Lisa can have lots of sleepovers whenever you want."

Jenny and Lisa erupted into squeals.

"Thanks for keeping Jenny. I'm sure she had a great time."

"Any time, Danny. I mean that."

Her sincerity reached his core. And he knew it wasn't just directed toward Jenny. Angela cared about him too. For a few seconds, his body relaxed, and he felt the warmth in the room. A smile crept across his face.

Grabbing Jenny's Barbie overnight bag, he left with her to go back home. She hopped, skipped, and avoided the cracks in the sidewalk on her journey. Danny envied her spirit, her playfulness, and innocence.

I wish I were seven again.

Tom was waiting in the kitchen when they entered, and Jenny ran straight into his arms. Watching his dad hug his sister made Danny sad. He'd never gotten much physical warmth from either one of his parents.

Boys don't hug, his dad had said years ago. *They shake hands.*

So, at five, he dutifully practiced the art of shaking hands and looking a person in the eye. Manning up.

"Where have you been?" Jenny demanded. "You just left me. Why couldn't I come?"

"Come here, peanut, and sit with me. I have something to tell you."

He sank down heavily on the green sofa. Jenny's liquid blue eyes widened, and she sat next to her dad.

"Lauren had an accident on her way down to school. She's in the hospital, and the doctors are taking good care of her." He was fighting to keep his voice from breaking.

"Why didn't Mommy come home with you?"

"She wants to stay with your sister until she's better. So, it will be just the three of us for a while."

"Oh, okay." Then, in total, unabashed innocence, Jenny turned to her brother.

"Will you come play Barbies with me? You can be Ken again."

"Sure, kid. Go get 'em ready. I'll meet you upstairs."

He texted Josh.

> *back home, again. gonna play barbies with my little sister. gotta keep her distracted. ltr.*

Up in Jenny's room, strutting a Ken doll across the carpet, Danny practiced his theatre voices, imagining he was in tryouts.

Jenny had set up the scene.

Barbie and Ken were sitting on a blanket having a picnic lunch when she turned to him and said:

"Doesn't Mommy like you?"

"What do you mean, Barbie?"

"I don't mean Ken," she said, looking up at him. "I mean you."

"Why do you think she doesn't like me?"

"Well, she's always doing things with Lauren, and she never does anything with you—like go to any of your plays. I think she's being mean. I hope she doesn't get mad at me 'cause I don't like the way she acts when she's mean."

She sees so much more than we give her credit for.

Shifting rapidly into Ken character, Danny offered Barbie some cake, deflecting the entire conversation.

Later, alone in his room, he thought long and hard about what Jenny said. *What have I done to piss Mom off so much? If she's not mad about something, she just ignores me. I gotta' get out of here soon, or I'm gonna' say something I'll never be able to take back.*

He reached under his bed for a quick shot of whiskey to make it all go away.

Four

SEPARATE LIVES BECAME the norm in the Foster household. Lauren and Rose in Christiansburg; Tom, Danny, and Jenny in Arlington. Weekends the ratio changed, and it was Lauren, Rose, and Tom at the hospital and Danny at home looking after Jenny. They were never together.

Lauren watched as doctors and nurses filtered in through osmosis: in and out, passing through the walls of the Foster family cell. One by one, she saw the bandages on her body get smaller and smaller. Only one terrible reality remained the same.

She couldn't feel her legs.

Desperately, angrily, she tried to wiggle her toes, convinced that with effort, she would see some movement. But her legs lay motionless beneath the sheets. She knew the doctors held out hope her condition might be temporary, but with each passing day, then week, the hope diminished.

And then the doctors spoke the words she had hidden in the dark.

"We need to start facing the possibility that you might be permanently paralyzed from the waist down. The swelling around your spinal cord has almost completely disappeared, but we haven't seen any movement yet."

Rose wailed and sank into a chair; Tom turned away to hide his anguish, and Lauren stared into the void behind the doctors. The air in the room was laden with unspoken emotions.

Moments later, Lauren cut through them and said, "I'm just glad to be alive," her thoughts turning to Maddy.

Her father stepped up to her side and placed an arm around her shoulders. "It's going to be okay." Rose was struggling to get up, glaring at the doctors. "I won't accept that. She's a fighter. She'll walk again—you'll see."

You're both in denial. Why can't you see what's right in front of you?

When the doctors stepped into the hallway with her parents, she was alone again with Maddy's arms around her.

You can handle this, she heard her say.

I want to for you, Maddy, but I don't think I can. I'm so sorry.

And when she looked up, Maddy was gone.

She rang her call bell, her thumb striking the button again and again—and again. When no one responded immediately, she yelled into the hallway.

"Someone, get in here now."

A team of nurses charged in.

"What is it?"

"I want to go home. Today. Get my mother."

One nurse approached her bed and produced a syringe. Reaching for the IV tube, she said, "You need to relax."

Lauren slapped her arm away.

"I don't need to go to sleep. I need to go home."

The nurse backed away.

"Let's get you settled in for the night," she tried to reason, "and we'll talk about this in the morning. We know how upset you are, Lauren. I promise we'll talk to your parents and figure this out."

"There's nothing to figure out. I want *out of here.*"

Emotions pent-up behind the anger burst, and tears spilled down her face. For the first time since she had heard about Maddy's death, she sobbed, her whole body shaking. Weeks spent dodging terrible, painful feelings collapsed into grief, and this time there was no real or imaginary Maddy to comfort her. No matter how hard she tried, she couldn't summon her back.

Her best friend in the world was dead.

Her last bit of strength depleted, she cried herself to sleep.

✧ ✧ ✧ ✧

The next morning, Lauren woke to see Rose breezing

around the hospital room, fluffing the pillows, filling her water jug, taking over for the nurses.

"I've made arrangements for you to go to a rehab center," she announced matter-of-factly. "Dad and I have spoken to the doctors, and they've agreed it's time for you to be discharged."

"Thanks for consulting me. I thought this was *my* life here. When did it suddenly become yours?"

"Don't be ungrateful. It wasn't easy getting you into this place. You were screaming at the nurses last night to let you out of here."

"Right—I want to go *home*. Not to some center with all the cripples."

"Honey don't think of yourself like that. You've just got some adjusting to do. Things are a little different now. You're going to be fine. It'll just take time."

Lauren glared at her mother. *What is wrong with her?*

Her mother would not accept that she would spend the rest of her life in a wheelchair. In her mind, there would be a magic cure. This was only a temporary setback, and life would resume as before.

Wake up, Mom. It's so not going to happen.

"So, I should just go to rehab? Let them poke and prod me all over again? Jab me with needles to see if I feel anything? Show me how to go to the bathroom by myself? Teach me how to get dressed?"

Her eyes were cold—haunted.

Minutes passed as each waited the other one out.

"Fine. I'll go wherever you want me to go. It doesn't matter anymore. Just get me out of here," Lauren finally said, shaking her head in defeat.

"Good," Rose said, smiling, winning the showdown.

"Mother, I want to talk about Maddy."

"Jenny sent down some drawings for you," Rose dodged. "They're in my tote bag. Let me get them for you."

ROSE'S CHOICE OF A FACILITY was impressive—new and brightly lit with live greenery everywhere. It was welcoming—for a rehab center. Even Lauren had to agree that it was a lot better than the hospital. And if she were lucky, her mother wouldn't be here twenty-four hours a day.

The idea of volunteering at a rehab center had once crossed her mind. She wanted to help the unfortunate, the maimed, the broken. The poor souls who struggled with their disabilities had touched her heart. But she hadn't had time. Now she had plenty of it; only she was on the other side—the needy side. And she hated it. Hated it and hated being forced to come here.

"Welcome, Lauren," said the head nurse, crouching beside her wheelchair, holding out her hand. Lauren held out a limp hand in response, conscious of the nurse's position in greeting her. She would have to get used to everyone bending down to talk to her.

"I'd like to introduce you to Warren, one of our top therapists."

She nodded toward a man in jeans and a sweatshirt who was stepping out of an exercise room. He headed toward them to greet his new patient.

"He'll be working with you to help you regain your strength. He'll also teach you the life skills you'll need when you go home. There's a whole team of us dedicated to helping you regain your independence."

"Independence? Seriously? I'll never be independent again."

"I know that's how you feel now," said Warren, greeting her warmly. "But you will get there, I promise. Now let's get you settled in your room, and we can get to work."

"Right now?"

"The sooner we begin, the sooner we can get you out of here."

Following the nurse down the hallway, Rose rushing behind, Lauren was struck by the clean, fresh air of the place. There was none of the antiseptic smell of the hospital. The walls were painted soothing blue-grey, not institutional green. Refreshing.

When she came to the room that would be hers for the duration of her stay, she froze.

"How do you like it?" said Rose, her face glowing with anticipation, waiting for her daughter's reaction.

She had re-created Lauren's dorm room. A lavender

bedspread, curtains, and a tan rug mimicked the last place she had lived before the tragedy that brought her here. Rose had even put up a picture of the girls taken on the day they moved in.

"How could you, Mother? How could you hurt me like this? How could you be so insensitive?"

Rose's face fell. "I don't understand, sweetheart. I thought you'd like it?"

"You don't understand *me* at all. Do you think I want to be reminded of the room I was sharing with my best friend—who's now *dead*? Get all of this out of here."

Grabbing the picture, the only thing she wanted to keep, she turned her chair and wheeled herself away.

Maddy, I'm so sorry. I wish I could bring you back.

As soon as Warren began to work with Lauren, Rose settled herself in a chair to watch.

"I'm sorry, Mrs. Foster," said the head nurse, "we prefer that Lauren work on her own with Warren. She needs to adjust to being alone."

"Well, she's not alone," Rose snapped back. "She'll always have me."

"I'm sorry, but that is our policy. You're welcome to wait in the lounge."

"I can't—I won't leave my child."

"I'm sorry, ma'am, she'll concentrate much better with just her therapist. She'll be with you soon."

Watching as her mother reluctantly left the room, Lauren realized how hard it was for her to let go. She was so used to being in charge. She almost felt sorry for her. The moment was fleeting.

Six

WHILE LAUREN was struggling with her therapy, Danny was miles away wrestling with college applications. Despite, or maybe because of, the family tragedy, he couldn't wait to get away on his own. Perhaps he'd finally find out who he was and where he stood. And hopefully, it was no longer second or third place.

The previous spring, he had drawn up a list of the colleges he planned to visit. He knew, of course, that his parents expected him to go to Virginia Tech to follow his sister. And he also knew that wasn't going to happen if he could help it. He had his heart set on The College of William and Mary to major in theatre.

After his success in *It's a Wonderful Life,* he knew he belonged on stage. It was the only place he felt good about himself, where he could escape into another character and pretend that he mattered.

But he also knew how his parents felt about his acting ambitions.

"We're not wasting our money if you're hell-bent on studying theatre. What in the world are you going to do with that degree?" his mom had said. "Do something useful with your life. Study languages. Look how good you are in French. There's always those little community plays you can have fun with if you have to."

The deprecating tone in her voice had cut right through him. You'll need to get a real job when you get out," piped in his dad. Look at your sister. She has her sights set on being a lawyer. A real career, not this pansy stuff."

There—it was out there—how his dad felt. No surprise. He knew his dad wanted to re-live his college days vicariously through him. But acting was certainly not what he had in mind.

Tom, regretting the word he had just used, softened his tone a bit.

"Why don't you study business or law, Danny? I'd love to have you take over the firm someday. Think about it. Foster and Foster up on the sign outside my office. Maybe go out for football or soccer, too. Join a Fraternity. Live a little."

"You and mom don't get it," he pushed back. "I'm an actor and a damn good one. Sorry, I'm not a jock."

It had fallen on deaf ears.

So, he waited until the last minute to spring the visit to the campus on them.

"Oh, that again. That's ridiculous," his mom said. "You need a career, not a hobby. We don't have time to take you everywhere. I've got to focus on getting everything Lauren needs when she goes away."

"Seriously, Mom?" She's not leaving for another four months."

"Well, there's no reason to visit schools anyway. You'll go to Tech like your sister—assuming you get in."

"Thanks a lot. What if I want to go to William and Mary?"

"It's out of the question."

And so it went. He knew if he wanted to go to William and Mary, he would have to apply on his own. He wasn't going to get any support from his parents.

And no way am I going to be at the same school as my sister. I'm in her shadow enough now. That would be suicide.

❖ ❖ ❖ ❖

Filling out applications was the easy part. The essay was the challenge. They wanted to know about him—something personal. So, Danny decided to write about the trials of growing up in the Foster house. Digging deep into his past, a past laden with emotions he often drew upon when he was acting, he opened the drawers with the memories and began:

From the time I was five, I knew I didn't belong. My older sister was the chosen one, the favorite. Even after my little sister was born, I still brought up the rear.

Now I'm having a pity party, he thought, as he crumpled the paper and tossed it into the wastebasket.

I always tried to please everyone, especially my parents. Whatever they wanted I gave them. But it was never enough in their eyes, especially my mom's. It was always Lauren, Lauren, Lauren.

Nah, they don't want to hear me whine.

And he tossed that one away, too.

Okay, here goes.

I was the only son, sandwiched between two girls, which was both a blessing and a curse. A blessing because I didn't get the hand-me-downs. A curse, because I had to do whatever the "girls" couldn't handle.

So, he lied his way through the essay, hoping for the best. The only thing that mattered was getting away.

Now, sitting home, his applications submitted, it was the long waiting game. Would they see the lies in the essay, or swallow them whole? With Lauren at the forefront of everyone's thoughts—even his own—he knew he was on his own for college.

Seven

JUST AS LAUREN WAS settling in and beginning to make progress with her therapy, Rose dropped a bomb, shattering her life again. She had taken matters into her own hands and arranged to transfer her daughter to a facility nearer home. Lauren's reaction was not quite what she was expecting.

"Why would you do that? I'm doing well here. I love working with Warren. He knows me. He knows when to push me and when to back off. I can talk to him about anything. He's more than a therapist. He's a friend. And now you want to take me away from the only person who understands my grief?"

"It's not easy for me being so far from home. I thought you'd want this, too."

"I'm so glad you're thinking of me," Lauren said, sarcasm lacing her words.

"I am thinking of you."

You're all I ever think about.

"I'm thinking of all of us. I've found a great place near the house where we can visit you all the time."

"Once again, Mother, I thought this was *my* life. Why aren't you letting me make any decisions for myself?"

Rose winced, her voice quivering a little. "I'm. . .I'm doing everything I can for you. I thought you'd thank me. Not blame me."

There it was—the guilt.

Lauren clenched her jaw and threw her hands up in defeat.

"Fine, let's just do it your way."

Rose immediately brightened. "You're going to love this place, honey."

"I'm sure."

Rose gave a deep, gratified sigh, and Lauren knew her mother had won—again.

Saying goodbye to Warren was the hardest part. He spoke gently to her as he wheeled her to the transport van, past the artwork and lush greenery which had greeted her on the way in and become such a part of her life.

"Hold onto your determination and strong spirit, Lauren. That's going to help you as much as anything in healing your whole body."

He leaned over to give her a light hug.

She squelched the tears forming in the corners of her eyes and steeled herself for the next phase of her uphill climb.

When the nurses safely secured her inside the van, it pulled out onto I-81, the first time Lauren had been back on the highway since her accident. Her hands balled up into fists as all the trucks barrelling by roared in her ears.

Instantly, visions of the accident blinded her, and all she could see was bright red blood coating everything—splashed all over the inside of the ambulance, staining the EMT's uniform, covering her hands, even her hair.

And when she looked at the nurse accompanying her, the only face she saw was Maddy's last terrified glance at her.

Is this what it's always going to be like, she thought. *Am I ever going to forget?*

Maybe I can't—or don't want to.

❖ ❖ ❖ ❖

"Daddy, can I go see Lauren now?" Jenny asked as soon as her sister was now close enough to visit. "I miss her."

She waited in the hollow silence, listening to the faint ticking of the wall clock.

"Daddy, did you hear me? I want to go see Lauren."

Danny watched his dad, who was pre-occupied as usual, fumble for an answer. Did Jenny know that her big sister was in a wheelchair? Would she understand it was forever? He listened to see what his dad would say.

"Jenny, you know that Lauren was hurt very badly in the accident and has to be in a wheelchair now, right? She can't walk."

"I know, you told me that already. It's okay. I can push her and get things for her."

"I'm sure she'd love that, pumpkin," he answered, finally present in the moment.

"I can take Jenny if you want," Danny offered.

"I think we should ask your mom first if Lauren wants any visitors."

"But, I'm not a visitor, I'm her sister," Jenny said, arguing her point.

"Okay, honey, maybe this weekend. But we'll check with your mom first anyway."

Danny caught the reluctance his dad had when it came to decisions involving Rose. Had he always bent to her will? Had there always been this weird kind of distance between them? Was there something in their past he didn't know about?

He turned around to see Jenny, wrapped up in her favorite pink Barbie blanket, huddled up next to her dad on the sofa.

"Want to play Barbies with me, Daddy?"

"No, honey, not now. Ask your brother. He makes a good Ken."

Danny caught the deprecating tone in his dad's words. It stung.

"Come on, Jen, I'll beat you up to your room."

He turned his back on the hurt, vowing to leave as soon as he got an acceptance letter from a college. Any college at this point. But he cringed at leaving Jenny in the middle of the drama he sarcastically called home.

Eight

"17. . .18. . .19. . ." Lauren counted her reps as she lifted weights to strengthen her upper body—the part of her that still worked. Progress was slow but steady, and as she worked to improve her muscles, she felt her resolve slowly returning.

With the help of the therapists and psychologists, she began to understand and accept that the accident wasn't her fault. Except when her thoughts turned to Maddy. Maddy's parents had cared enough to visit her when she moved closer to home to see how she was doing, making her very uncomfortable.

"I don't understand it, Mother. How can they even look at me, let alone care how I'm doing? I killed their *only* daughter, their *only* child. Why don't they hate me? I hate me."

"You know it wasn't your fault—the police proved that. And Maddy's parents understand that, too."

"Maybe they think they do now. I know they feel sorry for me. But someday they're going to realize that I'm still alive and Maddy isn't. Then what?"

"You can't dwell on that now. You still have a lot of work to do for yourself. Now, go for your therapy."

You'll never get it. This goes so far beyond you and me.

"Go home, Mother. You have other children to think about. I'll be just fine."

She spun her chair around and left the room.

Rose, recoiling from her daughter's stinging words, watched as she rolled away from her, the distance between them increasing with every turn of the wheels.

Her phone was ringing on her bedside table when she came back from her rehab session. She glanced at the picture of her and Maddy, the only thing she wanted to keep from her mom's failed attempt at normalcy. She never wanted to forget her—her eyes, her energizing smile, her voice. She feared that someday they would fade, and she wouldn't be able to remember her. Rising above the sadness covering her heart, she answered the phone. She heard a familiar voice.

"Hi, Dad. What's up?"

"Can't a dad just want to hear his daughter's voice?"

"Sure, but you never call for no reason. So. . .?"

"You got me. I do want to ask you a question. Jenny wants to see you. I talked it over with your mom, and she said it would be up to you. What do you think?"

What I think is, you're all at home together and coming to visit me here, in this place.

She had wanted to be away, but not here. She had wanted to be exploring a new life, on her own, and with her best friend.

"Honey, are you there? Did you hear me?"

"Sorry, Dad.

"Um, does she know what's going on—with me. I mean that I can't walk?"

"I've had a long talk with her, and she says she just misses you."

Silence whispered through the line as Lauren fought for control of her emotions. Could she face her little sister?

"Lauren, what's going on? Are you okay?"

"Sorry, Dad. I guess I just zoned out there for a minute. I'd like to see her, too."

"Danny said he would bring her over. Then you can see him, too. I think he'd like to talk to you about colleges."

Lauren's voice faltered before she could answer. She wasn't in college anymore.

"I'd like that too, Dad," she feigned.

Hanging up, she looked out the window to see the snow just beginning to fall, fat flakes rapidly blanketing the grass. Oh, how she had loved to make snow angels with her little sister. Her breathing slowed as the memory flooded in. They were laughing, catching snowflakes in their mouths.

She blinked, and it was gone. Pounding against her lifeless legs, she sobbed—for Maddy, for herself and for the things that would only ever remain a memory.

Jenny flew into her sister's outstretched arms as soon as she walked into the room. Danny hung back, still unsure of Lauren's feelings toward him—and his toward her. His were a tangle. He loved her, resented her, felt sorry for her, hated the attention she always got. He was on an emotional seesaw.

"Hey."

"Hey, yourself."

He awkwardly approached her until she held out her arms to him once Jenny let go.

"It's great to see you. Look, um, I'm sorry I told you about Maddy. I thought you knew."

"It's okay. I should have known. They should have told me when I asked about her. I guess I'll never understand why they didn't."

"They meant well. They didn't want to hurt you."

"How? By telling me the truth."

Changing the subject, realizing Jenny was homed in on the discussion, she asked, "How do you like my new wheels?"

Jenny's eyes flashed with delight. "Can I push you around?"

"Sure. That would be a big help. Boy, I've missed both of you so much."

I'm so alone here.

Warmth spread through Danny as love won the battle of his emotions. At least for now.

"When can you come home?" Jenny asked, jumping right to the point.

Danny was jealous of her innocent acceptance of everything. To her, Lauren was just Lauren, plain and simple.

"Wanna' see my temporary home?" Lauren asked.

"I'll push. Just tell me where to go," Jenny said, reaching for the handles of the wheelchair.

Danny followed, looking in awe at his older sister's composure. She seemed to have adapted. Or was she pretending? If she was, she was doing a hell of a job of it. Maybe she was the better actor.

He caught her eye for a moment when Jenny went to check out all the equipment in the physical therapy rooms.

"You didn't answer her question. When can you come home?"

"Soon, I hope. I've learned a lot here, but I know I'll probably still need a lot of help when I get home. I'm not even sure how I'll get up to my bedroom."

"Oh, don't worry. Mom's already taken care of that. She's

turned Dad's downstairs office into a new bedroom for you. She booted Dad up to your room."

Lauren lowered her eyes so Danny couldn't see the guilt pouring out of them. Just one more consequence of her tragedy. One more person affected by her carelessness. The weight pushed against her chest.

Jenny skipped back over to her sister, jabbering about all the great exercise equipment they had there.

"I wish I had some of this stuff at home. It's so cool."

You have no idea what it's really like.

"I'd better get you back home, Jenny," said Danny. "Good to see you again," he said, his eyes resting on Lauren. "I hope you can come home soon."

"Dad said you wanted to talk to me about colleges. What did you want to know?"

"Oh, it can wait for a while," Danny answered.

I can't make her relive that now.

Leaning over the wheelchair to hug her, the reality of the position, and the permanence of it struck him for the first time. So many adjustments they were all going to have to make.

Could they?

He passed his mom in the hallway of the rehab center when he and Jenny were on their way out.

"Take care of your sister when you get home. Make sure she does her homework, and she gets to bed on time."

So, what's new, he thought. *I'm always taking care of her now.*

Accepting his marching orders, he left.

On the drive back, Jenny, suddenly quite serious and subdued, asked her brother a pointed question.

"How's Lauren gonna' get dressed and stuff—I mean like go to the bathroom?"

"That's what they're teaching her at the rehab center. That's their job. And she'll probably have an aide to help her, at least when she first gets home. Don't worry."

Danny saw the look of concern cloud her face as she tried to digest his answer.

Poor kid.

When they pulled into the driveway, the house was blanketed in darkness. No lights to welcome them. It was eerily quiet. He wondered where his dad could be on a Sunday night. He was gone a lot lately.

I wonder if he's hangin' out at a bar somewhere to drown his problems. Wish I could join him.

Sneaking booze and pot with Josh was the only time, except for being up on stage, that he had been able to escape from his life, his family, his insecurities. And the pull was powerful.

He looked over at his little sister and sighed with resignation. He was stuck here, for better or worse. He had to protect her while he could.

"Go on up and get your jammies on, and then I'll read to you if you want."

"I can read by myself, you know," she teased. "But I like it when you use all your different voices for the characters."

At least someone appreciates my acting.

It was late when he heard his dad's car pull into the garage. He went down to greet him and noticed how drained he looked. For the first time, he saw the silver streaks piercing his dad's dark hair.

I guess this whole thing is tough on him, too.

"Hey, Dad. How's it going?"

Tom scrambled to compose himself. He knew he looked like crap and quickly diverted the conversation.

"Did you see your sister today? Did Jenny go with you?"

"Yeah. It was good to see her again, and she was so excited to see Jenny. She said she might be coming home soon."

"That's what we're hoping for, son."

Danny hadn't heard that term of endearment for a long, long time. It got his antenna up. Why the affection so suddenly?

He went on the offensive.

"Where have you been? I put Jenny to bed."

"Oh, just work. Thanks for taking care of her. It means a lot, especially now. I'll see you upstairs later. I have a little more work to catch up on."

Danny caught a look in his dad's eyes. Something was different. He didn't know what, but he suspected it had something to do with the tension between him and his mom. Or was there something else going on?

Nine

THE DAY LAUREN was released to go home, the overcast sky let loose with the season's first heavy snow. School was closed, and both Danny and Jenny were home waiting for her arrival.

Danny looked around at a house he barely recognized anymore. His mom had re-created Lauren's bedroom downstairs, where her father's office used to be. They had installed a ramp by the back door near the garage, so they could wheel her up and into the house. Spotlights lit the walkway to prevent accidents. All for Lauren. But he knew she deserved it. He just wasn't sure how she would adjust to a home that was now so different.

Jenny was outside making snow angels when her dad pulled the van in with Lauren and her mom inside.

"Look," she yelled when they helped Lauren out of the car.

"Remember when we used to make these?"

"Sure do," Lauren answered, so happy her sister still had such great memories.

Danny hadn't yet cleared the ramp by the back steps of snow, and the scathing look in his mother's eyes spoke volumes. No words were necessary—the message was loud and clear.

One of the drawers in his brain opened, and an old memory surfaced.

He was ten and helping to unload the dishwasher. A glass slipped out of his hand and crashed to the floor, shattering on the hard marble surface.

"For crying out loud," said his mom. "Now, go clean it up. 'Lauren, honey, watch your step. Your brother's made a mess."

He shut the drawer on the memory—this time locking it in with the others. He wanted to throw away the key.

As he finished clearing the ramp, his phone pinged with a new message. He pulled off his gloves to look at it. It was from William and Mary. His heart began racing and sweat broke out on his brow despite the freezing temperatures. He was torn between welcoming his sister home and finding out what his future would be.

"Danny, come here and help with this chair. The ramp is still slippery," said his mom, scowling.

He closed the e-mail without looking at it. It would have to wait. His sister's homecoming took precedence. He would wait until he was alone to absorb its contents—good or bad.

Once inside, he watched his mother begin to help Lauren off with her hat—and coat—and gloves. She wasn't that help-less. When was his mother ever going to back off?

"Mother, there's nothing wrong with my arms. I can do all this. It's only my legs that won't work," Lauren protested.

"Sorry, honey. I can't help myself. I'm only trying to help."

"I know, Mother, and I appreciate it. But my time in the rehab centers was all about teaching me independence. Trust me; there will be things I'll need help with. I'd appreciate it if you'd wait until I ask."

Disappointment descended down Rose's face, from her squinted eyes to her pursed lips. But Lauren knew she had to stand her ground if she was going to reclaim her life.

And as if on cue to break the building tension, Jenny grabbed the handles of Lauren's wheelchair.

"Can I show you to your new bedroom?"

"I'd like that," answered Lauren, praying that the bed-spread wouldn't be lavender again.

Rose seemed to recover from her rejection and followed them down the hall, hoping she had gotten it right this time.

"Wow, it looks just like my old room. I'm sorry you had to be booted out of your office, Dad."

"There's plenty of empty rooms upstairs for me, honey. I hope you like it down here. Consider it a trade."

"I'm going to love it. Thank you. I know this wasn't easy for either of you."

Danny looked at the attention pouring out for his sister's return and was happy for her. She needed this right now. He couldn't even imagine what she was facing.

Aware of the death grip he had on his phone, he remembered the unread message waiting to be opened. He slipped away quietly to his room for privacy.

Ten

>> Congratulations. We are pleased to inform you. . .

The words jumped off the screen. Danny read them, then re-read them again.

Flinging open his door, he took the steps two at a time until he reached the hallway. His parents' excited voices over Lauren's homecoming made him stop in his tracks.

Probably not a good time to share my news. I'll only catch flack for ruining Lauren's homecoming. But I gotta' tell someone—now. He texted Josh.

> got into w&m. stoked!!!

Ping pong balls bounced around in his brain. He was so happy to have his sister home, but this was big news, too. But he squelched it. It wasn't the right time. And sadly, he knew what his parents' reaction would be.

"Why don't you study something useful?"

"You need to stay home—you're needed around here now."

His five-year-old self returned carrying with it the rejection he always lived with. Just then, Josh texted.

way to go, man. congrats.

❖ ❖ ❖ ❖

"Don't just stand in the hall, Danny. Come on in and join in the celebration," said Rose waving him over.

Why can't she be this pleasant all the time?

Danny summoned up a smile for Lauren's sake and came into the living room.

"How does it feel to be home?"

"It's a whole lot better than where I've been the last couple of months."

Her words sucked the heat out of the room. She cast a downward glance at her legs, covered with a plaid blanket to keep them warm, pausing before speaking.

"Come on, everybody. It's supposed to be my homecoming party. Let's get some music on and dance. You can all fill me in on what's been going on." The irony of dancing caught in her throat.

Jenny was the first to start gabbing about what she and Lisa had been doing, about how their teacher could never find her glasses when they were right on top of her head, and about the new family in the neighborhood. The sheer abandon in her voice lifted the mood of the room immediately.

"So, Danny, tell me about college," Lauren said after Jenny ran up to her room to play. "Where have you applied? Have you heard from anyone yet?"

"You don't need to be talking about that now, honey," interrupted Rose. "There's plenty of time to talk about Danny. Today is about you."

Now we're back to normal.

But for once, Danny was relieved that his mom didn't want to talk about him—or to him. He would have to find the right time and place to tell them all that he would be leaving at the end of the summer to start a new life but now wasn't it.

Lauren settled into her new life—a life of re-learning how to live again. Therapists and home health aides came and went, slipping in and out like waves rolling onto the shore and back out again. Whispered comments and stealth glances filled the rooms.

How do you think she's doing?

Did you see the look on her face just then? I wonder what she's thinking.

Lauren heard it all. Did they think she was deaf, too?

The constant solicitousness was driving her crazy.

I wish someone would take me out of here.

Her dad was absent a lot, working longer and longer hours. She feared he was worried about the bills. He became further removed from the family. And something was going on between him and her mom. The snipes and snide remarks between them hurt her—she felt she was responsible for the tension.

"My God, Rose," she overheard her dad yell one day after the day's therapists had gone home. "Why can't you just leave her alone and let her do for herself?"

"How can you say that, Tom? She needs me. And how would you know the half of what's involved here? You haven't paid any attention to her therapy since she came home. Typical. You're always at work or on a damn business trip. Everything has fallen on me. It always has."

"Has it fallen on you, or have you taken it on? There's a difference."

The old familiar arguments came back to haunt him.

Rose shot him a look of contempt.

"I can see this conversation is going nowhere," he said. "I'll be in my office."

Tom left her room, closing the door behind him, and Lauren, listening at the foot of the stairs, rolled herself back to her room. Guilt wrapped itself around her once again. She now had more than just Maddy's death to feel guilty about. She was forcing a wedge between her parents.

Eleven

THE FORMAL ACCEPTANCE LETTER from William and Mary sat open on the kitchen island when Danny got home from school the next day.

"What's this?" Rose demanded.

"I was planning to tell you. I can't believe you opened it. Don't I deserve some privacy? It's exactly what it says. I applied to William and Mary and got in, and I'm going."

"First of all, I told you we wouldn't support you with this ridiculous major. The plan was for you to go to Tech. But that's a moot point now. You'll have to go to community college and stay around to help with your sister. Your father's always gone, and I can't do this by myself."

"What can't you do by yourself?" Tom asked, overhearing the tail end of the conversation.

"Your son took it upon himself to apply to William and Mary and now he thinks he can go and leave me with all the responsibilities of Lauren. You're never here, and I can't do it all."

"Hold on a minute, Rose. I'm here when you need me," Tom interjected, arms folded, a flush of anger spreading up his cheeks as he attempted to defend himself against her accusations.

He turned to Danny. "Did you get in?"

"Yeah, I did. And I'm going. Lauren went away, and I am too. And you can't change my mind."

Rose's face contorted with anger.

"And just where do you think you'll get the money?"

"You were planning to send me to Tech, so I'll take that money and go where I want. Where they want ME."

"Tom, are you going to let him talk to us like that?"

"Let it go, Rose. Let *him* go."

He just stood up to her. And stood up for me. Way to go, Dad.

"First you talked me into letting Lauren take the car and look how that turned out. And now this. Fine. Have it your way. I give up. Just leave me alone with this mess."

She turned to see Lauren sitting in the doorway, witnessing the entire conversation. If only she could retract her last sentence, rewind it and keep the words in her mouth. But it was too late. The pain in her daughter's eyes would stay with her forever.

Stunned with his dad's sudden support, Danny looked him in the eye, shook his hand, and said, "Thanks." Then his eyes met his sister's, and he read the words on her face. *It's okay,* they said.

So, I guess I'm a mess, Lauren thought as she gazed out the window of her room at the hydrangeas in full bloom. She had suddenly gone from being her mother's obsession to her burden. And there was nothing she could do to change it. A new kind of grief embedded itself in her soul.

Maddy and I would have just gotten home from our first year of college. We would be starting summer jobs. Maybe we'd have even found boyfriends down at school that we were already missing. Maybe. . .

She knew it was pointless to go down the road of maybes. Those maybes would never happen. Now it was her brother's turn to go away, find a great roommate, maybe even a girlfriend, and live out her maybes.

Twelve

"DAMN THIS CARPET," Lauren swore, attempting to navigate her way from her room to the kitchen for breakfast, getting stuck on the plush fibers.

"I'll help you," said Danny.

"I'll get it. Don't bother."

Backing away, fearing an outburst, Danny went back to his bowl of Cheerios. She had been very testy lately, and he wondered what had changed in the last few weeks. Then his mother's words, 'leave me with this mess,' echoed in his ears.' No wonder Lauren was upset.

"Want to talk about it?" he asked her, treading gently into her space.

"Nope."

Danny had been waiting for her euphoria over coming home to vanish as the reality of her life took its place. Despite making progress with her physical and occupational therapy, her spirits were going in the opposite direction. And Rose wasn't helping.

Watching her dote incessantly on Lauren had his hackles up, and he could only imagine how helpless it made his sister feel. And then to hear such scathing words.

Lifting her eyes, Lauren said, "Sorry. I'm just in a bad mood. Can I ask you to do something for me?"

"Anything."

"Can you get me out of here?"

"When and where?" he answered.

"Tomorrow at four, after you get home from school."

"Any place special?"

"I don't want *her* to know. You have to promise."

"It will just be our secret. Now spill the beans. Are you going to visit your friends?"

"My friends don't even come to visit me anymore. Why should I waste my time visiting them? No, I've made an appointment with a psychotherapist. I need to figure out how to deal with Maddy's death. I see her every time I close my eyes to go to sleep. I see the terrified look on her face. I see the blood. I see it all."

With those words finally out in the open, Lauren hung her head and sobbed. Danny reached out to comfort her, and for once, she gave in, allowing him in.

"I need help, Danny. I miss her so much."

Danny assured her of his silence. Their relationship had suddenly shifted.

He had just become her confidante.

Lauren waited while the therapist sat back in his black leather chair, pushing himself away from the mess of folders and sticky notes on his desk. When she had his attention, she spoke the words that had been festering in her.

Her body started to shake. In a moment she managed to say, "I killed my best friend."

"That's a painful statement," he replied, digesting her blunt, cold words. "What can you tell me about that?"

"I had an accident with her in the car. She died, and I was left like this," she said, motioning to her wheelchair.

"Can you tell me more about the accident itself? How did it happen?"

Fear and grief combined, causing her to tremble as she replayed the worst day of her life.

"We were driving back to school on I-81, and a tractor-trailer changed lanes and took us out."

She waited in the silence for him to respond. He sat with his fingers pressed against his face saying nothing, waiting for her to continue.

"If I hadn't begged my parents to let me take the car back to school—which irritated the hell out of my brother—it never would have happened."

"I see."

"Is that all you can say?"

"Why did it irritate your brother so much?"

"Now you want to talk about him?" Her voice was escalating, and her tone was becoming irrational.

"No, it's just that you mentioned him."

Not entirely understanding where he was taking the conversation, Lauren answered.

"Well, he was using the car for his senior year in high school, and I took it away from him. He was totally ticked."

The therapist leaned back once again, his chair squeaking on its hinges, making notes in her file. He glanced up to see Lauren biting her lip, waiting for him to say something.

"Tell me a little bit about your family, Lauren."

And so, the saga began. She told him about her brother and sister, then paused before launching into her mom and dad—especially her mom.

"Mom's obsessive. She's always pampered me—much more than the others—and now that I'm like this—she motioned to her legs again—she's become overbearing. She won't let me do anything for myself even when the Physical Therapist encourages me to. And just the other day she said I was a mess. Go figure. Dad's kind of okay, although I don't see much of him since I've come home."

"Does that bother you?"

"You mean about my mom or my dad?"

"Your mom."

"I don't know what to make of her. But that's not why I'm here. I can't stop thinking about Maddy. I miss her so much."

"Then let's talk about her—next week. I suspect we'll need more time than we have today. It's going to be difficult to dredge up something so painful, but our goal is to give you peace and acceptance. If we work together, we will get you there."

Fighting hard against the sadness filling every pore of her body, Lauren thanked the doctor and left the office.

When she came out into the reception area, she saw Danny absorbed in his French book. Hoping he wouldn't ask her any questions she began talking about what they would tell Rose when they got home.

"She can't know—you promised," she said as he gathered up their coats.

"I said I wouldn't tell, and I meant it."

"Thanks Danny. I need some privacy before she makes me crazy."

"Gotcha'."

He wheeled her out to the car, helped her in, and they drove home.

Rose was standing like a sentry waiting for them when they pulled into the driveway.

"Where have you two been? I've been beside myself with worry."

"I told you Danny was taking me over to see a friend."

"But you were gone so long. How was your visit?"

"It was fine, Mother."

"I'll be more than glad to take you next time, sweetheart. I'm happy to see you getting out."

Danny stepped in to get his sister out of a tricky spot.

"I'm glad to take her, Mom. I don't get much quality time with my sister. I have to take advantage of it since I'll be leaving soon."

His mom's eyes clouded over. She turned away with a parting comment. . . "We'll see."

Thirteen

TIME CHURNED ON, minute by minute, day by day, and as spring turned the world green again, Danny prepared for his graduation from high school. His remaining hurdle, final exams, would be his last hurrah. His mom had resigned herself to the fact that he was going away in the fall, but she never missed a chance to give him a guilt trip about it.

"I have so much to do today, Danny, and Lauren wants to get out for a while. I know you can take her now, but what am I going to do when you're gone?"

"Seriously, Mom. You're usually all over her. What's changed now?"

"Don't be so smart with me, young man. I do have a life, too."

"You might want to look into the special services the county offers. I know there are busses equipped for the disabled that she can take. I think Lauren would like to get out by herself for a change."

"Please don't use that word 'disabled' around her. She doesn't need to think of herself that way."

"I think she's way more realistic than you are. She's probably already got it all figured out. You need to loosen the strings a little, cut the umbilical cord, give her a chance to make her own way."

Danny saw a shadow cloud Rose's face. She had spent nineteen years keeping Lauren tethered to her, and Danny knew she'd dismiss his suggestion. His sister had stretched those strings as far as she could when she went away to school, but now, anchored back home, he knew she would never be able to break them.

Before he gave Rose a chance to react to his sermon, he changed the subject.

"I need to order my cap and gown for graduation. Can I have a check?"

Grateful for the escape from a conversation she didn't want to have, Rose reached for her purse and signed a blank check for her son.

"Thanks, Mom. Just three more weeks, and I'll be a graduate and ready to move on to my next phase in life."

Rose winced. Danny saw it and was glad she had lost this battle. He was leaving; she was not used to being defeated.

❖ ❖ ❖ ❖

The strains of *Pomp and Circumstance* filled the stadium as the graduates, regaled in their blue caps and gowns, marched in. Tom carried Lauren up into the stands so she could watch her brother get his diploma. When they called his name, she put her fingers to her mouth and gave out a shrill whistle.

Thinking back to the year before, she remembered walking into the same stadium, Maddy marching right next to her—Foster, Franklin—just as they had been alphabetically placed all through elementary school. They had their entire lives before them. So much had changed in one year, so much loss, so much sorrow, so much pain.

And now her fervent prayer was that her brother would fly free and be what she couldn't.

When the family exited the stadium where the graduation ceremonies had taken place, Danny was waiting for them. His blue eyes glinted as he held his diploma up for them to see. He was ready to get out into the world, away from the constant feelings of inadequacy he had been living with for as long as he could remember.

Remember your sandals next time.

Then he looked down at Lauren and saw the sadness in her eyes contrasted with the smile on her face. He knew she was happy for him, wanted the best for him. But she had lost it all—all the plans, the future ahead of her, the life she almost had. Her once bright green eyes were now dimmed, almost haunted. What could he—should he say to her? But, once again, she beat him to it.

"Hey, bud, congratulations. You look great holding that diploma. How does it feel to be finished with high school?"

"It's a big relief."

"Well, don't start slacking now. The hard work's only beginning."

Danny could see the wistful look on her face and knew she was remembering her first semester at Virginia Tech. She and Maddy were thriving on their own, out in the world for the first time. And now she was back in her own home, stuck back in the past, mourning for the future.

And missing Maddy.

Fourteen

AS THE HEAT and the humidity of the summer months raged on, Danny frequently took Lauren out on the porch out of earshot of everyone, especially their mother. Their trips to the therapist had brought them closer, and they were at last confiding in each other. How ironic that just when he was about to leave, he was making a connection with his sibling.

Their conversations always centered around Rose.

"I hate you, you know," Lauren said. "You get to get away from this mess we're living in. And away from *her*." She paused to steel herself for the admission she was about to make. "Can I tell you something?"

"Anything."

"I know I was a real bitch growing up. I saw how Mom ignored you for me. She did anything I wanted. And I loved it. I loved being the princess."

"That's okay," he lied.

"No, it's not. I hurt you just as much as she did. And I'm sorry you were treated so badly. It wasn't fair."

Danny looked around to make sure Rose wasn't listening.

"She always did the helicopter mom thing, especially where I was concerned. But this accident turned her into a mother bear protecting her cub. I get it. She wants to help. But she's always had this thing about me, this fixation. And it hurt you. Now I can see it. And I hate it. And sometimes I hate her."

Caught short by her statement, Danny, at last, admitted to himself what he hadn't been willing to accept up until then; his problem was not with Lauren, it was with Rose.

"I guess I thought it was my imagination. I never measured up to you. And I resented you for it. But it wasn't your fault. I'm sorry she's smothering you. I wouldn't mind a little more attention, but I'll be leaving in a month, so it really won't matter anymore. I just feel sorry for Jenny. I think she gets ignored a lot."

"Now that I'm home all the time, I'll make sure she gets attention, Danny. Not to worry."

She paused to digest the words 'home all the time.'

24/7.

With my mother.

Maddy, I need you.

She was suddenly so envious of her brother.

"Speaking of leaving, will Mom and Dad be taking you

down to school? I remember the big deal they made when I moved out."

You have no idea how much I remember.

It was all there as vivid as the day it happened.

"Why do I have to go? I'm going to miss a rehearsal. I can say good-bye just as easily here."

"This is not up for discussion. Now get in the car."

The car was packed, Rose making sure Lauren had every-thing she needed—and even a lot she didn't. But Rose was Rose. Comforters, rugs, curtains, and pictures were all crammed into the trunk. Danny, Lauren, and Jenny sat in the back, Jenny in the middle as a buffer between the older two. The girls chatted about how to decorate the new room, while Danny, glued to his phone, texted his friend, Josh.

> can't believe im on this stupid trip.
> waste of time.

When they finally arrived, Lauren waltzed into the room and threw her arms around Maddy, her best friend and roommate.

"Danny, go down and help your father bring up Lauren's things," said Rose, ready to plunge into the decorating.

Danny heard and obeyed the order. Once again, he was just a bystander—an errand boy.

"Let's get to work," Lauren exclaimed.

Turning his back on the charade playing out in the room, Danny went to explore the campus. When he returned, the girls had transformed the room into a brochure for prospective new students. There were matching lavender bedspreads and curtains, artwork already on the walls, and a tan, plush rug on the floor between the beds.

"Look, Danny," said Jenny. "Do you like it?"

He shrugged. He didn't care. He just wanted to get back home.

He glanced over to his mom and rolled his eyes at her forlorn look, and they hadn't even left yet.

And when it was time to go, the drama began.

"Are you sure you have everything, honey? We still have time to run out and get whatever you need."

"Mom, I'm fine."

"Maybe you and Maddy would like to grab something to eat before we go."

"Mother, Dad's waiting. It's time for you to be getting on the road."

"But. . ."

Danny watched as Lauren reached over and hugged her mom. Rose's fingers turned white as she clutched at Lauren's shoulders. Lauren pulled away gently.

"Everything will be all right, Mother."

The mother/child role reversal was profound.

The ride home was silent except for the sound of Rose's sniffling, tears falling in crooked lines down her pale cheeks.

"The house will seem so empty without her," she finally uttered, insensitive to the fact that her other two children were in the back seat.

"Where'd you go just then," Lauren asked.

"Oh, just thinking about something. What did you say?"

"I asked if Mom and Dad were taking you down to school."

Danny made a disgusted sound. "Are you kidding? I'm not even sure where Dad's gonna' be in a month, and Mom will never leave you alone. I'll get there by myself. It's fine."

"I'm sorry. I wish I could go with you."

Danny reached over and laid his hand lightly on her shoulder, realizing that they were trading places. He was getting away, and she was trapped at home. His heart sank.

Fifteen

DANNY HAD ALREADY shipped his footlocker down to William and Mary with most of what he would need for the year. Now, with Jenny sitting on the edge of his bed watching, he packed the one lone suitcase he would take on the bus with him.

"How come you're going by yourself? Couldn't we go too, to help?"

"It just isn't going to work now, you know, with all that's going on. I'll be fine. And I'll call you as soon as I get there. Now, run downstairs and see if my cab is here, okay?"

Glancing around at the posters he had tacked up on the walls to cover the Spiderman wallpaper he had aged out of long ago, Danny realized the years he had spent in his "safe place" were coming to an end. He was about to enter the real, blemished, unprotected world of college. And he would be free. Closing the door, he found himself whistling with satisfaction, relieved to be putting this part of his life behind him.

Lauren was waiting for him at the bottom of the stairs, a grim expression on her face, her hair pulled back. Maybe it was the tears she was fighting back, but today her intense green eyes bore straight through him.

"Where's Jenny?"

"I'm right here," she said, slowly making her way in from the kitchen as if delaying would make her brother stay a little longer. Her red-rimmed eyes told her story.

"Your taxi's here," she said.

Danny hugged them one by one, saving his biggest bear hug for Jenny.

"Be good to your Barbies," he said, ruffling her hair.

"Guess I'll see you guys in a few months." He forced a smile.

Turning to his mother, who had been observing his departure, he leaned over and hugged her. For the first time he could remember, she hugged him back—briefly. It was enough.

Dragging his suitcase down the steps, he glanced over at Lauren's ramp and said a silent good-bye to his old life, a shadow of guilt tinging the moment. He buried it with the past.

The bus sat idling, its exhaust fumes permeating the station as the travelers boarded. As Danny looked through the finger-smudged windows at the town he was leaving behind, he thought of all the people who had occupied these seats and gazed out of these windows.

Where had they all been going? What were their stories? Were they headed for new destinations? Were they running away from the troubles of their current lives? He was doing both.

In a half-hour, the bus was rolling down the highway, the engine humming to an inaudible beat, lulling Danny into a half-sleep. His eyelids became heavy, the strain of the past year sitting heavy on them.

Then the dreams began. Every time he closed his eyes, they appeared as though painted on the inside of his eyelids.

He saw his parents, dancing in the living room when they thought the kids weren't looking, then remembered holding his hands to his ears to block out their heated arguments.

He heard the praises his mom heaped on Lauren; then tried to erase her criticisms of everything he did.

And he dreamt of Lauren, the golden child, and the accident that changed her life forever and pushed him further into the background of his family.

He roused as the bus slowed to a halt at the Williamsburg Transportation Center. The restored historic brick building with its classic fluted columns and red brick pavers brought back memories of when he used to visit as a kid. He had always loved Colonial Williamsburg, and now he was getting to live here. He retrieved his suitcase from under the bus, passing other lives holding their secrets. Everyone had secrets.

The late-summer evening darkness was already falling on Williamsburg. The noise of bus engines and passengers disembarking intruded on the otherwise silent scene. After hailing a cab for the short distance to the school, Danny shifted uncomfortably in his seat, ants crawling inside his stomach.

Finally, I can be what I want, live how I want—and now I'm scared I'm not ready.

As the cab approached the campus, lights from the dorm windows shot out like lightsabers, brightening the darkness surrounding the buildings. Danny gazed at the place he would call home for the next four years.

Paying the driver, he retrieved his suitcase from the trunk of the car and walked into the dorm. The hallways were swarming with incoming parents and freshmen, a few of whom seemed more than ready for their parents to leave.

"Mom, stop arranging the pillows on my bed," Danny heard through one open dorm room door.

"You guys should get going. I'm fine. *Really*," came from another.

Danny pressed the elevator button, and when the doors opened, he was almost trampled by a crowd of girls exiting. He smiled.

Oh, yeah. Co-ed dorm. Almost forgot. Awesome.

For a split-second, though,

. . .he was back in the hospital elevator again, on his way up to see Lauren, not sure how bad her injuries were.

Palms sweating, he reached for the side of the elevator to steady himself.

The elevator rose interminably slow as Danny watched the digital green numbers light up. When the doors opened to let him out on the third floor, he inhaled the air in the hallway, calming himself down. His suitcase suddenly felt very heavy, so much of his life packed into an aluminum box.

He could see other kids with moms absorbed in decorating to make their rooms as homey as possible. There was only so much one could do with a loft bed and desk, but, then again, Danny didn't have anyone there to work the magic.

He remembered

. . .his mother going to town to trick out Lauren's room at Tech.

He convinced himself it was okay. He didn't want that kind of attention anyway—though a little help getting here and setting up would have been nice.

Locating his room, he walked into a scene of familial bliss.

A short, heavyset teen was busy helping an older couple set up his things. He had already chosen his side of the room.

"Hey, you must be Danny. I'm Chuck, and these are my parents, Frank and Linda."

"Nice to meet you." He saw them staring at his lone suitcase.

"We got Chuck settled in," said Frank, an older, taller version of Chuck. "If your parents are on their way up with the rest of your things, we can go lend a hand."

"Uh, no, they couldn't make it. I shipped most of my stuff ahead. I'm not sure where it got stored yet."

Acutely self-conscious now, Danny excused himself to go back down to the front desk to see if his trunk had arrived. A guy pointed him to the storage room behind the front desk.

How did things get like this? Why am I the only person moving in by myself?

In the lobby, a mother was holding it together to keep from getting emotional in front of her son. Danny remembered his mom's reaction to leaving Lauren at college, acting as though she would never see her daughter again, crying, clutching, refusing to be consoled.

It's a good thing she didn't come. That kind of stuff would have sent me over the edge. I don't need her. I don't need any of them.

A flash of Lauren's and Jenny's faces as he left home made him retract the last part of his thoughts.

He took a deep breath and arranged to have his things sent upstairs.

DANNY OCCUPIED A SEAT in the back of the hall, high up in the dimming light where he could observe the dynamics playing out in the cavernous space.

The first day of classes had just begun, with a current of anxious electricity. Scores of students, including Danny, had poured into the vacant lecture hall, rapidly filling in the stadium-style seats. Singles, doubles, and groups revealed the comfort level of the incoming freshmen just embarking on their four-year journey.

Danny felt so alone.

Then she walked in and his heart flipped. Long, brown hair and dark-rimmed oversized glasses completed a vision of perfection, knocking him off balance.

She sat up front, off to the side where he could see her profile.

Cute nose, with a small ridge. She seemed familiar.

Curious, he decided he had to see her up close.

When class ended, and he realized he hadn't heard a word of the lecture, he got up from his seat and approached her, trying not to look like he was staring.

Passing her seat, where she was still gathering her notes and books, his foot caught on the strap of her open backpack, dumping it over. The contents resembled Lauren's bathroom sink: lipstick, mascara, and hair spray spread across the auditorium floor. If he hadn't been so embarrassed, he might have laughed.

Damn.

"Sorry. I'll get these," he said, bending down and fumbling to collect her things, the lipstick tube rolling away from him.

"Hey, it's okay," she said, dimples dotting her cheeks when she smiled.

When he looked up, their eyes met—his blue, hers green. His mind raced—his thoughts careening against each other.

I'm sure I've seen her before—maybe in the dorm.

"I'm Danny." He felt the color drain from his face.

"I'm Kim. Why are you looking at me like that? Are you okay?"

"You look so familiar. Sorry if I was staring. Um, have we met before?"

"No, I think I would remember," she answered, suddenly aware of the flush creeping across her face.

"Well, again, sorry for the mess. See you next time."

Turning, he headed quickly for the door.

The encounter had only lasted seconds, but it left him dizzy.

Why do I feel like I know her?

Trying to recover from his embarrassing screw-up, he headed across campus. As he walked, he noticed all the groups of people chatting together like they had been friends for years. He wanted to fall in beside them—become part of their group—pretend. It had taken him the first two years of high school to find his crowd and make a few friends. And it was all so natural for them.

He stopped looking, his thoughts turning back to the alluringly familiar girl he had just met.

Classes were challenging. Always running in the back of Danny's head, like a bad recording, was his mom's comment that he would end up back home.

Not gonna happen. I'll prove her wrong.

But, as with all good intentions, there was always a crack—a convenient excuse—a rationale. And he jumped at the first one.

"Hey, how'd you like to come to a party this weekend?" Chuck asked.

His conscience fought with the devil, but in the end, the Danny, who was newly emerging won. He was finally free to do what he wanted. He didn't need permission. And without skipping a beat, he answered, "Hell, yeah. Just tell me when and where."

Two nights later, Chuck took him to an apartment off-campus. They could hear the sounds of raucous laughter and ear-splitting music from two blocks away. This wasn't just him and Josh sneaking booze and pot at Billie's when his parents were out. This was the real deal.

As they approached the brick house, a red cup landed on the sidewalk in front of him, spewing beer all around. He jumped out of the way and looked up to see half a dozen well-inebriated kids smoking and drinking on the front porch.

He and Chuck pushed their way through the crowd and made their way inside. The floor pulsed to the pounding of the music. The pungent smell of sweat and pot rose up his nostrils. Navigating past drunk and drugged kids, they made it to the bar.

"Here you go, man," said a tall, lanky guy with a sloppy grin on his face, pulling him a beer from one of the kegs lining the floor. It wasn't whiskey, but it only took a few swigs to kick in until all thoughts of his family, the accident, his sister—all of it—finally disappeared.

And he loved the rush it gave him. He was flirting with danger, and it shoved away any part of his conscience that tried to kick in. By three in the morning, Chuck was dragging him back to the dorm. He couldn't navigate the ladder to his bunk, so he just flopped down on the floor with a drunken grin on his face.

✧ ✧ ✧ ✧

As sunlight seeped its way through the blinds, Danny cracked one eye open. The light careened against his eyeballs, making his head pound.

I feel like shit.

Acid bile rising in his throat, he looked around for Chuck. Nowhere to be seen.

Oh crap, he thought. *I have a paper due Monday.*

Ducking his head under a cold shower, he grabbed his backpack and headed for the library. Afraid he wouldn't be in any condition to concentrate, his stomach turned to knots, adding to his nausea.

Some party guy I am—clearly a first-timer. Gotta' do somethin' about that.

Seventeen

DANNY SOON FOUND OUT that the lines between academics and the social scene at school blurred quickly. And it wasn't long before he slipped into the vacuum it created. His resolve to succeed promptly bit the dust as he succumbed to the parties and the booze. In short shrift, he was turning his papers in late, and he was missing play rehearsals. He was slipping, and he didn't even recognize it.

The latest party was in full swing, music screaming, liquor flowing, and Danny was feeling no pain.

Chuck shouldered his way through the crowd.

"Got something else you can try." He held up a small plastic bag with a little white powder. "If you want to party, you need some of this."

"Um, no. I'm good."

"Come on, loosen up."

"I'm pretty loose already."

Before Chuck could persuade him, his eyes locked on the figure making her way through the crowd. It was Kim.

What the hell's she doing here?

"Hey, Danny. What's up? I haven't seen you in class lately. Did you drop the course?"

"Nah. Eight o'clock's not my thing," he shouted over the racket in the room. "What are you doin' here?"

"Just passing by and heard all the noise. Thought I'd check it out."

With a good buzz on and totally chill, he threw one arm around her shoulders without thinking.

"Need a drink?"

She pushed the arm off and stepped back.

"No, thanks. I don't drink. They're passing around some bad stuff, and you're pretty wasted. You should go home and sober up."

"I'm good," he laughed. "Too bad you don't want to join me."

He stumbled away to the bar.

What a waste, Kim thought. *I thought he was cool.*

By the time she left with her girlfriends, Danny was sprawled on the front lawn, laying in his own vomit.

He woke up in his room, stinking of booze and puke, with no recollection of how he got there. Vague memories of a face hovering over him surfaced. The glasses. The eyes. Head pounding, he realized who it was.

Oh, crap. Why did Kim have to see me like that? What else did I do?

Swallowing hard, the acrid aftertaste of barf in his mouth, he rolled over, wishing for oblivion.

As a mountain of unfinished work, missed deadlines, and unattended rehearsals threatened to bury Danny under their load, he watched, as though from the sidelines, as his dreams of acting imploded. So, the summons one late afternoon to his faculty advisor's office came as no surprise.

The hallway was empty, the lights casting shadows on the walls and floor. The professor's office was down at the very end, and Danny found himself counting his steps again. 211. Keeping out of sight, he peered into the office. A small desk lamp was on, the professor hunched over his work. The dark, late-November sky signaled the end of the day, adding to the already gloomy mood surrounding Danny. He halted in front of the door, his fist hovering lightly above it. Professor Wilson looked up.

"Come in. Have a seat."

"Yes, sir."

"I'm sure you can guess what this is about."

"I know. I'm in trouble."

"I'm glad you at least recognize it. Some get in so deep they can't see what's going on.

"I saw and heard some good things about you and your talent before you got here. The information I'm getting back from your professors is dismal. Frankly, I'm disappointed. It's only November, and you're cutting classes, your grades are falling, and you're letting your producer down. He's on the verge of kicking you out of the production. I know you have talent, but I'm sure not seeing it."

Danny could not meet the man's eyes.

"You didn't just skate into this school. You're intelligent—and talented. I've seen bright young men and women go down quickly once they get away from home," he continued. "College will either make or break you. Which is it going to be for you?"

Danny wanted to fade away, to be invisible.

"I understand, sir. I'm going to turn it around. I want to be here."

"Thanksgiving break is coming up fast. I'll expect to see a turn-around from you before you go home."

Danny thanked his advisor and left the office, his cheeks burning with shame. He'd had enough of that when he was home. He didn't need to revisit it here.

Scrambling to make up for lost time, he hunkered down to catch up on his work. He skipped the parties, put in extra hours at play practice, and got his butt to every class.

His first Monday back in class after the fool he made of

himself, he avoided talking to Kim, embarrassed about the way she'd seen him, and how he'd blown her off.

"Whoa, what happened to 'eight o'clock's not my thing,'" she said. Her sarcasm smarted.

"I guess I deserved that. Um, listen, Kim, about that night. . ."

She held up her hand and stopped him.

"I've seen a lot worse. It happens. Don't worry about it."

"It's just—that's not really who I am."

He sounded lame even to himself. *She's giving me a pass. I should just shut up.*

"No problem. By the way, I stopped in to see one of the play rehearsals the other day and saw you. You're good."

"Thanks."

"Have you been acting long?"

"All through high school."

"Where are you from?"

"Arlington, Virginia."

"No, kidding? Me too. Where did you go to high school? I was at Wakefield."

"Washington-Lee."

She looked up. "The prof is ready to start. I'll talk to you later."

I guess I dodged a bullet there, he thought, dropping into a seat. *Not only is she hot, she's nice.*

When class was over, Kim caught him on the way out the door.

"How are you getting home for Thanksgiving?"

"By bus. That's how I got down here."

"I have a car here. Would you like a ride?"

"That would be great."

"Here," she said, handing him her phone. "Put in your number. Let's do this. Glad to have some company."

Score.

Eighteen

WITH DANNY GONE, and along with him, her transportation, Lauren was forced to tell her mother she was seeing a therapist.

"I still can't believe you've been going behind my back—and with your brother. How could you hide such a thing?"

"I knew how you would react, Mother—just like you are now. It's always a guilt trip with you. I just needed to do this by myself."

"You can talk to me. I'm sure I can help."

"You just don't get it, Mother. No matter what anyone says, I feel responsible for Maddy's death. I need to see a professional."

With her usual uncanny ability to switch moods as easily as changing her clothes, Rose answered.

"Well, at least now, with your brother gone, I can drive you to your appointments."

Lauren's eyes clouded over. More intrusion. She couldn't win. But now she had no choice.

The following Tuesday at Dr. Goldman's, Rose started to follow Lauren into the office.

"I'm sorry, Mother, but this is private."

"But. . ."

"Mother, this is *my* problem. Just let me deal with it."

Rose was deeply wounded, and let Lauren see it before she backed away. Realizing that her daughter had turned to her brother for help instead of to her, hurt. A crack was breaking open. She had to seal it before it got any bigger.

❖ ❖ ❖ ❖

"It's nice to see you again, Lauren," said Dr. Goldman. "How have you been?"

"I can't sleep. I keep seeing the accident. And I can't stop missing Maddy."

"Yes, let's talk about her. I gather you two were very close."

"She's been my best friend for most of my life. She is—was—like a sister to me. I needed her."

"What did you need her for, Lauren?"

"My sanity. My escape."

"Escape from. . .?"

"My mother. She wants to run my life. That's why I was

so happy to go away to school. She's obsessed with me. And now I'm stuck at home with her, and I'm going crazy. Sometimes I pretend Maddy's in the room with me, and I talk to her. Am I losing it?"

"How do you mean 'she's obsessed with you?' Is it possible your mother is just trying to be a good mom?"

"She's over the top. It's like she's trying to live vicariously through me. She practically ignores my brother and little sister. And now that I'm paralyzed—I can finally say that out loud—she won't leave me alone. You saw how she even wanted to come into the room with me. I have to fight for every minute of privacy."

Dr. Goldman took off his glasses and thought for a moment. "So Maddy represented freedom and the path to your own life. And now that 'bridge' is gone."

"Yeah. I guess that's right."

"And now that you're back at home, being cared for by your mother, you feel—what?"

Lauren thought. "Like I'm being pulled into this vortex. Like all my life is being sucked out of me. It's 'Lauren, let's do this together,' 'Lauren, let's spend time.' I'm drowning in my mother."

"And the rest of your family. How do they fit into this picture?"

"My dad's gone a lot. And now my brother is off to college. I'm left behind, feeling smothered and like I want to protect my little sister from being stifled by my mother, too."

More spilled out, as well. Memories from childhood when she used to enjoy the attention—but also felt guilty knowing her brother was being ignored.

"It's like this whole tangle of feelings I don't know how to deal with. Except I do know I can't take her anymore."

"We do have a lot to talk about, Lauren, but we'll sort this all out. Make an appointment for next week, and we'll continue then. Why don't you keep a private journal and see what comes up? You don't need to share it with me if you don't want to, but it may help you to get your feelings down on paper."

Open to anything that might ease her pain, she simply said, "I'll try."

When the door to his office opened, Rose leaped to her feet. Being excluded stung, and she inserted herself back into the scene.

"How did it go in there, sweetheart? Tell me all about it."

"No," said Lauren, her words biting the air.

Rose's face fell at her daughter's rejection. They rode home in silence, the crack opening wider.

Nineteen

BACK HOME IN HER ROOM with her door closed to salvage whatever privacy she could, Lauren searched for the journal Maddy had given her when they graduated.

"Just pretend you're writing to me," Maddy had said when Lauren protested that she wouldn't know what to put in it.

Finding it among a stack of books neatly lined up on her bookshelf, Lauren opened it to see the inscription inside.

For my best friend in the entire world. May we never be separated. Love, Maddy.

Lauren's shoulders crumpled under the weight of Maddy's words.

And now we are separated—forever—and I never got to say, 'thank you.'

Opening the small, floral-print journal, Lauren began.

Dear Maddy,

I know I teased you about your gift last June and never thought I'd use it for this, but I need to talk to you desperately.

I'm drowning—in grief for you, in smothering attention from my mother, and pity for myself and my condition. But, at least I'm alive to feel all these things.

My life is falling apart. My family is the same mess it's always been. Thank God Danny's finally off to college so he can live his own life—not that he wasn't doing that already here since mom and dad never paid attention to him anyway.

And speaking of Rose and Tom, there's a rift growing between them. I think it's because of the tension since my accident, but maybe it was going on before and I just never noticed.

I may never have told you this, but I always envied you. I wanted to be part of your family. I even fantasized that I was your sister. Crazy, huh?

I'm seeing a psychotherapist now, and he suggested I write down my thoughts and feelings to help me come to terms with everything. So here I am, turning to you once again for help. I know you're not here physically, but I feel you next to me all the time.

Please help me.

Your best friend forever,
Lauren.

Closing the journal, Lauren hugged it to her heart before tucking it into her bottom dresser drawer, hidden under the clothes, where she prayed her mother wouldn't find it.

Her thoughts turned to her brother.

I wonder how he's doing at school. I wonder if he realizes how lucky he is to get away from here. I hope his life is better than mine right now. He deserves to be happy and to have some respect.

Maddy was gone, Danny was gone, and she was wallowing in her own misery.

Get it together, Lauren. This is your life now.

Twenty

> leaving around 10 tomorrow morning if u still need a ride. meet in the parking lot behind my dorm. it's hardy.

> I'll b there. thx.

Glad that Kim was still willing to give him a ride after his embarrassing display of drunkenness, Danny knew he had to perform like never before to erase the impression she had of him. Sure, she acted like she was ignoring seeing him blackout drunk—but could she unsee it?

Grabbing his duffel bag from under the bed, he pulled a few things out of his closet to take with him. Passing by Chuck's dresser, which looked like a bag of trash had exploded on it, he spotted a small bag of pills partially hidden in the debris.

Chuck walked in and saw Danny staring at the bag. "Want some for the vacation? From what you've said about home, you need something to knock the edge off, and these'll do it."

Rose's face was staring at him. He tried to erase it. Then he thought about his little 'conference' with his advisor and knew what thin ice he was on.

"Nah, I'm good. Thanks, anyway."

"It'll always be here when you get back," Chuck said, opening the packet and popping a couple in his mouth.

"Hey, how are you getting home? Bus again?"

"No, I'm gettin' a ride with a girl I met in class. Turns out, we live in the same hometown. Just never met."

"Way to go, bud. It's about time you hooked up with somebody."

"We're not exactly hooking up. She's just giving me a ride."

"Is she hot?"

"Damn straight, she is."

"So, there is a man under that exterior somewhere. I say go for it."

"Yeah, we'll see. Have a nice Thanksgiving. See you when we get back."

Danny turned his back on Chuck, taking a backward glance at his dresser.

✦ ✦ ✦ ✦

"So, tell me about your family," Kim said once they were on the highway.

Not wanting to explain about Lauren's accident and condition, Danny just skimmed the surface.

"I have an older sister, Lauren, and a younger sister, Jenny, who's 7." Quickly moving on, he asked her about hers.

"I have a younger brother, Todd, in high school."

The conversation came to a halt as Danny tried to think of what to say to avoid any more personal questions. He wasn't ready to tell the rest of the story. Kim bridged the silence.

"I told you I saw you rehearsing the other day. I'll have to make sure I get to see the production."

Danny cringed not sure he would still be in it if he didn't clean up his act. Parties, booze, pills—and the escape they all afforded him—haunted him. There were so many people he would let down if he flunked out. And now he was adding Kim to the list.

"There's my house on the left, the tan one with the green shutters," he said, grateful for the reprieve of arriving home.

"Nice neighborhood."

For the first time Danny really looked around. The ground under the trees was blanketed with multi-colored leaves, a nod to the demise of fall and a bow to the coming winter months. Funny, he had never paid much attention to the beauty right in front of him. His concentration was broken with the sound of Kim's voice.

"Do you want a ride back on Sunday?"

"That would be great," he said, still not believing his luck.

"Text me when you're leaving, and I'll be ready. Have a great Thanksgiving."

"You too. I'll be in touch."

Her smile, so hauntingly familiar, warmed him.

As he got out, she seemed to be waiting for something. The promise of a phone call, an invitation to see a movie, or. . .?

"Oh, dang," he remembered, reaching into his pocket for a twenty. "Money for gas. I almost forgot. Sorry."

✧ ✧ ✧ ✧

Jenny was staring out the living room window when she saw the car pull into the driveway.

Ooh, it's a girl driving. I wonder if it's his girlfriend.

She went out to greet her brother, then paused on the front walk.

"What? No hugs?" Danny said.

"Well, I'm almost eight, you know."

"Oh, I see. Too old for that now, huh?"

Jenny's cheeks turned red before reaching up to hug him.

"How long can you stay?"

"Aww, I have to go back Sunday. But I'm looking forward to Thanksgiving dinner with everyone."

Well, almost everyone.

Jenny grabbed his arm and pulled him into the house.

"Look who's home," she announced.

Rose, busy with Lauren's PT schedule, pulled herself away from her computer and went down to greet him.

"Hi, Mom. How're things?"

"Good. Your sister is making progress and settling in nicely." No mention of him, how he was doing, how his classes were. No 'nice to see you.'

Just then, Lauren came in and reached her arms up to her brother.

"Hey, how's college, big bro? Hope you're having a good time."

Lying, Danny told her everything was great. He knew how shaky his position was, but there was no way he was going to let on to his mom.

"Where's Dad? Did he know I was coming home today?"

Lauren shot him a look that said, 'leave it alone.' Rose deflected the question by asking Danny about the girl who drove him home.

"I thought you were taking the bus?"

"She's just a friend from school, Mom. I'm getting a ride back with her on Sunday, too."

"Oh, that's nice. Why don't you ask her to come a little early so we can meet her?"

"Really, Mom? She's just doing me a favor. I don't think we need to have a social hour."

"I was only trying to be nice. You don't have to be so snippy."

"Sorry. It's just not a big deal."

Rose turned and left the room in a huff. Danny turned to Lauren when they were alone.

"So, what was that signal all about when I mentioned Dad?"

"I think something is going on between them. Mom's been avoiding him, and he's still staying out late. It's like he doesn't want to be here."

And neither do I, she thought.

"And what's this thing about some girl you don't want us to meet?"

"For God's sake, she just gave me a ride. Let it go."

It was the beginning of his secrets.

Just then, Danny heard the back door open and motioned to Lauren to cut their conversation short. Turning around, he saw a man he hardly recognized. His dad had aged tremendously since he left only a few months before. His eyes were sunken, and he needed a haircut and a shave.

"Hey, Dad, how's it goin'?"

Tom reached out to shake his son's hand. Danny took it and looked him in the eye.

"You're looking good, son. College must be agreeing with you."

Danny's face turned ashen, remembering his party nights.

"Yeah, Dad, everything's cool."

"Good to hear it. Now I'd better get to some last-minute work before I turn in for the night."

It was painfully evident to Danny that his dad hadn't even spoken to his wife.

Lauren wasn't kidding. Something's up.

He and Lauren locked eyes, a knowing understanding passing between them. The vibes in the house were different.

Twenty-One

DANNY KNEW the traditional Foster Thanksgiving was a ritual not to be messed with. Everyone dressed up for dinner, each person had a role to play, and it was all hands on deck with no exceptions. Rose's rules. She worked all morning on the turkey and side dishes, Lauren and Jenny helped set the table with the fine china and crystal, and Danny and his dad oversaw the carving and serving. For one day, they looked like a Norman Rockwell painting of the perfect, grateful family.

Part of the tradition was Rose's insistence that they all say what they were thankful for. The other 364 days of the year, they didn't even eat together. But Rose was Rose, and she wouldn't allow this tradition to die.

Jenny piped up first.

"I'm thankful I have my brother home again."

"Lauren, what about you? What are you thankful for?" asked Rose, oblivious to her daughter's plight.

"I'm grateful for my life," she said, casting her eyes downward, thinking of Maddy.

"Danny?"

"I'm grateful, for. . . ." he paused, gathering his thoughts.

"I'm grateful for second chances."

Rose glanced over to him, but he avoided her eyes.

She'd never get it.

Tom said he was grateful for having his family around him.

Lauren shot Danny a look that said. . .really?

"And what about you, Mommy?" asked Jenny, anxious to get to the turkey.

"Well, I'm grateful that Lauren is sitting with us here on this special occasion."

Crestfallen that she made no mention of his being home too, Danny looked up and said, "Let's eat."

"It's about time," Jenny whispered so only her brother could hear.

Danny gave her a wink as his eyes rested on the bottle of wine his dad was pouring. His body ached for anything to get him through this dinner.

With the last of the dishes stacked in the dishwasher, the family spread out in front of the TV to watch *Miracle on 34th Street*, another Thanksgiving tradition never daring to change. Jenny curled up next to Danny on the sofa.

"Did you get any parts in the plays down at school?"

"Yeah, Jenny, I did. Our first production is just before Christmas break."

"Can we go down and see it, Mom?"

"Honey, you know it's too far away, and that would be too long a trip for Lauren. Maybe another time."

"You never let us see Danny on the stage."

Rose shushed her as the movie started.

Jenny, with Barbie and Ken dolls in her lap, reached over to her big brother and handed him the Ken doll, never noticing her father leave the room. But Danny did. Discreetly following his dad into the kitchen, he watched to see him pull his phone out of his pocket and begin to text.

After four days of playing Barbies with Jenny and hushed conversations with Lauren, it was time for Danny to return to school. Anxiety set in as he realized that he'd have to erase Chuck, parties, and pills from his life.

Please, God, make me strong.

He packed up the few things he had brought with him, leaving his dress clothes in his closet. He would need them for Christmas, another day of tradition, and 'thanks.'

Correction. That makes 363 days of being ignored.

The ride back was more comfortable without the awkward pauses that punctuated the trip home, with Danny and Kim comparing their holidays. Hearing about Kim's family stirred a longing in Danny for some normalcy. For the longest time, he had just assumed that all families had their problems, but Kim's sounded like nirvana. He felt lonelier than ever.

As they parted ways, Danny thanked Kim for the ride.

"No problem. We'll do it again at Christmas break. See you in class."

Danny found himself looking forward to it. But that same gnawing feeling of knowing her from somewhere lingered in a far corner of his mind.

Twenty-Two

WHAT HAPPENED to us, Rose?

Tom's head was bent over November's monthly expense report, but his mind was elsewhere; he was troubled.

When did we fall out of love? Or were we ever really in love? He had thought they were, but maybe he was wrong. Those first few years of marriage were blissful—at least for him. He had hoped to make a new life for Rose—a life of love, acceptance, and belonging. Her early years had been anything but happy. But he knew she needed more than just him.

You needed a child, and I just wasn't ready. I thought we had it all—just the two of us. He wanted them to be everything to each other, at least for a while. She pushed, and he pushed back. He was growing the business and wasn't ready to be a father when she wanted him to be.

I guess I never realized how desperate you were to right a wrong. And slowly, a wedge grew between them, which he knew he couldn't fill.

But, Lauren did.

"Tom?—*Tom*?" He looked up to see Abby, his VP of sales, tapping lightly on his office door. Motioning her in, he nodded toward the leather chair in front of his desk.

"What can I do for you, Abby?" he said, riveted on her deep brown eyes.

"This isn't business exactly. I was just wondering how things were at home—with your daughter. I know she's home from rehab. I'm sure you're excited to have her there for Thanksgiving. Please forgive me for being so personal, but you look so down lately. All this must be quite a strain on you and your family."

He sat back in his chair, hesitant to open his private life here at work. But it also felt good to talk. And he knew from dinners on business trips that Abby was a good listener.

"It's been a big adjustment for everyone, Abby, but it's Lauren who's the real hero. Her resolve makes everyone else's struggle to adjust pale in comparison. She's a real fighter, and we're very proud of her. Thank you for asking."

"You have a beautiful family, Tom," Abby said, staring at the family picture on the corner of his desk. "I hope things improve for all of you—especially Lauren."

She rose from the chair and strolled toward the door,

glancing back momentarily, catching Tom's eye. He stared at her and swallowed the words he wanted to say.

As soon as the door closed behind her, he picked up his cell phone and called home. Rose answered on the first ring.

"Yes, Tom?"

"I'm just checking in on things. How's Lauren today?"

"We're just sitting down to lunch. I'll have her call you later."

"How are you, Rose?"

"Fine."

"Have you heard from Danny?"

"Not yet."

And that was their version of a conversation.

"I'll be home late. Don't wait dinner for me."

When he hung up the phone, he pounded the desk, his mouth filled with the unuttered words he had just silenced. He couldn't win. The wall was rising higher.

He walked down the hall to Abby's office. Standing where she couldn't see him, he took a deep pained breath, turned around, and walked away.

✧ ✧ ✧ ✧

Knowing he should restrain himself and put Abby out of his mind, Tom had succumbed anyway to the temptation to text her on Thanksgiving. He needed—no wanted—to share his day with someone who cared.

> Happy Thanksgiving, Abby. Hope you're having a wonderful day.

> It's been fine, Tom. How was yours?

> Great

he lied. No mention of his wife.

> See you at the office Monday.

Now what have I done, he thought.

Tom closed the office the Friday after Thanksgiving, but he went in as usual. He needed the quiet, the downtime, to think about his life with Rose and where they were headed.

Walking in from the parking lot, he spotted Abby's car.

What's she doing here on her day off?

He needed this time alone, without Abby.

Maybe I can avoid her.

Slipping quietly into his office chair, overly conscious of the creak it always made, he closed his eyes, hoping she hadn't heard him. A slight rap on the door told him differently.

"Come in," he said.

"Hi, Tom. I wasn't expecting you to be in today."

"Same here. Why aren't you enjoying the day off?"

136

"There's not much for me at home, Tom. Since my divorce, things are pretty quiet—lonely actually—so I find more comfort in my work."

Tom could relate. Although he wasn't divorced, sometimes he felt he might as well be.

Lightening the mood, she made a suggestion.

"You look like you're starving, Tom. How about we go out for a quick bite?"

He wanted to be alone, but the offer was too tempting. Maybe what he needed was to talk to someone, perhaps even share some of his troubles with someone who would listen. He hadn't known she was divorced. Maybe she needed an ear as well.

"Sure. That sounds great. I'll meet you in the lobby in five."

Watching the door close behind her, Tom squirmed. *What the hell am I doing?*

❖ ❖ ❖ ❖

The diner was old, and Tom wondered how many secrets the old cracked leather booths held—how many stories had unfolded across the scarred wooden table.

He slipped into one side, Abby, the other. For an instant, he was back in his college town, sitting with Rose. He blinked, and it was gone, Abby now in front of him, looking with the same piercing concentration Rose once had for him.

"Tell me what's going on, Tom. I don't want to pry, but you look like the weight of Goliath is sitting on your shoulders. I know things are hard with Lauren, but—"

She halted before she encroached into his private space.

He began to answer, then stopped.

I can't just dump my problems on her.

Turning it around, he asked how things were with her.

"I didn't realize you were divorced, Abby. How long were you married?"

"It wasn't that long, Tom. Five years. We just weren't a very good match. Different interests, different goals. It was for the best. But sometimes it gets a bit lonely."

Tom knew lonely. Even surrounded by his kids, particularly the antics of his littlest one, Jenny, he sometimes felt he was in a vacuum.

"I'm sorry to hear that, Abby. Life can be complicated sometimes."

Their eyes met briefly until they were interrupted by the waitress, bringing them the menus. Tom was grateful for the disruption. He was getting just a bit too comfortable.

Lunch was followed by innocent small talk until they realized it was three pm. Time had passed so quickly and easily. The comfort level between them was scaring Tom. It was all too easy.

They parted ways in the office parking lot.

"See you Monday, Tom. Have a good weekend."

"You too."

Tom paused to watch a young couple headed to their car, hand in hand. To their separate cars. Just like he and Abby had done—without the hand holding.

Don't go there, Tom.

Twenty-Three

ABBY WAS WAITING for him when he returned from an early morning meeting on Monday. When he caught sight of her sitting in his office, a torrent of mixed emotions seized him. He tried to squash the feelings he was trying so hard to ignore as he approached the door. He ran his hands through his hair and cleared his throat.

"Is there something I can do for you, Abby?"

"We need to talk, Tom."

"About what?"

"You know about what."

"I'm not sure I understand."

"Yes, you do, Tom. Look me in the eye and tell me I'm not getting signals from you. I see it in your eyes, hear it in your voice, notice it in your gestures. Am I wrong?"

Tom glanced at the picture of his family.

"Abby. . . ."

"Wait, Tom, before you answer. If I'm overstepping or misinterpreting things, I apologize. But you look so unhappy. If you don't sense what I do, then I understand. I know you have a family. Just do me this much. Think about it."

Turning to the door, she took one glance back to see Tom staring at her. She left him alone to think.

✧ ✧ ✧ ✧

Shit. Now what," he thought. *What am I supposed to do with that bombshell? I guess I'm not surprised. She's right. There has been something there—for a long time. I should never have texted her on Thanksgiving. I set this in motion.*

Tom thought of all the conversations he'd had with Abby over dinners whenever they were away at conferences. Bit by bit, he had let his problems at home seep into their discussions. And she had always listened intently as if he were the only person in the room. Never saying a word. Just a sympathetic look from time to time. Just like Rose used to do.

Slowly, she had changed from his VP of Sales to—what? What was she? What were they?

THEY. He had just used the word 'they.'

How the hell did I get myself here? I have a wife. Children. A life. He just wanted to rewind the day, take back the looks, unhear Abby's words. But he couldn't. They were already spoken and listened to. They had crossed a boundary.

Twenty-Four

WRACKED WITH MEMORIES of drunken, drugged nights, Danny returned to the dorm after Thanksgiving to begin a clean slate. There were only a few weeks left before the semester was over and he had a mountain of work to do. The conversation with his advisor rang menacingly in his ears. With chest heaving, he lay down on his bed, trying to close his eyes. Then the door slammed open. His roommate was back.

"Hey, bud," Chuck said, very obviously either stoned or drunk.

"Hey, yourself," Danny answered, temptation already swooping in.

"Man, I got to try some new stuff when I was home. It was a trip."

"That's great, Chuck, but I'm sober now, and I plan to stay that way."

"Well, you're no fun anymore."

"Just leave me out of your plans. I need to focus, or I'm gonna' flunk out. And that's not an option for me."

"Suit yourself. I heard there was a great party tonight in town. I guess I'll be going by myself. Be a good boy now and study hard," he said, gesturing with mock applause. He threw down his duffle bag and left the room.

Danny wondered if he should request a new roommate. This one wasn't working out very well.

On impulse, he texted Kim.

> r you doing anything for dinner.

What the hell am I doing? She's not interested in me—she only offered me a ride to be nice. Shit, how do I erase a text? Man, too late—it says delivered.

He just wanted to shrivel up.

His phone pinged with a message.

> nope and I'm starving. meet u in ur lobby in 5.

Knocked off his feet, he replied.

> great. c u downstairs.

Now what?" he thought. *Oh, hell, it's just a bite to eat. It's not like it's a date or anything.*

Danny had three minutes to change his shirt and two minutes to grab the elevator.

When he reached the lobby, Kim was already there.

"Where to?"

She turned around, flashing a familiar dazzling grin.

"How about that diner out in town? We can walk, catch a quick bite, then I have to get back to my paper for English class."

"Sounds good."

Over dinner, she asked about his roommate.

"Oh, he's okay, I guess. Why do you want to know?"

"Well, it's not my place, but he hangs out with a pretty wild crowd."

"Yeah, about that. I'm laying low now. I have to pull my grades up, or they'll kick me out of here."

Danny was grateful she didn't rag on him about how rough he was the night she saw him. Little by little, he was being drawn to her.

All she had to do was say the word.

Twenty-Five

RESOLVE OR NOT, the pressure in Danny's life continued to build. He missed deadlines for his papers, failed tests, and began forgetting his lines for the play. The pit he was in kept getting deeper despite his attempts to shore it up. And it all caved in when the producer replaced him with his understudy for the upcoming production.

"I'm sorry, Danny, but you're just not pulling your weight. I need to rely on you. You have a major role, and it's obvious your head is somewhere else. I hope you get your act together next semester. I see a lot of talent in you, but there must be something getting in the way. Good luck."

Grabbing his backpack, Danny stomped out of the auditorium and went in search of a party. It just didn't matter anymore. He was toast. On his way out of the building, he ran into Chuck. They had barely spoken to each other since Danny blew him off. He called out to him anyway.

"Hey, Chuck. Know of any parties tonight?"

"Whoa, you're back. Sure, there's one in town. I'll let you know when and where. I knew you'd get on board sooner or later."

Danny smirked.

It's not exactly the 'onboard' I was thinking of.

He remembered his conversation with Kim about Chuck.

Eh, he's not so bad. She shouldn't be judging him.

"Sure. I'll be there. I need a break."

The house was deceptively normal, until he went inside.

Darkness enveloped him. His vision clearing, he saw people leaning over old scratched coffee tables, lines of cocaine in front of them. Sleeping bodies were lying all over the place, on stained couches, numbed to their surroundings. Syringes littered the floor.

Man, this place sucks. This is hard-core. I'm not hooked that bad.

From a dark corner, a bearded man, much older than he, approached him and handed him something in a small bag.

"What's this?" Danny asked, his face turning pallid.

"Just some good stuff. Try it. You'll forget all your problems."

Danny did want to forget—home, his mom and dad, Lauren's wrecked life, the terrible feeling that he might flunk out.

He took the bag. Within minutes a kaleidoscope of weird, changing colors flashed on the walls, like lights bouncing off a disco ball. The sounds of muted voices washed like waves into his ears, sloshing and swimming, making no sense.

Then, mercifully, he passed out.

✧ ✧ ✧ ✧

"Hey man," he heard when he crawled up out of oblivion.

"You were so trippin' last night. First time?"

Danny, his head pounding, glanced up to see Chuck standing over him. His mouth tasted like an ashtray.

"Where am I? I gotta get out of here. Geez, this place stinks."

Looking around at all the wasted bodies, Danny vomited. Vague memories of contorted faces and bugs crawling up rainbow-colored walls came into a blurry haze. They were all there last night, along with the garbled voices—taunting him, swirling around on the walls, breathing in his face. It had to be a nightmare.

"Crap, Chuck, what did they give me?'

"Good, huh?"

"It was hell."

"Aw, you'll get used to it. How'd you like that girl you hooked up with?"

"What girl?" Danny answered, terrified of what he couldn't remember.

"That one over there," Chuck answered, pointing to a dirty blonde, her make-up smeared, lying in a corner.

Oh, god, please make this go away. Make this be a nightmare.

"Man, you were all over her. Looked like you were enjoying it, too."

Danny realized it was real. All of it. The drugs, the visions, the girl—everything. He had tripped out.

He scraped himself off the filthy couch and staggered out into the street. Now he had to find his way back to the dorm, navigating back through his nightmare.

Standing in the elevator, Danny realized he no longer felt claustrophobic. Nothing could compare to last night. Nothing could make him feel any worse. When the doors opened, his RA was standing in front of him.

"I think you'd better get to your room and sober up. You look like shit."

Turning down the hall, his eyes still unfocused, he found his room and opened the door, but not before a couple of girls caught sight of him.

"Heeey, Danny, have fun last night?" Then they erupted into laughter as he slammed his door shut.

Please tell me this isn't real, he muttered as he climbed unsteadily up to his bunk.

Twenty-Six

IT WAS OVER. After sleeping much of the next week away, Danny knew he had two choices. Flunk out and go home or withdraw—and go home. Either one landed him back in Arlington, washed up, defeated. He had broken through the thin ice his advisor warned him about and was drowning.

Taking a chance that his advisor would have some free time, he walked back down the long hallway to his office. He may as well have been on death row, the walls pressing in on him as he struggled to put one foot in front of the other.

Tapping lightly on the door, he heard a voice say, "Come in."

"I need some help."

"I suspected as much. What can I do?"

"I'd like to know if I can withdraw before I flunk out."

"There are rules. If you had come to me before the ninth week, there would be no problem. Since we're so far into the semester, you'll have to appeal, and it will depend on the circumstances. Tell me, Danny, is there something else going on in your life I should know about?"

Danny had never wanted to play the 'Lauren' card. He never wanted to admit he had harbored such hatred toward her, or that her accident had affected him so profoundly. And he definitely didn't want to talk about his mother. But now he had no choice.

The story flooded out—the accident, the conflicts at home, his mom's utter lack of faith in him—and even Kim. His nose-dive from alcohol into drugs. His shame.

"I wish you had come to me sooner. We have counselors here who could have helped you navigate these issues."

"I won't talk to a shrink."

"So be it, then. I'll help you with the forms, and you can petition the Dean for withdrawal for personal reasons. But I do hope you'll reconsider talking to someone. You need help."

"Thanks, but I'm good. Just tell me what to do."

Leaving his advisor's office with paperwork in hand, he did the only thing he could think of—find a party. No point in studying. That ship had sailed.

A week later, just before semester exams, his withdrawal was approved.

At least I don't have to say I flunked out. But I still have to go home—where it all started. Can't wait to hear mom's reaction.

Twenty-Seven

Dear Maddy,

I just talked to my brother, and he's coming home. The semester isn't over yet, so I don't know what's going on. He sounded awful, defeated. He wanted this so bad. He tried to get away—from this house, Mom and Dad, probably even from me. I think the only one he hated to leave was Jenny.

This whole family is a mess. My parents don't talk, my mom's impossible, and I'm going stir crazy. I wish you'd knock on the back door and come in like you used to. I'm drowning here—alone.

I thank God every night that I can still talk to you. I may not be able to see you, but I feel you all around me. I even felt you put your arms around me the other night when I was so down.

I miss you so much,

Lauren

A WINTRY MIX of snow, sleet, and freezing rain was falling as Danny climbed down the steps of the bus. The bus terminal was decorated with lights and a small tree to celebrate the season. Danny didn't feel like celebrating.

Hailing a cab to take him home, he waited by the curb as the passing traffic sprayed slush onto his jeans. He could hear Rose now.

Take those dirty clothes off in the mudroom before you come in here. I just washed the floor.

As though he were incapable of making that decision for himself.

"I wonder what else she'll have to say when she sees me?" Drop-out. Failure. No surprise. I've fulfilled her prophecy, and it didn't take me very long.

Kicking the snow off his boots, he opened the back door. Rose was sitting in the kitchen.

"Hey."

"Is that all you can say?"

Yup.

"Talk to you later. Gotta' take my stuff upstairs."

As his sentence trailed off, Lauren rolled in, followed by Jenny.

Jenny ran to hug him, and Lauren gave him a huge grin. Rose walked out of the room.

"I guess I saw that coming," he said. "I'll explain later, you guys. I need a little space right now."

"Come on, Jenny. Let's let Danny unpack."

"I'm open to talking any time, Danny. Whenever you're ready."

Grabbing his suitcase, Danny trudged up to his room. Back to Spiderman, back to his Marvel Posters. At least they weren't flashing.

✧ ✧ ✧ ✧

Showing up for dinner as if nothing had changed was a non-starter. He couldn't pretend. Waiting until everything was cleaned up and Lauren and Jenny were in their rooms, he approached his mom.

"Where's Dad?"

"I have no idea. He's always late. Now, what's this all about?"

Gathering every ounce of courage, Danny told her that he

had withdrawn to figure a few things out. He wasn't expecting a warm and fuzzy 'I'm sorry,' but he wasn't prepared for her next words.

"This is a hell of a way to figure things out."

"Look, Mom. . . ."

"Don't 'look' me. All that money down the drain, and for what? So, you could come back home with nothing to show for it?"

He had never seen her this angry.

"Don't even bother explaining, Danny. But now that you're home, I'll expect some help from you. You can take over where your father has failed."

Danny could see Lauren listening in the hallway. His eyes locked on hers. For a moment, he saw Kim. Then he saw Lauren put her finger to her lips, and he knew not to question his mom's blatant declaration. He would ask about it later.

Twenty-Nine

THE LONG MAHOGANY TABLE was set with bottles of water, notepads, and pens, ready for the board meeting.

Tom had avoided Abby since her bold statement in his office. He averted her eyes as the flow charts and PowerPoint presentations were rolled out for the participants.

After the meeting, she skirted to the door, but he called out to her.

"My office, please, Abby."

"Close the door, please," he said as she stepped in.

"Look, Tom, I'm sorry. . ."

He interrupted before she could finish.

"You're right, Abby. I do feel something for you."

"No, Tom. I was out of line. It was inappropriate. If you would like, I'll turn in my resignation. I crossed a line."

Tom put a finger gently to her lips and reached behind

her to close the blinds to his office. Taking her in his arms, he kissed her.

All the emotions he had been holding so tightly inside rushed to the surface as she melted into his arms and responded passionately to his kiss.

Suddenly, pulling away, she questioned him.

"Where does that leave us now, Tom? You're married with a beautiful family. I can't compete with that."

"There is no competition, Abby. My marriage has been dead for a long time, long before Lauren's accident. I don't know how to proceed from here. I only know what I feel now. I'll have to figure the rest of it out."

He walked behind his desk, gently brushing the picture frame as he went. His broad shoulders sagged with the weight of his actions. He turned to see Abby opening the blinds and slipping quietly out, leaving him alone with his thoughts.

Tom was caught in a vise. Life with Rose had once been good. He had been a faithful husband and father. But Rose began to turn away from him, shutting him out of her life as Lauren took his place in her affections. Part of him under-stood—would always understand. But she had gone too far. He was now husband in name only.

Entering this new territory with Abby frightened him.

He was struggling with his feelings. But the kiss, the passion pouring from her lips and her body were undeniable.

Was it his heart or his body that was aching? What would an affair do to his kids?

Dammit. I don't know how to do this.

Rose may have been hyper-focused on her older daughter, but Tom knew she was no fool. One of the things he had loved so much about her was her keen observation of things. He knew she hadn't missed the signs.

Never home for dinner, more frequent overnight business trips, sleeping in the guest room, "so he wouldn't disturb her when he came in late."

What he didn't know was that Rose already knew—about Abby.

One evening, one of his rare moments of being home early, she threw her gut punch.

"How's your girlfriend?" Rose said, as nonchalantly as if she were asking him what he wanted for dinner.

"What are you talking about? What girlfriend?"

"Do you take me for a fool? How long has it been going on with Abby?"

"This is ridiculous, Rose. Abby's my VP, that's all."

"I saw your text to her on Thanksgiving, Tom. You left

your phone on the table in the kitchen, and the screen was still lit."

"Wait, Rose—"

"No." She cut him off. "It's all suddenly become very clear. I want you out of here. You just dug yourself a hole you can't climb out of. Go—take Abby with you—just don't come back here. I'm sure she'll help you find a place to sleep."

"Wow! I can't believe you just threw me out. You're just as responsible for the distance between us as I am. You've shut me out of your life. The only person in this house you care for is Lauren. There's no room for me anymore."

"How dare you accuse me of being responsible for your affair. That's all on you. Now, leave me to deal with Lauren alone. And you might want to have a word with your son before you go. He's just as much of a mess as you are."

Rose turned her back on Tom, her marriage, and her old life.

Leaving Tom to pack up his things, Rose debated what she would tell the children. Or maybe she would leave that up to Tom. Let him squirm while he explained it to them. Starting that day, December 11th, they would become a family shifted—separated. Tom was moving out, and Danny was moving back in. She would be in charge—of everything.

The sound of drawers slamming, and suitcases being

dragged out of the attic startled Rose out of her thoughts, and she looked into the hall to see her three children staring at her.

"What's going on, Mother?" asked Lauren. What's all the shouting about? What's dad doing?"

An awkward silence ensued. How much should she share? Would it be cruel to mention the affair? Had they suspected something was wrong before she did?

"I'll let your father explain when he comes down. It's complicated."

At that moment, she heard the bedroom door open and watched her husband of twenty-five years drag suitcases stuffed with memories of their life together down the stairs and into the foyer.

"Daddy?" Jenny stammered. "Where are you going?"

"It's okay, honey. I'm just going away for a little while. I won't be far, and I'll see you all the time. Danny, Lauren, your mother and I are taking some time apart. Everything will be alright."

Rose shot him a look of contempt.

"You can leave your key on the console table," she said, motioning to his key ring.

She watched him hug his children one by one and walk out the front door to his car. She turned off the porch lights after him.

Thirty

Dear Maddly,

I can't believe what just happened. Mom threw dad out of the house. I knew they weren't getting along, but this is extreme. There must be something going on that they can't—or won't say.

Jenny's. . .

Before Lauren could finish her entry, Rose barged into her room, carrying folded laundry. No knock, no consideration for her privacy.

"Mother! How about letting me know before just assuming you can come in."

"What could you possibly be hiding that you can't share with me? Is that a diary?"

Flashbacks to her childhood diary roared in before Rose chased them away.

"It's nothing, Mother," Lauren said, slipping the journal under a stack of books on her desk.

"Careful what you put down on paper."

"Leave it alone, Mother. It's my business what I write."

You'd never know by her mood that she just threw her husband out of the house.

"Fine," said Rose, puffs of frigid air escaping her mouth. Putting Lauren's 'personals' in her drawers, she turned to hang up her other clothes in the closet. She glanced back over at the desk to see some of Lauren's textbooks from her first semester at school.

Her voice now suddenly dripping with warmth, she said, "why don't I put those away for you, sweetheart. You won't be needing them now."

A sinking feeling rushed into Lauren's body.

"Maybe later, Mother. I'm a little tired. I think I'll take a little nap. Can you help me to bed?"

Lauren stretched out with her flowered comforter, feigning fatigue. She would have to find a safe place for her journal. Her mother was just too nosy.

Moments after her mother left the room, Lauren heard her footfalls going up the steps. She slipped out of bed and into her wheelchair.

Whew, that was close, Maddy. Mother just barged in as usual while I was writing to you. Honestly, that woman hasn't got a courteous bone in her body. I guess my life is just fair game.

Anyway, like I was saying, Mom threw Dad out of the house. Jenny's beside herself, crying all the time, asking when he's coming home.

I'm still not sure why Danny dropped out of W&M, but part of me is glad he's home. We three have to stick together now. I hope he'll confide in me. We were getting close before he left. I hope we can get that back.

I miss you,

Lauren

Thirty-One

AFTER DRIVING aimlessly through the streets for hours, Tom found himself parked in front of Abby's apartment building, ten miles away from his home in Arlington.

The View at Liberty Center was a high-end apartment complex in the Ballston neighborhood minutes from D.C. and the Orange Metro Line. And only minutes from their office. Its convenience to everything made it highly sought after—and very expensive.

Tom's emotions were twisting inside him like a funnel cloud about to touch down. He just didn't know where. His resentment toward Rose had driven him straight to Abby. But his love for his kids had him trapped in the car, on the street, paralyzed.

Convincing himself that this was his only option, he approached the sharply dressed doorman and asked for Abby's apartment number.

"Your name, please, sir?"

"Tom Foster."

Turning to the intercom, he buzzed her number.

"Ms. Mansfield, there's a Tom Foster here to see you."

Tom heard her inhale and pause before answering. He knew this was a mistake, but it was too late—the doorman had already announced him.

"Please have him come up, Harold."

"Yes, Ma'am," he politely answered and ushered Tom inside.

Crossing the lush lobby to the elevator, past the luxuriously modern furnishings, Tom found it hard to take a deep breath.

This is a bad idea, he thought, pulling his hand away from the UP arrow just as he was about to press the button. *I'm just reacting to Rose's impulsiveness. She'll rethink things in the morning and let me back home.*

The door slid quietly open, and a man, woman, and two children stepped out. Tom moved aside to let them pass, and hesitating, he watched the elevator door close, and the numbers begin to rise. The apprehension he felt reminded him of standing in front of the hospital elevator on his way up to see his daughter, not knowing how serious her injuries were.

The guard at the security desk eyed him suspiciously.

"Can I help you with anything?" he asked, striding toward him, his gun strapped to his side. His eyes were cool, calculating, sizing Tom up.

"Uh, no. I'm good. I just realized how late it is, and I'm not sure I want to bother the young lady at this hour. It can wait until tomorrow."

Tom backed away from the elevator, his eyes lowered, and walked out through the lobby, heels lightly tapping the tiles.

Approaching the doorman again, he asked him to buzz Ms. Mansfield back. "Send my apologies. I'll see her at the office tomorrow."

Pulling the collar of his overcoat up against the night chill, he walked back to the parking garage. It had cost him $7.50 to change his mind and run scared.

The nearest hotel was a stone's throw from Abby's apartment. Checking in, Tom took the elevator up to his room. He pulled the key card from his trouser pocket and passed it over the lock, watching the light turn green.

He should have put the brakes on when he saw the barriers piling up against him. He should have put Abby in the rearview mirror as soon as she opened the Pandora's box and told him how she felt.

But he didn't. He succumbed to her freshness, her sincerity, her openness. He hadn't protested when Rose threw him out of the house—or at least not as much as he should have. He let it all happen. Somewhere in the back of his soul, he had wanted this, had welcomed it even.

But what about the children? He had a son who was drowning, a daughter mired in grief, and a little one who needed her daddy.

Looking at the king-sized bed enveloped in lush bedding, he thought of Rose and their bed at home that he had barely slept in these past few months. He blinked, and a vision of Abby lying there waiting for him pushed its way in.

Nausea rose in his belly. He still had choices. And the path of his life depended on the decision he was about to make.

Tom stared at the ceiling most of the night, unable to sleep. He had expected to hear from Abby after the doorman had announced his arrival and then departure. And then he began to read his own words written, scrambled, on the stark white ceiling.

My marriage has been dead a long time. You're right, Abby, I do feel something for you.

Perhaps it's best this way. She doesn't know I've been kicked out of my own house, and if she invited me to stay with her, I'm sure I'd cave to the temptation. It's too early—too many circumstances and emotions to sort through. Maybe I need to try harder with Rose. Try to be a real family again. And I still don't know what she meant about Danny being just as much of a mess as I am. I hoped he had gotten what he wanted when he went away. I guess none of us really does get away.

It was 4:37 when her text came in.

> Why were u here? Why didn't you come up? Please call me.

> Taking a few days off. Don't worry.

Tom needed this time to determine which path of life he should follow—if he even had a choice with his family—and Rose. He had broken a sacred seal, although he had never slept with Abby. But it didn't make any difference in Rose's eyes. She considered him a cheater.

Maybe that's what I am at least in thought if not yet in deed.

Thirty-Two

"SO, I GUESS your dreams of Broadway have gone up in smoke," Rose said to Danny the next morning. "Didn't you get a good enough part?"

"Stop, Mom. I don't want to talk about it, okay?"

"You can't just trot back into the family without an explanation."

"You call this a family? I just watched Dad pack a suitcase and leave. I don't know why, and I don't want to know. All I know is that we're even more messed up than I thought we were. You're obsessed with Lauren, and you ignore Jenny. You want to know why I dropped out? Here's why. I got in with the wrong people, 'cause I wanted to belong somewhere. I sure never belonged here. I didn't want to flunk out, so I withdrew and said it was for personal reasons. You happy now?"

Watching his mom's face turn crimson, her lips a rigid

line across her face, Danny feared he had gone too far. He had never spoken to Rose that way before.

"So now it's my fault that you couldn't be the person you all wanted us to believe you were? I warned you about overinflating yourself. Now you'll have to suffer the consequences. And one way or another, you'll pay back every penny we wasted on you."

Rose turned her back on him once again.

He texted Josh.

> i need to get out of my head.
> meet u at our spot.

❖ ❖ ❖ ❖

"Man, I didn't expect to see you home so soon. And you look like shit," said Josh as Danny scuffed his feet across the cracked concrete and kicked the broken beer bottles out of his way.

"I feel like shit, too. First, home was hell; then, I got kicked out of the play for not showing up. I got hooked bad, and now I'm back in the same house where it all started. And now it looks like my mom and dad have split up. You gotta' help me, man."

"No shit. They split? Yeah, no sweat. I found some good stuff when you were gone, but it's not cheap. How much you got?"

"I'll get it somehow. Just help me over the edge, 'k?"

Looking around for cops, and seeing none, Josh passed him a packet.

"You owe me."

"You're the best. Promise, I'll get you the cash. Later, man."

"You're sure you don't want anything stronger. I can get my hands on some fentanyl."

"If I go down that road, I'll never come back up. I can't. Thanks, anyway."

Turning away, Danny realized he hadn't gotten away from Chuck. He had just replaced him with Josh.

✧ ✧ ✧ ✧

Arriving home, Danny slipped quietly up to his room. The buzz from Josh's stash had him feeling pretty good. It wasn't even close to what he felt at that ill-fated party at school. Just enough to mellow him out. He thought about the fentanyl and wondered how that would make him feel. No doubt it would solve all his problems.

I can't. I won't. That would be the end for me. I'll never go there. My life would be over.

For now, he just had to figure a way to pay Josh back. He needed a job.

Lying back on his bed, high on this new cocktail, he

thought about Kim. He hadn't even told her he was leaving. He considered texting her, but what would he say?

Hey, Kim. I'm busted. Had to drop out before they kicked me out. Text me when you get home for Christmas.

Riiiiight. Can't imagine that happening. I might as well kiss her good-bye.

✧ ✧ ✧ ✧

The daily paper lay open on the kitchen table, black circles ringing possible job opportunities. Desperate for money with Josh at his heels and his mom's threat to 'collect' his wasted school debt, Danny had to act fast.

A position at a local convenience store a few blocks away caught his attention. He was desperate enough to take anything, including stocking shelves. Slipping on his jacket and pulling a ball cap low over his eyes, he walked to the corner to inquire.

"I've come about the position in the paper," he said when the clerk asked if he could get anything for him.

"Oh, you'll want to talk to my dad about that."

Just then, the door to the storage room opened, and a man about Danny's father's age came up to the counter.

"What can I do for you—it's Danny, isn't it? I'm Bill Hudson."

"Yes, sir, Mr. Hudson. I came about the ad for the stock boy you had in the paper."

Thoughts of his next drug buy and the money he already owed Josh put an edge in his voice. Not wanting to appear desperate, he shoved his trembling hands in his jeans' pockets.

"Well, we certainly could use a hand around here if you don't mind some manual, menial labor. It's just the two of us here most of the time when Andy here isn't at school. What hours can you work?"

"I'm open for anything, sir, including nights. I live a few blocks away and can walk or catch the bus, so transportation isn't a problem."

"I'm sorry, what did you say your last name was again?"

"Foster."

Bill Hudson's eyes flickered in recognition.

"I'm sorry about your sister."

"Thanks, Mr. Hudson. She's doing better now, but my mom needs me around. This job will help."

"Then it's yours. Can you start tomorrow morning around eight?"

"You bet. Nice to meet you—and you too, Andy."

His lungs expanding with relief, Danny texted Josh.

> got a job. will have ur money soon.
> hook me up with ur supplier ASAP.
> talk tonight.

Thirty-Three

> hey. haven't seen u. need a ride for Xmas?

Danny stared at the text from Kim. The one person who had seen him bottom out still seemed to care about him.

Maybe I should ignore her. Nah, she was nice to me. She deserves better.

Groping through his thoughts for the right words, he copped out and placed the blame on his family troubles.

Although that's not far from the truth. It all started at home, and I'm right back there again.

> had to drop out. needed at home. maybe c u over the break.

He didn't expect an answer.

> ill txt when i get home. hope to c u.

Rattled with her quick response, Danny panicked.

How long would he be able to keep up his charade about being needed at home? She wasn't stupid. She'd figure it out. She had seen his "crowd"—even voiced her concerns—and disapproval. She'd seen him shit-faced.

Why does she even care?

Jenny's persistent voice broke his train of thought.

"Earth to Danny. Did you hear what I just asked you? You were really on another planet."

"Huh? What did you say?"

"I said, can we go to the mall to get something for Mom and Dad for Christmas?"

I wonder if we'll even see Dad at Christmas. Damn, I don't even know where the hell he's living.

"Sure. How about tomorrow? It's Saturday, and I don't have to work at the store."

"Can Lisa come, too?"

"Uh, huh."

His thoughts turned to Lauren. She needed to get out too—away from the house, out among people. He found her in the kitchen, browsing through some recipes.

"Where's Mom?"

"Upstairs. Why?"

"I'm taking you to the mall to do some Christmas shopping tomorrow. I'll let her know. I'm taking Jenny and Lisa, too."

"You're a lifesaver. I can't take much more of her

undivided attention. Do you think she even misses Dad? It's life as usual for her. She hasn't missed a beat."

A hint of sadness clouded her usually bright green eyes.

"I miss him," she said.

"So do I," he replied.

✧ ✧ ✧ ✧

The mall was a madhouse on steroids for the holidays. Parking was a challenge, but Danny had the handicapped sticker in the car and was able to get up close to the building.

"This is so cool," Jenny said to Lisa. "We get to park way up front."

Danny shot her a look of disapproval, but Lauren waved him off.

"She's just a kid, Danny. She doesn't mean anything by it. Let it go."

Danny watched as the light in her eyes grew even dimmer.

The mall was ablaze with lights, ornaments, and greenery everywhere. Massive silver stars hung from the rafters, and in the center was a two-story Christmas tree trimmed with gold and red balls. In the distance, they could hear the melodious sounds of carolers serenading the shoppers.

Danny was thirteen, Lauren fourteen, Jenny only three. The house was festively decorated with Santas, and angels adorned the fireplace mantel. Wrapped packages spilled out from under the tree.

The teenagers dragged themselves from their beds in the early hours of Christmas morning, amid squeals of surprise coming from Jenny who still believed that Santa had come down the chimney and deposited the wealth of presents.

One by one, the gifts were opened to smiling faces accompanied by shrieks of delight from Jenny.

Only Danny counted the presents, comparing his to Lauren's.

When the little girls were out of earshot, Danny spoke openly.

"This is the first time we've ever bought Mom and Dad separate gifts. I guess there's no point in getting a joint present when they're living separately now."

"Do you think this is permanent? I mean, are they done with each other?" Lauren asked.

"It doesn't look good. Let's face it; it didn't come as a complete surprise. I don't know what tipped them over the edge. Especially Mom. I've never seen her rail at him like that. I couldn't hear what they were saying, but it sure sounded like all hell broke loose."

"It stinks. But whatever happened between them must be bad. I'm just afraid that my accident made everything worse. It pushed the wedge deep between them."

"You can't take that on, Lauren. The blame rests on them.

They did this—whatever it is—to each other. And my disaster with school sure didn't help. I'm a huge disappointment to them."

"Cut it out. You're great at what you do. I don't know what happened down at school—and you don't have to tell me—but I'm on your side. We just have to make sure Jenny isn't scarred from their separation."

Her eyes met his, and an understanding passed between them.

"Now let's get on with this shopping. We still need to find something for Dad."

Leaving the store where they had picked out a handbag for Rose, Danny halted in his tracks, a lady almost running into him from behind. Up ahead, he saw Kim coming in their direction. He attempted to distract everyone, but Jenny was the first to spot her.

"Isn't that the girl who drove you home at Thanksgiving?" Jenny asked.

Lauren looked where Jenny was pointing. A girl wearing stylish ripped jeans and a sweater was coming toward them.

Kim spotted Danny first before she saw who was with him. He had never told her that his sister was in a wheelchair.

How awful. I wonder what happened.

Making her way through the crowd, she locked eyes with Lauren. Her skin prickled.

Lauren watched her coming toward them and smiled.

That's when it clicked for Danny.

That's why she looks so familiar. It's her smile—it's almost like Lauren's.

Danny was at a loss. He did the only thing he could—he introduced them.

"It's very nice meeting all of you."

Jenny was the first to blurt out the obvious.

"If you had lighter hair and took off your glasses, you'd sorta look like my sister."

"Don't be ridiculous," said Lauren, looking twice at Kim. "She's lovely. And I look like—this."

Realizing that a wall of awkwardness had just dropped between them halting the conversation, Kim took the lead.

"Well, I guess I'll get going with my shopping. Hey, Danny, text me when you have time, so we can catch up."

Turning her back on the discomfort, Kim melted into the crowd. Meeting Lauren was—different. She felt like she could see inside her—like there was a current between them. Her scalp tingled.

"Let's get going, guys. We have lots more shopping to do," said Lauren, still trying to process the encounter. She shot Danny a look that said, *we've got some talking to do.*

Thirty-Four

WHY DID *I have to run into her? It just brought everything back—school, the theatre—and her.* A current of shame and self-loathing returned. He had no one to blame but himself.

I had it all and threw it away. And for what? A little bit of escape, a little bit of acceptance, a little bit of belonging?

He didn't know where he belonged anymore. Everything he thought would give him peace he had squandered. Maybe it was right that his mom always preferred Lauren over him. She was everything he wasn't. She'd lived their dream for them. And he didn't. All he'd ever done was disappoint them. And now he was stuck back home feeling like crap.

He needed something to put him back on his feet.

He texted Josh.

> got money. meet u same place.
> 1 hour.

✧ ✧ ✧ ✧

The transaction was brief: money for drugs.

"Thanks, man. You're a lifesaver."

"You're sure you don't want anything stronger? I can still get ahold of some China White."

"Yeah?"

"It'll cost."

"Maybe."

"What happened at school? I thought you were living your dream."

"I screwed up. How'd you get in so deep?"

"Shit happens. Tonight, at Billie's? He's got the good stuff."

"Yeah, later, bro."

✧ ✧ ✧ ✧

With every paycheck squandered on the addiction of the day, Danny withdrew further into himself and away from reality. Josh became his lifeline. He was living in a vacuum, losing himself daily in an alcoholic or drug-induced haze. Time centered around his next fix.

"When was the last time you showered, Danny. You look pretty ripe," Lauren said when he finally made an appearance in the kitchen scrounging for something to eat.

"*Phew*, you stink," said Jenny.

"Stuff it."

Grabbing some leftover cold pizza, he left the room, lifting his armpit as he walked past his sisters.

"Gross. What's wrong with him?" Jenny jeered.

"I don't know. He's probably just ticked off over some girl."

"Maybe it's that girl, Kim, we met in the mall. Maybe she is his girlfriend."

"Well, if she is, she sure won't last long with him looking like that. Anyway, are you seeing Lisa today?"

"Yup. Her mom's coming over later to watch us 'cause mom has to go out for a while."

Us. Does she think I need a babysitter, too?

Livid that her mother thought so little of her ability to take care of herself, Lauren snapped.

"Mother," she yelled through the house. "Where are you?"

Rose appeared in the doorway within seconds.

"Oh, thank God you're all right. I thought you were hurt."

"Stop it, Mother. Just stop it. I'm sick to death of being treated like a baby."

"I don't mean to, honey. I'm just concerned about you."

"Jenny said Angela's coming over to babysit while you're out. Are you kidding me?"

"She's coming just to watch the girls."

"As if I can't?"

"Well. . .if something goes wrong. . . .""

"I give up. You're never going to let me forget that I'm damaged. . .that I'm not whole anymore. . .that. . .oh, forget it. It will be good to talk to someone else for a change."

Rose attempted to interject, but Lauren threw up her hands and left the room.

"Wow, that was tense," said Jenny under her breath, as she watched her mother's face go from pink to white in the space of two minutes.

"I think I'll just go get my Barbies and wait for Lisa."

Rose was left standing alone.

Dear Maddy,

I've had it. My mother just asked Lisa's mom to come over to watch the girls while she goes out. She didn't even ask me if I would do it. She doesn't trust me. I'm not that broken. If she doesn't let me do for myself, I'll never get any independence and get away. That's all I want to do—get away.

Danny's a mess. I think there's more going on with him than just leaving school. I'm pretty sure he's into drugs. I've seen that look—you did too when we were down at school. You could always tell just by looking at them—the sunken eyes, the runny noses. I don't want to think that of him, but he looks awful.

He's always kept his feelings buttoned-up, hidden inside where they couldn't be seen or *touched. But today, he lashed out with Jenny in the room. I know he adores her, but he snapped. I wish I could help. Maybe I need to confront him.*

If you were here, you'd tell me what to do. I guess I'll have to channel you and listen.

Lauren

Lauren finished her entry to Maddy just as the doorbell rang. She had nothing against Angela; in fact, she liked her a lot. She had been a godsend to Jenny, especially right after the accident, and had shielded her from the worst of the trauma by having her over often to play with Lisa.

If only Mom would pay as much attention to her youngest child.

Lauren went into the family room just as her mother was going out the door. She and Angela looked at each other, and each knew the awkwardness that passed between them.

Angela spoke first.

"Look, Lauren. . . ."

"It's okay, Angela, I'm fine. This is something I have to get used to with my mother. I'm not sure when she'll be able to trust me or realize that I'm okay by myself. But I do appreciate your coming over."

She hesitated before continuing.

"Can I ask you something?"

Angela shifted uncomfortably. "Of course. Anything."

"For as long as you've known our family—what right after

Danny was born—has my mother always been this way about me? And did you ever sense anything that would indicate that my parents would separate like this? I'm sorry if I'm putting you in a bad spot, but I'm trying to figure her—them—out."

Carefully dodging the question, Angela lied.

"Honestly, Lauren, I'm as surprised as you that they separated. But all families have their troubles and secrets, so I couldn't say. Hopefully, they'll work things out. Now, shall we get some lunch for you girls?"

Angela had become privy to some tidbits about the family because of Lisa's friendship with Jenny. Whenever the girls played with their Barbies, the "conversations" the dolls had were often telling.

"You're never home anymore," said Barbie to Ken. "You don't care about us."

and

"Where have you been, Tom? You're late again."

and

"Lauren, honey, let me do that for you."

Bits and pieces of the Foster family life as seen through a seven-year-old's eyes. But she kept these things to herself, nurturing Jenny along with her own daughter.

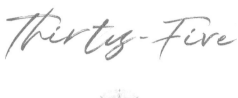

DANNY STARED at the China White hidden inside his nightstand. That night at Billie's, he had succumbed and bought some. So far, he hadn't tried it. But now the devil was taunting him, tempting him. His hands trembled as he reached for it. The coke wasn't good enough anymore. He needed a better high.

Just this once, he rationalized. *Just to get through this day, then I'll quit. I just jumped all over my sisters. They don't get it. Nobody does. I've lost everything.*

He laid out the lines on his desk and snorted. Within minutes he was euphoric. He crawled back into bed.

He woke to the thundering jolt of a fist banging on his door. "What the hell. Who is it?"

"It's me," said his mother. "I thought you had to go to work today."

Rolling over to look at the neon numbers on the clock, Danny realized he had missed an entire day. Blacked out. Unconscious. Trashed. He checked the texts on his phone—and the missed calls. His boss had been trying to get in touch with him. He hit redial.

"Hey, Mr. Hudson, it's Danny."

"Where have you been. You missed work yesterday, and you're late again today. I've been trying to reach you. I depended on you, Danny."

"I was sick," he lied, "and I slept all day. I didn't even hear my phone. I'm so sorry. It won't happen again. I'll be there in an hour, okay?"

"I'll be waiting. I hope you're feeling better."

Danny crawled out from under the tangled covers of his bed and made it over to the bathroom. One glance in the mirror propelled him back to the last party at school with Chuck. He saw the wasted bodies, the ashen faces, the gaunt expressions compressed into one image, and it was staring back at him. He had become one of them.

Jumping into a cold shower to jolt him out of his stupor and black out the image he had just seen, he imagined himself back up on stage, disappearing into another character, playing a role to hide behind. Maybe he would get out of the shower and realize that it had all been an act, a scene in his play, that he wasn't an addict.

Nice try, Danny boy. I couldn't even dream this up. It's real,

*and I'm bottoming out. And now I have to get to work, pretend
I'm fine and make some money to pay Josh.*

For the first time in months, he was petrified.

❖ ❖ ❖ ❖

Cleaned up as best he could, he went downstairs to make
his excuses to his sisters for his outburst the day before. He
was hoping he could lie his way through it. Lauren was waiting for him.

"Hey, um, listen. . ."

"Danny, it's me. Talk to me. What's going on? And don't
tell me you're just sick. How long have you been hooked?"

"Huh, what?"

"Don't, huh, what me. I may not have been at college for
long, but I saw enough. Hell, I saw it when I was still in high
school. You can't hide it, Danny. Maybe Mom is oblivious, but
I know the signs of drugs when I see them. I want to help.
Just talk to me."

His face turning crimson, Danny forced the tears from
spilling over.

"I can't talk about it now. I'm late for work. But I will.
Promise. Please don't tell Mom."

"Of course, not. But I do want to listen. You've been here
for me, and now I want to pay the favor back. Tonight, okay?"

Lauren reached out her hand to him, but the shame
wouldn't allow him to take it. Grabbing his jacket from the

187

peg on the mudroom coat rack, he walked out the door. Lauren watched his hunched shoulders recede into the morning sun. She knew there was no sun left in her brother's life anymore.

We're both in the shadows now.

Thirty-Six

Hey Mads,

Remember when I told you I wished I could live at your house? Well, now I wish I could live with the Franconi's.

Angela was here all afternoon yesterday, and she was such a breath of fresh air compared to my mother. She never once asked if I needed help with anything. We just sat and talked like we were family.

I finally got up the nerve to ask her if my mother was always like this with me, and if she knew of any problems that would have caused my mom and dad to split. She said she hadn't noticed anything, but I saw the look in her eyes. I know she was holding something back.

She also asked about Danny and why he was back home. I really couldn't go there with her although I wanted to. She's so easy to talk to, and now that I can only speak to you on paper or in my mind, I could use a good ear. It would be nice to have a confidante, someone I could trust with my feelings. I tell them all to Dr. Goldman, but he's a shrink, and that's his job. I'd just like a friend.

Anyway, it didn't turn out so bad having her here after all. Lisa's a lucky girl to have her for a mom. I wish Jenny could feel as loved. But, maybe she's too young to notice not getting so much attention. She's happy in her own little world. But someday she'll grow up and see what's going on in this family.

Talk to you later.

L.

THE JINGLING BELL over the door to the store reverberated like a gong in Danny's ears. The fluorescent lights overhead stabbed at his eyes. The tapping sounds of metal—the noise of cans being stacked and rearranged—pounded in his ears

Peering over the top shelf, Bill Hudson watched Danny come into the store more than an hour late for his shift.

"I'm so sorry, Mr. Hudson. Here, let me take over there."

"I'll give you the benefit of the doubt this time, son, but next time—if there is a next time—I'll expect a call from you if you're sick. Andy's in school until three, and it's difficult for me to stock and run the store at the same time. That's why I hired you. I need you here when I schedule you."

"I understand, sir. It won't happen again."

As Bill turned the rest of the stocking over to Danny, he took notice of his trembling hands.

"Are you sure you're all right now? I don't need you collapsing on me."

"No, I'm fine. It must just have been the flu that knocked me down. I feel better."

The lying was becoming second nature. It all came so easily. Just like learning lines from a play, he was learning the cop-outs, the excuses, anything that would fly.

At the sound of the bell, he glanced up to see one of his neighbors breezing through the door. Crouching down to the lowest shelf trying not to be seen, he tuned in to the words flying haphazardly from her mouth.

"I don't know, Bill. Something sure is strange over at the Foster's. I haven't seen Tom for ages, and I know that boy of theirs is back home from school. I don't know if he flunked out or what. I've seen Angela Franconi there a few times lately. I'll have to see if she knows anything when I see her."

Bill Hudson let her ramble, not wanting to comment on the private goings-on of a family he knew, especially when Danny was working for him. Quickly checking her out at the register, he glanced over to see Danny hovering, stalling, until she left. If there was something unusual happening with the Fosters, he would wait for Danny to tell him. He had no use for rumors.

Danny sagged against the shelves, his knees almost buckling beneath him. When had his family become the hot topic of the neighborhood? Wasn't anything private anymore? Did anyone know about his addiction?

He heard garbled words swimming around him as if he were underwater.

"She sure is a talker, isn't she?"

"Huh? Oh, yeah. I heard what she said about my family."

"It's your business, Danny. No one else's. All I ask is that you show up when you're supposed to and do the work I expect. Every family has its troubles and problems to work out. I like you. If there's anything I can do, ask. In the meantime, Andy will be getting home soon to take over. I suggest you go home and get some rest. You're still looking pretty shaky."

"Thanks, Mr. Hudson. But I'm fine. I appreciate the chance you're giving me. What she said, you know. . ."

"Danny, forget her. As I said, it's your family's business. I know things have been tough since your sister's accident. Don't let town gossip get under your skin. That's all it is—gossip. Now, go home, take care of yourself, and I'll see you tomorrow morning—on time. Okay?"

"You bet. See you in the morning."

With all the acting ability he could muster, Danny pushed back his shoulders, exuding confidence he no longer had, held his head up high, and left the store, the bell ringing with his departure. This time, instead of a gong, it sounded more like a death knell.

Thirty-Eight

"TOM, IT'S ROSE."

Hoping Rose had had a change of heart, Tom answered, his knee bouncing rapidly under the table.

"Yes, Rose. What can I do for you?"

"Christmas is next Friday, and Jenny asked if you could come over. Come after one, after we've finished dinner, and visit with the children for a couple of hours. I don't want to ruin their Christmas just because you've ruined mine."

Stomach clenched, his hopes dashed, Tom agreed to her terms so he could see his children.

It's worse than I thought. She wants me out of her life.

With a last-ditch effort, he gave one last attempt.

"Can we at least have dinner together?"

"No. Just come later for the children."

Rose hung up the phone.

Tom dialed Abby. Rose had made up his mind for him.

✧ ✧ ✧ ✧

This time with his anger and disappointment giving him courage, Tom had the doorman announce him. He needed to be needed.

As the elevator approached Abby's floor, Tom tried to piece together what he was going to say to her.

I care for you.

I need you.

I love. . . .

Tom knocked gently, and the door opened immediately. Taking one look at Abby, it all spilled out:

"I care for you. I need you." He couldn't get out the word 'love.'

Searching deep into her eyes for a reaction, Tom knew he was ready to break his vows.

"Are you sure, Tom?"

"I've never been surer."

She reached out her hand and led him to the bedroom, the ambient light from the bedside table casting a sultry glow on the silk sheets.

"Why. . .? She began to say before he laid a gentle finger to her inviting lips.

"We'll talk later," he responded, taking her in his arms and softly lowering her onto the bed.

The air suddenly shifted, and Abby sat up.

"Wait, Tom. Why now? What's changed? Why did you come the other night and then leave?"

"Rose kicked me out the other night. She found out about us. She saw the text I sent you on Thanksgiving. She was just waiting for the right moment for maximum impact to confront me. She refused to listen to me and just told me to leave. I needed to see you and then got cold feet, so I went to a hotel."

"There's no 'us' for her to find out about. We haven't done anything wrong—at least not yet." Abby flushed at where her thoughts were taking her.

"I want you in my life. I need you. I care deeply for you."

Abby was acutely aware of the absence of the word 'love.'

"As much as I want you, I can't do this now. You're on the rebound from what may be a 'heat of the moment' reaction from your wife. I need to be sure that this is real. I've been down this road before, trusting in something that wasn't real, and it hurt. Please take more time. If you're sure this is what you want—that I'm who you want, then I'll be here for you. I can't take this lightly. It's not the kind of person I am."

Tom, overwhelmed with her honesty and convictions, drew away from her and walked over to the bedroom door.

"Thank you."

"For what?"

"For making sure this isn't a mistake. But know this. When I do come back—and I will—I will be sure."

"And I'll be here. Goodnight, Tom."

Thirty-Nine

A SCARCITY OF wrinkled Christmas paper lay beneath the eight-foot tree on the first Christmas morning since Lauren's accident and the first one without Tom present. Lauren's make-up and new cell phone, and Danny's iPad and gift cards fit tidily into gift bags, creating a streamlined gift exchange. With one exception.

Jenny, now eight, and teetering on the verge of questioning how Santa could come down the chimney without getting his butt burned, had a mountain of gifts. Arts and crafts kits, whatever the latest "must-have" fad was, books, and yes, Barbies, spilled out in a wide radius from the Santa tree skirt. And the most prized possession of all was Barbie's Dream House, which had held the place of honor at the top of her wish list since September.

"When's Daddy coming? I can't wait to show him Barbie's house."

"He'll be here after dinner. Now, why don't you take your things up to your room so we can clean up here," said Rose, her efficient nature not even diminished by the excitement of Christmas morning.

"I wish she had let him come for the gift opening at least for Jenny's sake," whispered Lauren to Danny out of earshot of her mother.

"Yeah, it would have been nice for him to see the look on her face. They could have at least Facetimed. But he'll be here for a little while. You know, I don't even know where he's living right now. All we have is his cell phone number to get in touch with him," answered Danny.

"I didn't want to tell you, but I overheard part of their conversation the day she told him to leave, and I distinctly heard him mention Abby, his VP. Do you think they're having an affair and that's why Rose got so mad?"

"Your guess is as good as mine, Lauren. It would make sense, though—his late hours, his long business trips, his lack of connection with us."

"I'm not sure I'd even blame him. I know that's hard to hear but think about it. Mom doesn't give him the time of day since my accident—hell, even long before that. I wouldn't blame him for turning to someone else."

"That's harsh, Lauren. I can't believe he'd jeopardize the family by having an affair."

Their conversation was cut short when Rose called them to the dinner table. Roast beef, mashed potatoes, green bean casserole, rolls, and butter adorned the buffet. Rose insisted they sit and say grace before passing around the food.

She acts as though everything is the same, Danny thought, his dad's empty chair at the head of the table, glaring at him.

The conversation was stilted until Jenny broke it open.

"I can't wait to show Daddy my Barbie Dream House. It is the best, best, best present ever."

"Well, I'm sure your daddy will be happy for you. And I'll just bet he'll have some presents for all of you, too," said Rose, realizing how much seeing her dad meant to Jenny. And to all her children.

As Tom approached the house, the bushes gleaming with white lights that Danny put up in his absence, he caught a glimpse of the family just finishing up with dinner.

This is where I belong, at least with my children. I can't believe she wouldn't even let me be here to watch them opening their presents on Christmas morning.

Packages bundled in both hands, he reached out for the doorbell. A shriek came from inside as Jenny scrambled to open the door for him. Tom placed his presents on the step and swooped his little girl up in his arms.

"Merry Christmas, sweet girl. Was Santa good to you?"

"You bet, Daddy," she answered, not wanting to dash his belief that she still believed when she wasn't quite sure herself.

Danny and Lauren greeted him with outstretched arms, ushering him into the family room.

"The tree looks great, kids. You did a wonderful job. Hello, Rose."

"Tom."

A hush enveloped the room, an awkwardness making everyone acutely aware that life was not as it once was.

Jenny smashed through the ice beginning to form.

"Daddy come see my Barbie House. It's the best thing ever."

"Wait a minute, honey. I have some things for all of you, too."

With warmth returning to the room, Tom passed out gift cards for his oldest two and a Special Edition Collector's Barbie for Jenny.

"Here's a little something for you, too, Rose," he said as he handed her a small bag.

"I didn't get you anything, Tom."

"That's fine, Rose. Under the circumstances, I didn't expect anything."

Tom turned back to the children and listened intently to all their news. Not wanting to question Danny too much on his decision to come home from school, he focused instead on his new job and how much he appreciated the help he was able to give around the house now. Danny exhaled softly with relief, keeping his secret deftly hidden.

"Well, Tom," Rose said, after a couple of hours, "I guess it's time for you to be going. Thank you for coming by. I know it meant a lot to the children."

"Rose, could we. . ."

"Not now, Tom. There's nothing to say right now. Just go, please."

Turning to his children, Tom hugged them one after the other, his eyes liquid with repressed tears.

"I'll see you guys soon. Call me anytime. I want to know how you're doing."

Lauren caught his eye as he reached the door.

"Dad, where are you staying?"

"Oh, I've taken a furnished apartment near my office. It's nothing glamorous, but it's fine for now. Take good care, Lauren, and call me anytime if you'd like to talk. I love you more than you know. I love all of you."

Tom turned away from his family. As soon as he reached his car, he pulled out his phone.

Merry Christmas, Abby. Can I see you?

Forty

FAT FLAKES OF SNOW blanketed the ground creating the perfect Christmas card. All the tinsel, lights, presents and family did nothing to make Tom want to celebrate. It was blatantly clear that Rose did not want him in her life. She was convinced he was having an affair.

But it's not an affair, he rationalized. *It's not physical, at least not yet, thanks to Abby's level-headedness and self-control.* But it was an affair of the heart. He understood her caution. *She doesn't want me ruining her life while I'm still mired in my old one. And I have to think of my children. What a shitty mess.*

Pulling into the parking garage of Abby's building, Tom was terrified of making the wrong choice.

Was he just desperate to be needed? Was he going to regret falling into the arms of another woman—a woman he was passionately attracted to, a woman who was the polar opposite of his wife? His wife. He was married. *I'm not an adulterer. And if I choose that path, what will it do to Abby?*

The elevator door closed on his thoughts. He was numb. He twisted his wedding ring around on his finger.

Abby answered the door at his knock.

"You came back."

"Yes, I did."

Before he could wrap his arms around her, Abby turned to the bar and offered him a drink, sending a clear signal that she wanted to talk.

"You know how I feel about you, Tom. It's painful for me not to lead you straight back to that bedroom. My body aches for you."

"That's why I'm here. I need you, too."

"It has to be more than need for us to take that step and not regret it. I'm no angel, Tom. I'm not self-righteous here. I never imagined myself having an affair with a married man. But, I'm not sure you have this all figured out. I think it's all too raw for you right now. I want you to want me for the right reason, not to ease your pain. I want you to love me. What happened between you and your wife? Or is that too private?"

"I know I don't love Rose anymore, and she doesn't love me. We lost that connection a long time ago. All she ever does is shut me out."

"It's a two-way street, Tom. You can't lay all the blame on her. You have to settle this. What if she knows that we're

NOT having an affair? Would she take you back? Would you want to go back?"

Tom was swept back to the early days of their marriage when their passion was so intense. He saw Rose's body molded so perfectly into his. Until Lauren slid up the middle.

"Tom? You went somewhere just then. Was it back to Rose?"

"It was back to a life that no longer exists. I want my life to be with you now."

"Then go take care of business and come back to me when you're truly free. Only then will you know if this right. I'll wait, but not for long. Just be sure this is what you want."

 Tom brushed aside her hair and gently kissed her forehead.

"Thank you."

"For what."

"For making an honest man out of me."

Tom closed the door, hoping to open a new one when he was ready.

Forty-One

A GUT-WRENCHING ACHE racked Danny's body. He wouldn't have enough money for another fix until he got paid—if he managed to keep his job.

Rummaging in his nightstand, he greedily swept up the traces of spilled powder, desperate to get enough to get him through the rest of the day.

Jenny heard him go into his room and called out to him. "Can you come play Barbies with me?"

One more round with Ken and I'm gonna' puke.

Garnering his strength and composure, he walked down to her room. The explosion of Pepto Bismol pink on the bed, the walls, the curtains, and the area rug turned his stomach. He picked up the Ken doll to begin the play.

Barbie: What's wrong with your son? He's so mean to his little sister.

Ken: He must be upset about something.

Barbie: But I don't like the way he's acting.

Ken: Leave me—I mean him—alone.

Barbie: He yelled at her the other day. I won't have that in my house.

Hearing the words coming from her mouth crushed his already throbbing body. It was the last nudge in his cascade of failures. Anger raging inside him, he threw the Ken doll across the room and, with one violent swipe of his hand, smashed his sister's new prized Barbie dollhouse, launching plastic furniture and parts into the air. One of the pieces knocked over Jenny's treasured kaleidoscope, dropping shattered bits of colored glass everywhere.

Jenny wailed.

"Daddy gave me that kaleidoscope, and now you broke that too. It was so beautiful, and now it's ruined."

"I'm sick to death of this—of all of you. Grow up. Barbie's are for babies. Get a life."

Pushing himself to his feet, he flew out of the room, stepping on the jagged pieces of glass and leaving his sister hysterically in tears crying for her mother.

"What's going on up there?" Rose screamed, hearing Jenny's uncontrollable sobbing. Bounding up the stairs, she saw her daughter sitting in the middle of shards of plastic and glass."

"I hate him," she screamed. "I wish he'd just go away again."

Those were the last words Danny heard as he stormed down the back steps, slamming the door behind him.

Desperate, not knowing where to go, he had one last phone call he could make.

"Dad, it's me, Danny. Can I come over?

Forty-Two

APPROACHING the old apartment building, Danny found an empty parking spot in the back of the lot. He climbed the dark, narrow staircase and stood outside apartment 4B. Muffled voices seeped out of closed doors to his right and left. His hand hovered over the door before he knocked.

This is a bad idea.

But desperation took over like a guiding force, and he reached out with his fist. As soon as the door opened, he saw his father's eyes open wide with surprise—or was it disappointment. He knew how awful he looked. He reached out to shake his dad's hand, but Tom grabbed him by the shoulders and hugged him.

"Is everything okay?"

Danny was not used to seeing his dad any place except

home, and the sparsely furnished apartment sucked the breath out of him. He looked around and saw a family picture, the only nod to his dad's former life.

Danny wasn't sure where to begin. He was still angry with his dad for not understanding or even taking the time to understand him. But things were so bad with his mom that he had nowhere to turn, so he just let the words fly out of his mouth.

"I'm in trouble, and I don't know where else to turn."

In the silence that ensued, he knew his dad was waiting for him to continue.

"This is so hard for me to say."

"You can tell me anything, son."

"Can I? You've never listened before."

"I guess I deserved that. But I'm here now."

"I dropped out of school."

Again, silence.

"I got hooked on alcohol and then drugs. I was about to flunk out, so my advisor said I should withdraw. But that's not the worst. I just blew up at Jenny and smashed her new dollhouse. I'm scared, Dad. I don't know what's happening to me."

He wasn't ready for Tom's reaction.

"Geez, Danny. I thought you were smarter than that."

"See. I failed again."

The timer on the oven beeped, distracting them both.

When Tom got up to turn it off, Danny started toward the door.

"Wait. Don't go. I'm sorry. I shouldn't have said that. Talk to me, Danny."

Running his hands through his unwashed hair, still smarting from the words he just heard, Danny jumped into new territory.

"Did *I* ever mean anything to you? Did you ever care about anything I did? I know Mom sure as hell didn't."

The color drained from his face revealing a scared little boy. All at once, the room clouded over with emotions long held hostage to propriety. Tom's voice trembled as he fought for composure.

"How could you ask such a thing? You mean the world to me. You're my only son."

"Well, you sure never acted like it. You were always gone, Mom was obsessed with Lauren for some reason, and I was out in left field. That's why I had to go away. I had to prove myself to you even though you hated the idea of my acting. I know I've been a big disappointment.

He was seven, his ear pressed against the wall trying to make out the words being said:

'. . .why does he always. . .'

'. . .not what I hoped. . .'

'. . .still young. . .'

'. . .look at her. . .'

He thought he had forgotten those muffled fragments, but they still haunted him.

That same voice rang clearly this time as Danny saw a look of. . .what; fear, sadness, hurt, anger. He couldn't read his dad's face.

"I love you, Danny. I have a lot to make up for." Tom made a motion in Danny's direction but backed off when he saw him pull away.

"You could never disappoint me. I guess I never let you know."

"I was never what you wanted me to be."

Staring his dad in the face, he realized how much his words hit home.

"I don't know why you and Mom couldn't have given me a chance to succeed at what I wanted, not what you wanted for me. It's as bad as Mom wanting to run Lauren's life."

"About that. . ."

"Look, Dad, I don't want to talk about Lauren and Mom right now. I need help. I'm drowning—and I'm scared."

Becoming a little boy again, he fell into his dad's open arms and sobbed.

Hushing him as he did when he was an infant, Tom cradled his baby boy.

"We'll fix this," he said.

Forty-Three

HE WOKE DISORIENTED on his dad's sofa. Nightmares of his one night of tripping out at school swam around him. He fought the urge to find Josh. His whole body was on fire. Vague traces of a conversation with his father, of admitting to his addiction, of asking if he was ever wanted, surfaced. He wasn't sure what he was feeling—shame, remorse—maybe both. But there was also a strange feeling of comfort and acceptance, easing his pain.

"Hey, did you get any sleep?" Tom asked, shuffling into the living room.

"I guess. Look, Dad. . ."

"It's okay, Danny. I know last night was difficult—for both of us. There's so much more I want to say, but we have time for that. The most important thing is that we've got to get you some help. It's time for me to step up and be the father I never was to you."

Tears rolled from Danny's eyes onto his sunken cheeks. As awful as he felt, he also felt safe and hopeful for the first time in months.

"What am I gonna do, Dad? I'm scared."

"Of course, you're scared. I'm scared for you. But this, what you've become, is not the real you. You're smart, talented, ambitious, and stronger than you think. We've all failed you. But that's going to stop right now. You can do this, and I'll be there for you—if you want me. I'd certainly understand if you didn't want to have anything to do with me. I've disappointed you. Please let me help now."

"How? Where? It hurts so much."

"Let's get some breakfast first. I researched some local de-tox places you can check into right away. Don't worry about the cost. You're worth every penny it will take to get you better."

"Could I. . .stay here with you for a while? I can't face Jenny and Lauren right now, and mom would be furious if she knew."

"For as long as you want."

When Tom went into the bedroom to get dressed, Danny almost bolted to the door. Withdrawal, fear, shame, guilt, were all tearing at him.

What made me even think I could do this? My whole life is trashed.

Grabbing his jacket, he reached for the doorknob. From

somewhere deep in his consciousness, he heard Kim's words: *I stopped in to one of the play rehearsals the other day and saw you. You're really good.*

I was good, wasn't I?

His dad's voice jarred his thoughts.

"Let's go, Danny. You can't get off this stuff by yourself—it's too dangerous. Let the professionals handle it. We'll stop by the house and pick up a few things for you."

Tom put his arm around Danny's shoulder and ushered him out the door.

✧ ✧ ✧ ✧

"I can't go in there, Dad. I hurt Jenny so badly, and now she hates me. Can you grab a few things for me?"

"Of course. I'll be right back."

Tom left Danny in the car, curled up in a ball trying to hold himself together. Peering in the kitchen window, he saw Rose at the table sipping her morning coffee. Realizing he should have called first, he knocked, hoping she would let him in.

He saw her look up and glare at him as she got up to answer the door, her expression telling him she was still unyielding in her anger.

"What do you want, Tom?"

"Hi. Um, Danny came over last night and wants to stay

for a while. I came to pick up a few things for him. Can I come in?"

"Why couldn't he just come in himself? Oh, that's right. He just broke his little sister's heart."

"He's not feeling so great today. I'll only be a few minutes. Are the girls here?"

"Jenny's already gone to school and Lauren's sleeping. Just do what you came for and leave."

"Look, Rose. . ."

"Not now, Tom. I don't want to hear any lame excuses. You made your bed. . .and you know the rest."

"It's not like that."

"It's way more than that, and you know it."

"What's that supposed to mean?" Tom retorted. "Are you forgetting your part in all this mess? When are you going to be honest with yourself and everyone else?"

"I can't get into this now. Please, do what you came for."

Tom slipped quietly up to Danny's room. Looking around, he realized how seldom he had been in his son's room the last few years. He never knew the rock groups his son loved, as he surveyed the posters now covering up the dated wallpaper. He looked at the framed pictures of Danny and his friends, especially Josh, and realized he never took the time to get to know them.

Walking towards the desk, he spotted a newspaper clipping tacked to a bulletin board. It was a review of Danny's high school performance in *It's a Wonderful Life*—the one they had scoffed at. Rose's words rang through his head.

You mean when you were wearing that angel costume? Couldn't you get a better part?

And here it was—a reporter's glowing words:

Delivered with such great poise and depth by such a young actor.

While I spent all my time trying to make you into what I wanted, I never took the time to know the real you.

Regret gnawed at him over the lost time he could never retrieve.

Forty-Four

DIFFERENT HOSPITAL, different admissions desk, different child. But the fears were the same. Tom was here with a hurt child, and nothing could lessen his anxiety. But this time, there was no Rose crashing her way through, pushing the guards, making her demands. He was in charge of this.

Approaching the Admissions desk to check Danny in, he took note of the people waiting for admittance to the clinic. He saw every walk of life represented—teenagers, professionals, tidy, unkempt. This disease, these addictions, didn't discriminate. And it had chosen his only son for its latest victim.

Tom began talking to the nurse, but she interrupted him.

"I'm sorry, sir, but your son is considered an adult now, and he must take responsibility. If he is still under your insurance, I can give you those papers. The rest he must do for himself."

"He's in pretty bad shape."

"I'm sure. That's why he's here, and you must be very proud that he has taken this first step. I'll be here to help him with the forms."

Hearing his name called, Danny uncurled his body from the waiting room chair.

Why did they have to say it so loud?

Gathering all the strength he had left he walked the endlessly long hall to the desk—counting his steps once again.

Maybe I am crazy. I can't stop this incessant counting.

With trembling hands, he signed the reams of paperwork handed to him. But he wasn't prepared for what came next. A guard approached him and searched him to make sure he didn't have anything illegal on him.

Tom stood to the side mortified. This was his son they were patting down, turning his pockets inside out, emptying his backpack. It was all surreal.

How did this happen? How did I not see any of this coming? What kind of a father have I been? I can't blame all of this on Rose.

Tom caught his son's red-rimmed eyes and saw the humiliation pouring from them. But he held on to the fact that Danny was in the right place for help. Reaching out toward him, he said the only thing that he could—the only thing that made sense.

"I'm so proud of you, son."

He wiped away the salty tears from his son's cheeks—and his own.

It was 2 a.m. by the time Danny was admitted to the hospital.

"He'll be in detox for several days, Mr. Foster. We'll make him as comfortable as possible. There will be intensive in-patient therapy followed by several days—or weeks—depending on the individual—of out-patient counseling. It will be hard work, but I know he wants to get better, and we'll work to have him be successful."

"Thank you. I can't believe this is happening."

"No one does, least of all the patient. No one wants this. But he's doing the right thing, the best thing for him. He's not alone. We're here for him as much as you are."

Turning toward the sliding glass doors, Tom tried to remember the last time Danny was in the hospital.

He was ten and broke his arm playing baseball—a game I made him play. I wanted him to be a jock like I was, but it was never what he wanted. But he did it anyway to please me. I'm so sorry, Danny.

He didn't know where to go. Back to the apartment, alone? Or could he run to Abby for consolation? She had made it clear that she only wanted him if, and when, he was completely free. But he desperately needed to talk to someone.

And then the utter shame of the situation, of Danny's situation, pushed against his heart.

What kind of man am I? Am I embarrassed by my own son's plight? Am I that low?

Getting into his car, he broke down, sobbing into his hands, and in a half-hour drove home alone.

❖ ❖ ❖ ❖

Tom showed up for work in body only the next day and the next. He was able to speak to Danny in the evenings, after his counseling sessions, and knew that they—he—had made the right decision to seek help. If only there were a clinic for him to figure out his own life.

Realizing Abby was keeping her distance, most of their business dealings were done by e-mail or text, avoiding any personal encounters.

I'm not sure what I could even say to her. She's pulled back and left the ball in my court. And I can't keep running to her to unload my problems. What did he want? Was he falling in love with her or just in love with love again? If he had the chance to go home, back to his family, would he take it? Abby was right. He played a part in the death of his marriage. It wasn't all Rose. He had ignored her fears, her insecurities, her past. If he went to her, if he admitted his selfishness a long time ago, would she take him back? Or was it too late?

Forty-Five

REHAB WAS PAINFUL; Danny was alone and frightened. But with the proper medication to help him detox, combined with group and individual counseling, he began to heal. He still couldn't forgive himself for what he did to Jenny, though. She was the one person in his life who never judged him, and he had destroyed the bond they had. He knew the words he had uttered in anger could never be taken back. But, no matter how long it took, he would make it up to her.

Weeks after he checked into the hospital, the doctors and counselors were ready to discharge him into outpatient therapy. But to where? He knew he would never be welcomed back home, and he didn't know how he felt about being with his dad—if he were able to stay there.

Shakily, still suffering the effects of withdrawal, he called Tom.

"Hey, Dad. They're discharging me tomorrow. Can you pick me up?"

He knew his father could hear the hesitation in his voice.

"Of course. That's excellent news. What do you have to do next?"

"Can we talk about it at home? Um, I mean, your place?"

"I'd like that. I'd like you to stay with me, but only if you're comfortable."

Danny exhaled, his shoulders relaxing.

"I'd like that, too. I'll see you in the morning. . .and thanks."

Tom heard the faint sound of sniffling as he hung up.

Returning to his dad's apartment after his stay in rehab, Danny still felt out of place. Gone were all traces of the man his father had been, replaced by a big sign that said, "Temporarily Under Construction." He didn't know if he was hoping that his father would make it more comfortable or realize that he needed to move back home. But, with his mom so angry, that option seemed remote.

Awkwardness surrounded them as Tom showed Danny to the room he had cleaned up for him. Clean towels and sheets lay on the pull-out sofa Tom had found at the Salvation Army for $25.

"Sorry, it's not much," he said as Danny stood in the doorway.

"It's fine, Dad. It's all I need."

But you deserve so much more.

"Come on into the kitchen, and I'll fix us something to eat. You can tell me what the next steps are for us."

Danny fought the temptation to hug his dad. Tom was trying so hard to make things right, but Danny had spent years never feeling part of the family. Now he was finding it hard to fill in the place marked 'son.'

"Thanks for the 'us,' Dad, but I'm on my own for this. I have a strict regimen of medication and counseling to follow if I have any hope of turning myself around. This past week I've started to dig deep to figure out how and why I am where I am."

"It sounds pretty intense. Are you okay?"

"Pretty much. I have to come to grips with what I've become, just like Lauren had to accept what happened to her. We're grown up now, Dad."

And I've missed all the growing.

"Dad, can I ask you something?"

"Of course. Anything."

"Why does Mom love Lauren more than Jenny or me? I know it's not my imagination. It's so obvious."

Tom tried to extricate himself from answering such a loaded question, so he deflected.

"She's just concerned about her well-being. After she lost

Maddy and became paralyzed, nothing was the same for her anymore. And Mom wants to help, that's all."

Opening the little drawers, Danny let his memories float out.

"No, Dad. She's always been that way. Lauren has always been number one in her life. Jenny and I come in way down the list. Me especially. That's why I asked you if I was ever wanted? I mean, I did come along just a year later. Was I just an accident? Did she resent it when she got pregnant with me? I'm just trying to understand this big, like, *canyon* there is between us."

Tom squirmed, wanting to steer Danny away from this issue.

"It sounds like therapy has you digging deep."

"It's all part of how I got here, Dad. I accept full responsibility for crossing the lines, but I need to understand why. That's why I'm asking. I know there's something between Mom and Lauren that's blocking the rest of us out—especially me. And then there's this gulf between the two of you. Why did she throw you out like that? Aren't you in love anymore?"

"Relationships can get very complicated, Danny. Things happen in a marriage that husbands and wives don't always see the same way. And sometimes a rift grows, which can be hard to overcome."

"Is it Abby? Are you in love with her?"

Caught short, Tom went silent. The sound of a faucet dripping somewhere kept time with the seconds on the clock.

Finally, with a deep breath, he decided to level with Danny. Suddenly he had difficulty seeing him as the curly, dark-haired little boy who loved to pretend he was Superman.

He loved acting even back then. And I never even gave him a chance.

"This is so difficult for me to talk about. But you've just told me you're an adult, with adult problems and you deserve as honest an answer as I can give you. Abby has begun to fill a hole in my life. I'm very attracted to her. But we are not having an affair. She's an honest woman and does not want to be responsible for breaking up my marriage. She won't be the 'other woman.' I admire her a great deal."

"So, is that a no? You don't love her?"

"I'm not sure what I feel right now. But I do know that my children need me—at least I hope they do, and I have to get my head back in the game and be there for all of you. Do you understand how much I love you?"

"I love you, too. I just don't know if I'm ready to forgive you." Danny bit his lip and looked away.

Forty-Six

Hey, Madds,

I haven't talked to you for a while. Things are shifting around here. Danny admitted the other day that he got caught up in alcohol and drugs before he dropped out of school. I think it's bad.

He exploded last week, lashed out at Jenny, and broke her new dollhouse. She was terrified. And he hasn't been home since. He went to stay with my dad. I hope he's getting him some help. He needs an ally right now, and Mom sure isn't going to be it.

Speaking of Mom, I need to get her off my back. I've been doing a lot better, though I still miss you terribly. My counseling sessions are helping me come to terms with the accident, your death, and my paralysis. But the best thing is still writing to you.

I'd love for her to go back to work. I can take care of Jenny after school, and I need her to focus on something other than me. I know it's always been this way, and I'm not sure why, but I'm so over it. I want to start taking some online courses to get my life back, and it would be so much easier if she weren't snooping over my shoulder every minute of every day.

What do you think? Do I dare bring it up? Will she go ballistic on me? Maybe I can talk to Lisa's mom when she comes over next time to drop off her daughter. Maybe she can subtly ask her about going back to work. Maybe it will work. If not, I'm going to bite the bullet and see what happens.

Love you lots,

L.

Lauren closed her journal, wondering why her family was such a mess.

Forty-Seven

LAUREN HAD REHEARSED her words carefully, couching them so it would seem like a spontaneous idea, maybe even making Rose think it was her own. She put down her bagel and coffee and interrupted her mom, who was reading the paper—her usual morning routine.

"Whatcha looking at, Mother? Job listings?

Wow, so much for being subtle.

"Whatever would make you think that? I have a full-time job right now, being here for you."

Lauren winced.

"Come on, Mother, surely I'm only a part-time job now." A forced smile worked its way onto her face.

"Can I get you something else to eat? Maybe some eggs? Or pancakes?"

"You're doing it again, Mother—changing the subject when you don't want to talk about something. Why can't you just leave me alone for once? I don't need your help anymore."

Lauren saw the effect of her stinging words scrape across her mother's face, but she continued to fling them.

"What is this obsession you have with me? And don't deny it. I feel like I'm always under glass, so I don't break. It's not normal. You need to get your own life and stop living mine. Maybe you need some counseling."

Seeing the devastation in her mother's eyes, she retreated. But she couldn't apologize. She had finally been able to speak the truth.

Rose's blue eyes turned gray, and she turned from the room.

M.

I got up the courage to suggest that my mother go back to work. It didn't fly. She had her lame excuses about how content she was looking after me. I want her to leave me alone and let me get on with my life.

I've been thinking a lot about how peculiar my relationship with her is. I used to take for granted the mother/daughter thing. You know, doing things together, leaving out the "boys." But, as I got older and saw how she shut everyone else out when we were together, I knew something was weird. I think she's disturbed. I don't know what kind of relationship she had with my grandma because she died before I was born. But something must have happened for her to have such a skewed view of motherhood. I'm probably just spending too much time in therapy myself. I'll just shut up now.

I'm going to continue putting the bug in my mother's ear about work and hope that she gets the message. This is getting too intense. I need to start my new life.

L.

IN THE ESSAY he had written to get into William and Mary, Danny's mother and father were solid as a rock, his older sister was bravely defeating the demons from her accident, and his little sister was the delight of the family.

The truth? They were a dysfunctional mess—except maybe his little sister, Jenny.

And, unbeknownst to him back then, he would be the one to start the explosion that would blow them all out of the water. Now, 365 days later, immersed in intense therapy and counseling, Danny was beginning to emerge from the rubble, his courage breaking through.

His phone pinged with a message. Not wanting to break his train of thought, he ignored it. He would check it later.

"Dad, I think I want to go over to the house tonight when Mom and the girls are home. It's time I talked to all of them about me."

"Are you sure you're ready?"

"My therapy's been pretty intense, and one of the steps I have to take is to apologize to all the people I've hurt. Especially Jenny. She didn't deserve how I treated her, and she should know why."

"Would you like some company?"

"That's okay. I need to do this by myself. I'll be fine."

"You're a fine young man."

No, I'm not—at least not yet. I have a lot of work to do first.

Pulling up into the driveway at home, Danny wondered how others saw the house when they drove by.

Who was inside?

A mother, father, three children—one half-paralyzed, one an addict, one an innocent little girl.

Were they happy?

No.

What were they like?

Total mess.

You never know what's behind closed doors.

The back door was open to let in the warm May air. He peered into the kitchen and saw Lauren pulled up to the kitchen table engrossed in her laptop. Without knocking, he let himself in, startling her.

"Hey, bud, what a nice surprise. You look really good."

He chuckled. "Well, I guess since the last time I saw you, there must be an improvement."

His mind circled back to his appearance and actions the tragic day he destroyed his little sister's dollhouse, shattering their relationship in the process.

"Is Jenny here?"

"Yeah, she's upstairs playing. Do you want to see her?"

"Yes, but I'm not sure she wants to see me. I wanted to see both of you—and Mom, if she's here, too."

"What's this about? Is everything okay?"

"It's much better than it was before I went to Dad's, but I wanted to explain it to you. Would you ask them to come in here? If they hear my voice, they won't want to see me."

"Don't be stupid. We've all missed you."

"Hard to believe after the way I've treated everyone. Anyway, can you get them to come down?"

Lauren rolled to the bottom of the stairs and called up to her mother and sister, asking them to come down to the kitchen. She waited to hear the panic she usually got from her mother, who was forever afraid something was wrong. This time there was silence.

"Mother, Jenny, can you come here for a few minutes?"

The sound of doors opening broke the quiet. Rose and Jenny appeared.

"Ken was just about to propose to Barbie, and you

interrupted him," Jenny cried, her voice crackling with annoyance.

Just then, Danny poked his head around the corner, and when she saw him, all thoughts of the impending marriage disappeared. Brother and sister hadn't spoken since that fateful night when he, in a fit of despair, had destroyed her trust.

"You came back," Jenny said, her voice flat, unsure.

"Not for long, sweetie, but I need to talk to all of you about something."

Rose stepped through the doorway into the room like a freight train arriving.

"Well, look who finally graced our home with his presence. I hope you're here to apologize to Jenny. Your behavior was uncalled for and downright mean."

"Hi, Mom," Danny said, ignoring her caustic, sarcastic tone.

"Um, can we all go into the living room for a minute. I have something to say."

Lauren was the first to go, followed by Jenny and finally Rose.

Danny asked everyone to sit down so he could get off his trembling legs. Lauren, catching his nervousness and hoping he wouldn't have a panic attack, spoke first.

"You look good, Danny. Doesn't he, Mother?"

"Why are we here?" came her unsympathetic answer.

God, grant me the serenity to accept the things I cannot change. . . .

Drawing on the prayer he had learned in his rehab program, he began.

Forty-Nine

"ARE YOU TELLING ME you were doing drugs here under my roof?" Rose bellowed.

Her sudden outburst startled Jenny.

"Mommy don't yell at him. He's just being honest with us."

Danny wanted to hug her.

"Honest or not, we have an eight-year-old living in this house, and you brought drugs in here. How irresponsible is that?"

Danny was acutely aware that this was her only concern. Yes, she had a right to be concerned about Jenny. But she made no effort to try to understand him and what he was going through: no compassion, no tolerance, just anger.

"I know that was wrong, and I'm sorry. It's just hard to explain where my head and body were. If you let me, I'll tell you as much as I can."

"I just don't understand how your father could have kept this from me."

"He didn't know until I was pretty far gone. I didn't know myself how bad I had gotten until I hurt Jenny so much. I'm so sorry for what I said and did."

Rose, the color gradually receding from her cheeks, seemed to digest what Danny was telling her. She knew about addiction, about kids who abused drugs, but until it hit home, she condemned them. Now it was her son who was suffering. She needed—no, wanted—to understand.

"So, what is this program you're in all about? Jenny, why don't you go up to your room to play while we talk to your brother."

Danny knew what the kids were learning in school about drugs and felt she should hear it all. But he deferred to his mom. There was no need to go against her wishes and rile her even more.

"Mommy. I'm not stupid. I have friends whose brothers and sisters have done drugs. If Danny wants me to hear this, then I want to stay."

Danny looked at her closely and realized that Jenny was not just the sweet, innocent little girl he'd pegged her for. She knew things. She *wanted* to know things. Playing with her Barbies was only masking the maturity lurking within.

✧ ✧ ✧ ✧

"Are you planning to go back to your father's?" Rose asked.

"I think so."

"If you promise never to do drugs again, you can come home."

"Mom, you know I can't make that promise. It's what I want with all my heart, but addiction is a daily battle."

Rose swallowed hard. Fear for her two daughters set in at the thought of Danny relapsing and bringing drugs back into the house. She couldn't do it.

"If you can't make that guarantee, I can't have you here. I'm sorry, Danny. I just can't do it."

Danny thought of what a counselor had told him—about how difficult it was for people who didn't understand, or were unwilling to understand, addiction. But this was his mother.

Hurt rose in his chest.

"I'm sorry. I'll miss you and the girls, but Dad's been a major force in my recovery, and I'd like to be with him—for now. Maybe someday things will change with us."

He glanced over to Lauren.

Maybe they'll change for you, too.

Purged and exhausted, Danny turned to see Jenny's face in the window as he descended the back steps to go back to his father. She seemed so strong listening to him come clean about his addiction, but he worried about how it would affect her later. Would she come to hate him—or worse yet—fear him? After his destructive actions, she would have every reason not to want to see him again. He smiled at her, hoping she would remember all the times he played Barbies with her, read to her, took care of her. The good memories.

Fifty

BRAKE LIGHTS were all Kim could see for miles. Cars stretched out as if strung together with an invisible thread lining the route from Williamsburg to the DC area. The typically congested roads were now peppered with college kids returning home for the summer. Impatient, tired drivers struggled to stay alert.

She missed Danny's company. The ride was lonely and tiresome without his words filling the silence. Just before she packed up to leave the dorm, she had texted him to see how he was doing, hoping for a response and maybe a meet-up. She still hadn't heard back.

What is it about him? Why can't I shake him off? He had hit the skids pretty hard, pretty fast. She knew he had talent, so she didn't understand why he went off the rails. But she couldn't get him out of her head. *And then there's this feeling I have about his sister, Lauren. There's a connection there, and I think we could be good friends.*

A blaring horn shook her out of her musings.

Come on, people. Honking your horn isn't going to make this traffic go any faster. Some people have no patience.

A message popped up on her screen. The traffic had come to a complete stop, so she looked over at her phone.

> can I c u.

> anytime, she replied.

> know where Metro Diner 29 is on Lee Hwy? Friday at 11?

> perfect. see u then.

✧ ✧ ✧ ✧

The diner was familiar—an old favorite of Danny's family when he and Lauren were younger before Jenny came along. It was a classic—cold, shiny steel outside—warm and comfortable inside. Timeless booths lined the sides under the window, marred tables with history filled the middle, and a gleaming counter faced the kitchen.

They met in the parking lot. Her intoxicating smile went right through him.

"Hey," she said.

"Hey."

She watched his eyes focus on her ball cap.

Crap. I'm wearing my William and Mary hat. Nice goin', girl. Nothing like rubbing it in.

Glancing up at the angry clouds filling the sky, Kim said, "Let's get inside before the deluge begins."

"Sure."

Holding the door for her as he had been taught, he uttered, "Booth, counter or table?"

"How about a booth?" she answered as she took in the cushy red leather seats. "It's by the windows, and we can watch the storm. I love the rain."

"Yeah, me too. I think I was born under a cloud."

Distracting themselves from the awkwardness, they reached for the menus snugged against the ketchup, mustard and salt and pepper shakers. A middle-aged woman, her white tennis shoes hushing her approach, appeared almost immediately.

"Hi, my name's Alice, and I'll be your waitress today. Can I get you started with some drinks?"

"Iced tea, please," said Kim, taking the lead.

"Me too."

Glancing at the menus, they gave their orders to Alice, the distance that had opened between them starting to close.

"How are. . ." they both began at once.

Danny laughed. "You first."

"How are things at home?"

"Not so great."

"What's wrong?"

God grant me the serenity. . .

And the words came tumbling out of Danny's mouth. The whole story—Lauren, the family, the drugs—hit the space between them, sucking out the oxygen.

The second hand on the clock ticked slowly, one notch at a time, as he waited for Kim's reaction. It would be all or nothing. She would either get up and walk away, horrified by his words, or she would take them in and, hopefully, not judge him.

He looked into her green eyes, attempting to read what was behind them. They softened, glistening with moisture, as she reached out and took his hand.

"That was pretty courageous."

Memories of the hurt she had so often seen in his eyes suddenly made sense. She realized then why he was such a good actor. He had always been playing a role. His life had been a play, and he the performer tucked away in the pages of the script. Her heart hurt for him.

"I'm so sorry, Danny. I had no idea."

"It's fine—well, it's getting better. Now, it's your turn. How's school?"

"It's over for the summer," she said. "Now, I have some decisions to make."

"About what?

"I'm trying to decide if I'll go back next year. I'm a little homesick."

A glimmer of excitement sent a sliver of light and hope into him. If she stayed here, he could see her.

"What would you do? Where would you go?"

"Let's not talk about it now. But I wanted to ask you about Lauren. I felt a real connection with her when I met her at Christmas. I feel like we could be friends. Do you think she'd want to see me, or would she think I was bothering her? I mean, she doesn't know me."

Knowing how desperate Lauren was for companionship—anything to get away from Rose—he didn't hesitate.

"I think she'd like that—a lot."

Kim smiled.

Finishing their breakfasts—he pancakes, she bacon and eggs—Danny looked out the window. "Well, the rain's let up. Maybe we should get going. I'll give your number to Lauren so you can talk."

Hesitating, he tried to find the right words. "Thanks for being such a good friend." He wanted to say more but now was not the time.

Kim smiled, looking back over her shoulder as she walked to her car.

Outside, the heavy rain had let up, a few left-over drops still spitting on Danny's windshield. He sat in the car watching Kim pull out cautiously onto the wet streets, still slick with fallen leaves from the storm.

The awkward space between them had begun to shrink.

Fifty-One

AS HIS STRENGTH and courage slowly returned, Danny's outlook on life turned more positive. Gone were the hangovers and shakes he felt every morning. His head was clear, and he started to think about the future. And he had heard from Kim.

There was still a multitude of decisions he would have to make: where to live, how to support himself, whether to try to go back to school. But he was ready. He was strong, yet still faced with the pull of addiction he would always live with.

He was back at his first AA meeting after finishing his outpatient rehab. He slunk in, still mortified at being there, and bumped into Josh.

"Hey," Josh said, pulling his ball cap lower over his face

"Good to see you, man," he answered, reaching out with a fist bump.

As Danny and Josh took their seats, the leader, who said his name was Kyle, asked if there was anyone new who would like to introduce themselves. Pulling on the resolutions he had made to himself to tackle this problem full steam ahead, Danny stood.

"I'm Danny, and I'm an addict."

"Hi, Danny," came the unanimous reply from the participants.

Kyle asked if he would like to address the group with his story.

"Um, not just yet, thanks."

"In time," Kyle answered. "We're all here in the same situation. Sometimes it's just good to let it all out."

Danny had been through this with his counseling sessions. He knew there was nothing to be ashamed of, so he stood and told his story. Out came everything:

I was always second best.

My parents hated that I wanted to be an actor.

No one gave a shit about me.

"So, I left home, went away to school, hit the skids, and dropped out."

He was interrupted by a young girl with an apparent hangover.

"So, none of this shit is your fault? You're just an innocent victim? How lame is that?"

Kyle interjected. "Hannah, remember, there is no blame here."

"But it sounds like he had it all and threw it away. Some of us had nothing to begin with. That's all I'm sayin'."

"She's right," Danny interrupted. *"I know I gotta' accept some of the blame. That's why I'm here—to face up to my faults and make amends. Thanks for reminding me, Hannah."*

"Sure, man."

So, he began the 12-Step Program, the foundation of AA, got a sponsor, and began the hard work of turning his life around.

❖ ❖ ❖ ❖

He knew it was okay to stay with his dad for a while longer, so the next task he had was to get his job back. With his newfound confidence, he pulled into the parking lot of the convenience store to face Mr. Hudson.

The familiar jingle of the overhead bell threatened his resolve, but as soon as Mr. Hudson appeared, he knew what he had to do.

"I came to apologize—and to offer you an explanation for my behavior a couple of months ago."

"I'm listening."

"I got myself into some real trouble with drugs, and they took over my life. When I came to work for you, I was desperate for money. I took advantage of your generosity and kindness and was irresponsible. I know I can never make up for how I let you down. I just wanted you to know that I've been in rehab and I'm clean now. If you can't forgive me, I hope you can try to understand."

Bill Hudson took a step forward, staring Danny straight in the eyes.

"I believe you, Danny. I can see it in your eyes. It took a lot of courage for you to come to me, and I appreciate it. I can't tell you how happy it makes me to see a fine young man like you pull yourself up and start over."

Danny's shoulders relaxed from where they were shrugged up under his ears.

"How would you like your job back? I could still use the help. Andy's busy with after school sports most days, and I'm still struggling to keep this place together."

Danny didn't know what to do except nod his head and offer his hand to Bill.

"I won't let you down again, Mr. Hudson. I'll be here early tomorrow morning."

His pride pulling his shoulders back, he walked out into the sunshine.

✧ ✧ ✧ ✧

Exhausted from the effort it had taken to put on a good front and face his issues head-on, Danny drove back to his dad's apartment to chill. A parking spot opened up just as he pulled in off the street, and he acknowledged the driver with a quick wave as he swerved in to take his place.

Kim's smile had stayed with him since they left the diner, that spontaneous flash of perfectly aligned teeth reminding him so much of his sister.

Lauren. I need to call her and let her know Kim wants to see if they can get together. She could use a good friend to talk to since Maddy's death.

As if by serendipity, his cellphone rang with its opening four notes of Beethoven's Fifth Symphony. He had gotten so razzed by Josh after he had programmed it.

"Seriously? Beethoven? What are you, a geek?" he had mocked.

"Got your attention, though, didn't it?" he had replied without missing a beat.

Warmth spread over him, thinking of Josh in AA with him. Once again, they were friends, not cohorts in crime.

The persistent strains of the music brought his attention back to the present. He glanced at the caller ID and saw that it was Lauren.

"What's up?" he said, finally answering on the fourth go-round of BA BA BA BUM.

"I was just thinking about you," she said, a welcome lilt in her voice traveling through the line.

"Well, imagine that. I was thinking about you too. I've been talking to Kim, and she asked if she could stop by and visit."

"Why?"

"'Cause she wants to. She felt a good vibe when you met and thought it would be nice to hang out for a while."

"Yeah, she was cool. Sure. Send me her number, and I'll text her. I could use someone to talk to besides Rose."

Did she just call our mother, Rose?

Acutely self-conscious of her condition, she asked her brother one more thing.

"Oh, and could you be here when she comes? At least just for a few minutes?"

"You bet."

Yes!

Fifty-Two

"READY?"

"I guess so."

"You'll be fine. Just be yourself, and you and Kim will have a great time getting to know each other."

As soon as the words left Danny's mouth, the doorbell rang. He walked through the living room, noticing for the first time how many baby pictures of Lauren were on the mantle. How had he not seen them before? Or were they new since the accident?

Wow. Even back then, mom was fixated.

Opening the door and seeing Kim standing there, he tried to figure out what was different about her. The glasses. They were gone. Then she smiled, and he got that strange feeling all over again.

"Wow, you look different. And your hair is lighter."

"Yeah, I decided I needed a change—got my hair highlighted and got contacts. What do you think?"

"I think you look great," Lauren interjected, a little weirded out with the changes.

"Hey, Lauren, nice to see you again."

"Same here. Danny, would you stop staring and invite her in?"

Aware that he was mesmerized and zoned out, he pulled himself together and ushered Kim in. Standing on the threshold of the living room, the light from the window pouring over her, he thought she looked like an angel.

"Hey, guys, if you'll excuse me, I have some things to do. Um, Kim, would you text me when you get home?"

Giving him the thumbs up, she turned her attention to Lauren.

"So, how did you and my brother meet?"

"We were in a big lecture hall together, and he tripped on my backpack."

"That sounds about right." Lauren chuckled.

The back door opened, and Lauren heard her mother come in.

"Mother, we're in here."

"Who's we?" Rose called back, putting her bags on the counter and walking toward the living room.

"Kim's here. Danny's friend from school. She came to visit."

Rose rounded the corner to see the girls laughing, enjoying themselves.

I haven't seen her this happy in a long time.

"Mother, this is Kim. Kim, this is our mother."

As soon as Kim smiled, the light dimmed in Rose's eyes.

"It's nice to meet you, Kim. I'm sorry to break this up, but Lauren has some physical therapy to do."

"I can do that later, Mother."

"Best get it over with before you get too tired.

"Thank you for coming over to see Lauren. Maybe another day will be better."

Puzzled, Kim said, "I'll call you, and we can get together again."

"I'd love that," said Lauren as Kim turned to go.

As soon as the door closed behind her, Lauren lit into her mother.

"How could you be so rude? I finally have someone I can talk to, and you practically threw her out. You're impossible."

"There's no point in getting to know someone who's going to be going back to school, is there? You'll just be left alone again. Remember, you can talk to me any time about anything. Now, let's start those exercises."

"Forget it, Mother. I'll do them when I damn well please."

Lauren rolled down to her room, pulled out her phone, and texted Kim.

> pls forgive my mother's rudeness. another time?

> u got it, girl. name it.

Fifty-Three

M.

Danny's friend came over today, and she's great. We got along really well. We just seemed to connect somehow, like we'd been friends forever. I mean, not like you and I are friends, but meeting someone you felt you'd known before. It's hard to explain.

Anyway, my mother came in and was unbelievably rude. She practically threw her out. Honestly, I think she's afraid of anyone coming between us. It's totally irrational. She's my mother—not my buddy. If she starts to do this with everyone, I don't know what I'll do.

Sorry if I haven't talked to you much lately. I've been talking to Danny more, and I go down to the rec center when someone can take me, and I've started making friends with other disabled people.

It's amazing how some of them cope. It's very inspiring.

Anyway, I just needed to vent.

Talk to you later.

L.

Fifty-Four

THE GENTLE, STEADY HUM of the air conditioner was the only sound breaking the silence in the room as Lauren pored over YouTube videos. Thinking about going back to school, she was exploring Paraplegic Car Transfers and handicap-equipped cars. She desperately wanted to be able to go somewhere by herself, get her own car, and learn to drive.

Her occupational therapist had been working diligently to teach her to get in and out of her wheelchair to get into bed, and she felt ready to take the next step with a car. Her only obstacle would be her mother.

Rehearsing the words to make her case and cataloging the YouTube videos to show how feasible her idea was, she braced herself for the conversation. Her attempt at suggesting Rose go back to work had backfired, so this one had to be convincing.

Choosing her moment carefully after sizing up her mother's mood, she took her laptop into the kitchen.

"Good morning, Mother."

"Well, look at you—dressed and ready all by yourself."

Lauren caught a glimmer of something coming from her mother. Was it pride or panic?

"I told you one day I would surprise you. I've been working hard with my OT to get to this point. It's easy once you get the mechanics down."

Pushing away the increasing encroachment of independence she was beginning to see, Rose said, 'Congratulations.'

"Now, let's get you some breakfast."

"I'm good. I got something before."

There it was again—the space growing between them.

"Can we talk?"

"Of course. About anything in particular?"

Opening and closing her hands to mask her nerves, Lauren pulled up the videos on her laptop.

"There's something I'd like to show you."

Without letting her mother interject to distract her, she hit PLAY.

As soon as Rose saw the car, she blurted out, "don't even think about getting in a car."

"I was actually thinking about driving the car myself."

"Over my dead body. Look what happened the last time you drove."

Seeing the shadow cross Lauren's face, Rose retreated from her tirade.

"I'm just worried about you, that's all. You've seen how anything can happen on the roads out there."

"If I don't get back on the horse, so to speak, I'll never drive again. If you would just take the time to watch these videos, you'll see how doable it is. I've got all the information; statistics, advice from psychologists about how important it is to get back to a normal life after a devastating event, it's all here. You just have to look at it.

"I know it's hard, and I've had to wrap my head around it too, but it would mean so much. I could take classes at the college instead of online, I could get out to see my friends, and even go over to see Dad as long as he can get me up the stairs. He even mentioned getting a ground floor apartment to make it easier for me to visit."

"You've already spoken to your father about this?" Rose said, once again feeling excluded.

"Yes, and he can see how much I want to get on with my life. He believes in me. Why can't you?"

Please let me go.

The words 'believe in me' cut deep. Is that what she had been doing—not believing in her daughter?

The past year Rose didn't believe in much of anything. She didn't believe how serious the accident was—her daughter would walk again. She didn't believe Lauren would be able to do anything for herself ever again. She didn't believe she was capable of throwing her husband out of the house.

Yet, she had succumbed to it all.

"Go ahead, start it again. I'll watch what you want me to watch. But I'll make no promises."

Sitting beside her daughter, it all hit. First Kim, now this. She felt the cords coming loose.

❖ ❖ ❖ ❖

"Boy, do I have things to tell you," Lauren said when Danny called later that afternoon.

"Yeah? Like about Kim?"

"Well, that too. But first, let me tell you about my conversation with Rose."

She said 'Rose' again.

Lauren recounted her exchange with her mom, almost word for word.

"Did she really say, 'over my dead body?' Seriously after what happened with Maddy? That was flat out cruel."

"Oh, I know she didn't mean it that way. She's scared, Danny. She's scared of me driving, but most importantly, she's scared of losing me. I think her life IS me. Like there's no separation between us."

Danny thought about the conversation he'd had with Rose when he told her to cut the umbilical cord. They were all aware of what was happening. All but Rose.

"But in the end, she watched the videos with me. I could tell there was an interest there, but I didn't push. It's best left for a while so she can digest it all. She wasn't thrilled when I told her dad knew. Just pray she considers it."

"You know you are an adult and can do this without her permission."

"I know. I don't want to hurt her. She's lost, Danny."

"I know.

"So now, what about your time with Kim."

"It was great—until Mother walked in. She was SO rude. She couldn't wait for her to leave. I really lit into her. I know I just said I feel sorry for her, but she's becoming overbearing. I want to see Kim again—but not here. Can you take me over to her house?"

"Sure. When?"

"I'll text her to see when she's free. I know she was planning to start her summer job next week. I'll let you know."

"We'll work something out. If there were an elevator here, I'd bring you over, and you could meet here. But I don't think I could get you up the stairs."

Lauren clutched when she heard his words. So many simple things she had taken for granted, like walking up the stairs, had been taken away from her. Whenever she thought she had come to terms with her condition, something like this would happen.

I'm determined more than ever now to drive again.

"I'll let you know, Danny. And thanks."

"Anytime."

Lauren hung up the phone and made an agreement with herself. Beginning today, she would accept the past and look to the future. Picking up the catalog of courses from George Mason University, she began circling what she planned to take.

And she would keep seeing Kim no matter what her mother said or did. She wouldn't let her run her life anymore.

What was it about that girl that made me react that way? Rose thought as she was putting some of Lauren's clothes away. *Was it her voice, her look. . .? Something threw me—scared me. Oh, I'm overacting. I don't want her coming around anymore. It's not good for Lauren to make friends with people who will only make her regret what she can't do for herself. I'll nip it in the bud.*

Pushing the scarves around in the bottom drawer of Lauren's dresser to make room for some new things she had bought for her, Rose uncovered a flower-covered book tucked into the very back.

She picked it up, the pull to open it intense. It was a journal.

Hesitating, feeling it must be private since it was hidden, she put it back where she found it and proceeded with the task at hand, although her eyes frequently drifted to the floral cover. So tempting.

Lauren appeared in the doorway just as her mother was shutting the bottom drawer of her dresser.

"What are you doing?" she asked, eyeing the drawer.

"Just putting away some new things I bought for you. What are your plans for the rest of the day?"

Deftly turning over the college catalogs she had placed next to her laptop, she replied.

"Not much. Going to get some reading done. Later would you take me over to the rec center? I thought I'd try out the wheelchair basketball they've got going on over there."

"Are you sure you're ready for that?"

"The docs say I'm fine, and it would be good for me. Remember that conversation?"

Rose had chosen to ignore the doctor's advice that Lauren move on with her life. She was still afraid, still thought her daughter was too fragile.

"Of course, honey. Just let me know when you want to go. I'll be upstairs finishing the laundry."

Just when Rose thought the crack between them was sealing, she had to face that Lauren was gaining her independence. There was much about her oldest child she wasn't going to be a part of. She forced those feelings away.

❖ ❖ ❖ ❖

As soon as Rose left her room, Lauren searched for a new place to keep her journal. Her private thoughts to Maddy were just that—private. The times when they confided in each other, knowing that their secrets were safe, were treasured moments. They were nobody's business, least of all her mother's.

The built-in bookshelves above the desk in her room were too high for her to reach, leftover from when the room used to be her dad's office. It was apparent that the dresser was a bust now. She rolled over to the closet, searching for a hidden location. Most places would still be visible, but she spotted a box in the lower-left corner. Curious, she reached down to pick it up.

Taking off the cover, she discovered it held a surprise of its own. Inside were two envelopes marked LAUREN. Nothing else. Realizing they weren't sealed she opened the first.

Tied in a beautiful pink ribbon was a lock of hair—her hair. Stroking the hair, she realized how blond she was even as a newborn.

She opened the second envelope. Carefully unfolding the letter contained within, she discovered a Birth Certificate.

LAUREN ELIZABETH FOSTER

Just before re-inserting it into the envelope, she noticed the place of birth—St. Francis Medical Center, Trenton, New Jersey.

Wow, I never knew I was born in New Jersey. That must have been before we moved here. I have to ask mom.

Wait. Why is this hidden in the back of the closet? Where are the birth certificates for Danny and Jenny?

Her mother's obsessive behavior towards her all her life had begun at birth. Why was she so different? Was it because they had waited so long for her? She knew her parents had been married for five years before she was born. Her dad wasn't this way with her. Why was her mother so over the top?

She replaced the box back in the corner of the closet and tucked her journal in with it—secrets lying together.

Fifty-Five

want to meet up?

sure. when and where?

how bout at our favorite diner.
have some news. five-ish?

see you then.

✧ ✧ ✧ ✧

This time Kim and Danny chose to sit at the counter. Suddenly, he was a kid again, sitting in the diner down the road from the beach. This time the memories were good. His dad had swung Jenny up onto the stool, her little legs dangling off the edge. Lauren, busy slurping her milkshake, sat beside him. His dad was teasing his mom about the white rings around her eyes from where her sunglasses had perched all day.

His feet weren't burning.
And now he was here with Kim.

"So, what's this news you have?"

"Wow, right to the point, aren't you?"

"Well, you can't just drop that bomb in a text and not spill the beans."

"Fine. I've decided about next year. I'm not going back." Danny's eyes widened.

"So, what are you going to do? Where will you go?"

"I've transferred to George Mason—so I'm back to stay. I can live at home and save all sorts of money."

Kim hesitated to tell Danny that he was part of her decision. She still had to feel him out, try to read him.

A softness shone in Danny's eyes. Did he dare hope?

"Um. . ." Words stalled on his tongue.

"Um, do you think we could see each other now?"

"Stupid. Why do you think I told you? I was hoping you'd say that." Kim's green eyes turned a deep shade of emerald when she laughed.

Danny, unabashed, reached over and took her hand.

"I'd really like that."

"Me, too."

"Oh, by the way, I picked this up over at the library. Thought you might be interested."

Pushing the paper toward him, Kim slid off the counter stool and brashly gave Danny a quick hug. She got no push back.

Danny turned the flyer over.

Auditions for Our Town

By Reston Community Players

July 20, 21, 22 8 PM

RCP Rehearsal Hall

Sunset Business Park

266 Sunset Park Dr.

Herndon, VA

His mother's words, 'You can always try out for community theatre' came back to him. Here was his opportunity to get back on stage, maybe show his family where his heart still was.

How subtly Kim had nudged him. How she *got* him. Like no one else ever had.

He folded the flyer and shoved it in his back pocket. Maybe all his days of doing voice-overs for Ken would pay off.

Fifty-Six

LAUREN, STILL DISTURBED by her mother's treatment of Kim, tread lightly around the subject when they were together. But she did bring it up in conversation with Dr. Goldman the following Thursday at her appointment.

Rose, still driving her, had conveniently disregarded mention of a car, of driving, of moving on. Lauren suspected that her theory was if she didn't bring it up, maybe Lauren would forget about it.

Like hell I'm going to forget it.

With her mother once again parked in the waiting room, Lauren went in to see her therapist.

"How are you, Lauren. It's been a while. I'm assuming that's good news then."

"I've been doing much better. Thanks."

"Are you still keeping your journal—writing to Maddy?"

"Yeah, but not as much lately. I've been able to talk to

my brother more now that he's home, and I've made a new friend."

"Tell me about her."

"She's Danny's girlfriend. He met her at school, and now she's transferring back here to George Mason. She wants us to get to know each other better. We've both felt like we've known each other all our lives. Strange, huh."

"Not so much. There are people in this world that we instantly connect with, who we're drawn to. I'm happy for you. You need someone to take over where you left off with Maddy. I hope that doesn't sound cruel."

"I'm so afraid of losing her, my connection with her, but I know she's gone, and I have to cherish the memories of us while I make new memories with other people."

"You've come such a long way, Lauren. I'm pleased to see that you're ready to get on with your life. You will always cherish your memories with Maddy, but it's time to store those away with your journal and pull them out only when you need them.

"How is your relationship with your mother?"

"Suffocating, but I'm trying to create a little space between us—very gradually. I know she's alone and lonely, especially since Dad left. And I know she's terrified of losing me. I wish she'd realize that just because I want to move on with my life doesn't mean I don't love her."

"Have you ever asked her why she needs you so much?"

"Not exactly. I've hinted that she could go back to work

now, that I could learn to drive again, go back to school. It all seems to terrify her. I don't want to hurt her—I do love her—as a daughter loves her mother, not as a possession. I'd love for her to see you for herself. I think there must be a great deal of baggage in her past for her to be acting like this."

"Your mother is not you, Lauren. You're separate people with separate issues in life. You must move on, even if it hurts her. She'll come to terms with it, or she'll seek some help. I'm very proud of how you've turned your life around."

"Speaking of turning a life around, my brother is clean and sober since he's been home, has himself a job, and a girl-friend. He's doing great and I'm happy for him."

"Do you know what his turning point was?"

"Yeah. He hit rock bottom at Christmas and smashed Jenny's dollhouse. He turned to our dad for help. That ticked my mother off, but she didn't want him in the house because he couldn't promise ever to do drugs again."

"Is your dad still living somewhere else?"

"He has an apartment. I don't know if he and Mom will get back together. I suspect there's more to their issues than just my accident. But I've learned that I can't take that on either. It will be what it will be."

"Do you still want to keep up with our sessions? You're doing so well."

"Maybe not as often, but yes, I would. It helps me to talk things out with a real person—someone objective."

"I'll leave it up to you to make an appointment whenever you want. My door is always open."

"Thanks, I'll remember that."

"Is your mother waiting outside?"

Lauren rolled her eyes. "Of course. But I plan to do something about that soon, too. See you next time."

Fifty-Seven

JULY OOZED IN with intense heat and humidity, coating everything and everyone in beads of moisture. Temperatures hovered in the 90's with little cooling off at night. Air conditioners hummed 24/7 to keep up with the heat seeping in.

"We need to plan a 4th of July barbeque," Lauren said to her mother while they were enjoying a rare relaxing moment on the porch, the overhead fan whirring like a helicopter about to take off.

"It's a little late for that, Lauren. We only have a couple of days to plan."

"Oh, Mother, it's not a big deal. We could have Danny come over and grill, make some side dishes, and we'll be all set."

"Who do you plan to invite at this late date?"

"Well, the Franconi's for one. Dad, of course. And Kim.

She and Danny are seeing each other now. Did he tell you she's transferring to George Mason?"

Uneasiness made Rose shiver despite the heat.

"Oh, I think we should keep it to family. The Franconi's of course because they're almost like family. But, there's no need to invite that girl. We hardly know her."

"That's the point, Mother. I want to get to know her better. We clicked when we met. And besides, if she is Danny's girlfriend, she should be here. Why are you so against her? You only met her once, and you know how I feel about how you treated her. Think about someone other than yourself for once."

As soon as the words left her mouth, Lauren regretted saying them.

"I'm sorry. I didn't mean that. It's just that everything's different around here now with Dad gone and Danny working so hard to stay on the straight and narrow. We need to start over, branch out, welcome new people into our lives."

Rose sat very still, ruminating on Kim. *Why am I so against letting her in?*

Lauren could see her wheels turning and knew she was taking in everything she was saying.

"If that's what you want to do, I'll leave the planning up to you. Just remember this is pretty last minute so that girl might not be able to make it."

"Mother, that girl has a name—Kim. And Danny likes her, and so do I. Give it a rest."

Leaving those harsh words to hang in the stifling air, Lauren left the room to make some phone calls. Every time she thought she was getting somewhere with her mother, the ax would fall, separating them even further.

✧ ✧ ✧ ✧

What's wrong with me? Why do I keep suffocating my daughter? Why do I still try to run her life?
Because she's special.
Painful memories seeped in. She shoved them out.
She had been pushing her away with that love, but she didn't know how to change.
I know I have to let her go to get her back.

✧ ✧ ✧ ✧

The patio was cleaned off, tables washed, chairs scrubbed from the spring pollen that had accumulated, and umbrellas raised. Lauren took care of the menu: chicken, ribs, hamburgers, and hot dogs along with side salads. Angela offered home-made potato salad, Tom said he'd bring some coleslaw, and Lauren planned to cut up a watermelon for dessert.

Before long Danny had invited Josh and his family, too. Their friendship had withstood some pretty rocky times and survived unscathed. Then he thought about how good Mr.

Hudson had been to him, taking him back at the store, and he added him and his family to the list.

Extra chairs were added to the patio as the list expanded, and the grocery list grew exponentially. Danny's only request was that they not serve alcoholic beverages, thinking not only of himself but of Josh. So, they bought cases and cases of soft drinks, lemonade, and iced tea from the local Costco.

"Mommy, can we get some sparklers?" Jenny begged.

"I'm not comfortable around them, Jenny, but you can ask your father. If he's okay with it and will monitor their use, it might be fun."

Lauren overheard the conversation and noticed how much her mother was loosening up.

She was twelve, Danny eleven, and Jenny just a baby. They were lined up on the sides of the street watching the 4th of July parade. Tom had Jenny up on his shoulders so she could see better. The local high school marching bands were parading down the street to the cheers of the crowd. Everyone was so happy and excited to see the fireworks later that night. Rose was smiling and laughing, one of the few times Lauren remembered her enjoying herself.

Did she dare hope that some of that was returning? Was there even the slightest hope that they could become that family again?

Danny's voice interrupted her memories.

"Mom, I want to invite Kim's family? This party has grown, and I hate to leave them out."

"Do you even know them?"

"Not really. I mean, I've heard all about them from Kim. I think it will seem strange with all the other families here to have Kim here alone."

"Have you thought that maybe she might like to spend the holiday just with her own family?" Rose hedged.

"Come on, Mom, I've already invited her, and she said yes. What're three more people?"

Feeling backed into a corner, Rose relented. Maybe if the girl's family were here, she wouldn't focus so much on Danny.

"Fine."

What have I gotten myself into now? Rose thought. *This whole thing has snowballed, and now I have all these people I hardly know or don't know at all, coming to my house.*

And then that girl will be here with her whole family. What is this—a meet the family event? Maybe we should invite some of Lauren's new friends from the rec center to come, too. Since she's so determined to get herself out and away from me, maybe I can steer her in that direction. Damn, why do I have this feeling?

Fifty-Eight

THIS IS EXACTLY *what we've all needed*, thought Danny. A party. Lauren's getting out, I'm sober, Dad's coming—and Kim will be here.

Reaching into his pocket, he retrieved the flyer Kim had given him in the diner. Flashbacks of his times up on the stage, slipping into someone else's shoes, transforming himself, pulled heavily. God, how he missed the theatre.

I've got to give this a shot. Kim believes in me. Now I have to believe in myself.

He tacked it up on the bulletin board in the kitchen, where it would stare down at him, not letting him forget.

On his way out to shop, he took notice of an announcement on the lobby bulletin board for a two-bedroom condo for rent on the other side of town. It was on the first floor. His dad had talked about moving so that Lauren could visit more without needing to be carried upstairs.

It must be so humiliating for her.

He jotted down the number to give to his dad and hoped he was still welcome to stay with him. Otherwise, he would be homeless. He couldn't afford a place of his own plus pay for school with the money he made at the store. With Kim transferring to George Mason, he hoped to go there too and that would cost even more. He was navigating new territory and it was unsettling.

Thoughts of getting his family back together tended to seep in when Danny was unaware. But visions of a long time ago, when he was a child, were unsettling. Nothing was right as far back as he could remember. Yes, there were those moments when he remembered his mom and dad enjoying each other. But it seemed so long ago. Most of his memories were of tensions, arguments, and his parents just tolerating each other. The marriage had been in trouble for a long time.

Danny had become very introspective as part of his recovery. He learned in counseling how everyone's past influences how they grow, who they become. What could be in his parents' past to make them the way they were? Or was it just a bad match?

Twenty-five years and three kids later, it was all coming apart, and he wasn't sure what the survival rate for them would be.

The phone rang for so long Danny almost hung up.

"This is Countryside Rentals. How may I help you?"

"Yes, I'd like some information about the two-bedroom condo advertised. When is it available and how much? What's included?"

The click of the keyboard tapped through the line as the agent pulled the information up. She gave Danny the details and asked if he would like to schedule an appointment to see it.

"I'm inquiring for my dad, so I'll have to check with him first. Has there been much interest?"

"Quite a bit, so I would act as soon as possible while it's still available."

"Thank you. I'll get back to you as soon as I can." He hung up the phone and placed the ad and the information on the kitchen table.

Fifty-Nine

DESPITE THE WRECK his personal life was in, Tom's business was thriving, and he began working longer and longer hours. And he didn't have Rose to register her disapproval. Danny was on the right path, and Lauren, more confident, was confiding in him more. And, of course, Jenny was still playing with her Barbies, although not as much anymore. She and Lisa had moved on to constant phone conversations begging to get their own phones.

Coming in early one Monday, he saw an envelope addressed to him marked PERSONAL. He recognized Abby's handwriting. Uneasiness clutched at him. They had kept their distance around the office, interacting strictly for business purposes. The secretive presence of this letter was ominous.

Reaching for his letter opener, he sliced through the flap and began reading.

Tom,

Enclosed, please find my letter of resignation. I have been offered a position in New York, which I plan to take. Working for you has been a boon to my career, but it is time I moved on.

This has been a difficult decision to make, given our personal relationship. After a great deal of thought, I realized that it would never come to fruition. There are too many obstacles.

I'm sorry to do this in such an impersonal way. I am putting in my two-week notice and taking two weeks of vacation, so I will not be returning. It's better this way.

I wish you all the best and hope that your family issues can come to a successful conclusion. My best to your daughter, Lauren, on her future.

Regards,
Abby Mansfield

The letter slipped slowly from Tom's grasp fluttering to the floor, another part of his life slipping away.

Stung, confused, Tom pulled the blinds, shut off the lights and sat at his desk to think. But there wasn't much to think about. Abby had already made the decision for them. He understood. He couldn't keep her in limbo while he figured his marriage out.

He replayed the last conversation they had.

"Did you get things straightened out with your wife?"

"She doesn't want to have anything to do with me, Abby. She's still harboring a lot of anger over something way in our past. She's never going to come around."

"Does she have a right to her anger over this 'something'?"

Taken aback by her accusing tone, Tom had put up a shield. He didn't need Abby's wrath as well as Rose's. But she continued.

"You seem to think that everything is Rose's fault. I hate to say it takes two to tango—that's such a cliché—but it's true. Have you had a heart to heart with yourself about your part in this mess you're in?"

Tom heard Rose's words reverberating in his head.

You don't understand how much I hurt.

You're only thinking of yourself.

Do you have any idea how much this means to me?

Do you even care?

In such a brief period of their 'relationship,' Abby had dissected him. She had cut to the chase about things he wouldn't admit to himself—he had been a bastard twenty-five years ago, and Rose had never forgiven him. And she was right. He hadn't even tried to understand what was driving her. It wasn't until after Jenny was born so many years later that he truly fell in love with all his children—with Lauren.

"I don't know what to say to you, Abby. You're right? You got me?"

"I never wanted to hurt you, Tom, but you have to take some responsibility for your failed marriage. And until you do, I can't be a part of your mess. I need to protect myself. I've been hurt before. I won't be hurt again."

Tom had reached out for her, but she had backed away. He had never seen such strength in her before. He had grossly underestimated her.

She turned and left his office, not looking back, the sound of her clicking heels receding into the distance.

That was when he knew he had lost her. He had squandered his chance at happiness and made to look at himself for what he was—a coward, a selfish coward. Perhaps if he had apologized to Rose for his selfish behavior way back, had been more sympathetic to her struggles and needs, his marriage might not have failed. But Rose's secrets hadn't helped either one of them.

And now he re-read Abby's resignation letter imprinted boldly on his memory.

Her last words in the letter were so cold.

Regards, Abby Mansfield.

All business. Impersonal. Final.

The realization that he needed to solve his fractured

marriage overwhelmed him. There were so many under-lying issues that he and Rose had never resolved. And one was explosive. Kept under wraps for so many years, he was terrified of what would happen if the bindings came undone.

Sixty

WHEN HE COULDN'T FIND a parking spot at the apartment complex Tom's frustration mounted further. He was sick to death of this place. Crammed into 840 square feet with Danny sleeping on the pull-out in a tiny room, he regretted what had become of his life: broken marriage, emotional affair, estrangement from his kids, and secrets.

He trudged up the stairs to his apartment, checking the mailbox on his way. Nothing but junk. Most of his mail was still going to the house. The key turned in the lock, and the smell of this morning's sausage greeted him. Danny must have made himself breakfast.

He's really turned his life around. I wish I could turn mine around, too.

There was a note on the table for him.

Check it out, was all it said.

Tom scanned the information about the condo. First

floor, two bedrooms, 1200 square feet. Partially furnished. Two reserved parking spaces. Price—negotiable, followed by a phone number. The reserved parking clinched it for him.

If this is the life I've been relegated to, this is a no brainer.

He pulled his phone out of his pocket and dialed the number.

Finding the condo, he pulled into the parking space. It was a dream come true—right in front of the building—perfect for Lauren to visit.

The space was a corner unit, airy and full of light. Each bedroom had a bed, and there were a couch and two chairs in the living room. All he would need was a table and chairs, some lamps, and end tables. Tom's heart thumped. This was serendipitous.

The owner's last tenant had left suddenly, breaking his lease, and he was anxious to get it re-rented—thus the negotiable price. It took no longer than 15 minutes for Tom to make up his mind. This was meant for him. Providence was on his side for a change.

Putting his signature to the rental agreement, Tom shook the agent's hand, walked the few steps to his car, and drove away, a smile filling his face. He couldn't wait to tell Danny. Danny. The son he was just beginning to know.

✧ ✧ ✧ ✧

"Hey, Lauren, it's Dad. Give me a call when you get the chance. I've got some news I hope you'll like."

Next, Tom texted his son over at Hudson's Convenience Store.

> Deal done. It's perfect. Thanks. You're the best. See you for dinner and we can go see it together.

With a major decision made, moving his life forward instead of stagnating in the present, Tom still knew he had to deal with Rose, with the past, with their marriage—or what was left of it. Abby had released him from his confusion. Their relationship was over. No more tug and pull about doing the right thing.

She was everything Rose was not. She just came at the wrong time.

Everything for the barbeque was ready—except Rose. As the partygoers began arriving, her anxiety spiked. Always guarded, she felt exposed. Since she had left work, since the accident, her world had shrunk. With Tom and Danny gone, her universe was Lauren—with Jenny on the fringes. Now she was going to be on display to everyone, including strangers. She turned to see Tom approaching.

"Hello, Tom."

"Hello, Rose. How are you?"

"Fine," she feigned, still trying to keep her apprehension from showing.

"You've done a great job here. Thanks for letting me come."

"You are their father. You should be here, especially for Lauren."

"And Jenny. Don't forget about her."

"Don't start."

"Start what? It was just a statement of fact. She's growing up and needs more attention, that's all."

"Leave it alone, Tom. Go put the coleslaw on the table and have Danny start the grill."

Who am I kidding? Nothing's changed. This is never going to work.

Glancing back at his wife, he saw the scowl he was so used to, return. Following her gaze to the side of the patio, he saw a family he didn't know come across the lawn.

Must be new neighbors since I left.

Then he watched his son pull apart from talking to Josh, stride over and hug the girl.

This must be the Kim he's been talking about lately. How lovely is she? I must have seen her around somewhere—she looks so familiar.

Her smile warmed him immediately.

And he watched as Rose turned away to talk to Angela.

What is it with her? I know there's a softness behind that exterior, but she just won't let it out.

They were newly married, madly in love, going up the steps to their new apartment. A ball rolled into the street, and Rose, anticipating a child coming right after it, spun around, ran out to get it, and handed it to the little boy.

Such compassion she had back then. How, when, did it all go wrong.

He saw Danny shake hands with the girl's dad and heard him say, 'nice to meet you.'

Tom put down the coleslaw and went over to be introduced, taking the first step to ease the discomfort he saw on Danny's face.

"Welcome, to our home," he said, the irony of 'our home' not escaping him.

"Thank you for inviting us, said Sarah, Kim's mother. This is lovely."

"Come on, Kim. Let me introduce you to my buddy, Josh."

And the mingling began.

Sixty-One

"WHAT'S WRONG with you, Mom?" Danny let fly while they were cleaning up. "You didn't even come over to say 'hi' to Kim and meet her parents and brother."

"Oh, there were just so many people here, I guess I just missed them."

"Bull shit. That was on purpose. Lauren told me how rude you were to Kim the first time you met her. And here you go again. Well, just so you know, we're dating now, and she's going to be part of my life.

So, you'd better get used to seeing her."

Rose, astounded at his anger, suspected the worst.

"Are you on drugs again?"

"Thanks for the confidence, Mom. And no, I've been clean for months, thanks in good part to Dad."

"I'm sorry, Danny. I shouldn't have said that. I must just be tired. Let's forget this conversation happened."

"Fine," he answered, tucking her words away into one of his drawers.

Why does that girl rattle me so much? I'm sure she's very lovely. And smart. And she likes my son. Why do I dislike her?

Throughout the party, Rose had kept her distance from Kim, but observed her closely. She watched her interact with Danny and then with Lauren. She fit right in.

Something was nudging in the back of her brain, but it wouldn't come forward. Something she couldn't quite put together. At first, it was just an annoyance. But it morphed into uneasiness. And now Rose was scared of something she couldn't put her finger on.

Turning back to her son, she tried to apologize.

"I guess that was rude of me. I don't know what makes me react to things the way I do."

"Look, Mom, I know it hasn't been easy for you with Dad gone and adjusting to how things have changed around here. I get that. But Lauren and I are both grown now, and we both need to make our own decisions and expand our horizons— meet new people, do new things. You have to let us go."

Danny looked over to see tears filling Rose's eyes. Back peddling his words, attempting to suck them back into his mouth, he said, "We love you, Mom. And we know you really love us. It just has to be a different kind of love now."

Danny saw her glance at the scar on her arm, her reminder of that fateful day that changed things for everyone. He knew she had heard him. But would she be able to do anything about it?

Reaching out to put his arms around her to say goodbye, he felt the chords on the back of her neck stiffen. It was then that he realized there was so much more he didn't know about her. What drove her? What made her react the way she did? What made her treat her children so differently?

His mother was a complicated mess of emotions, and he needed answers.

Sixty-Two

THE 5TH OF JULY DAWNED, and all traces of the party were gone. Danny had stayed late to help clean up and, with extra chairs stacked and tables put back into place, he finally crawled into bed around one.

As Mr. Hudson was leaving the evening before, he told Danny to take a break and come in late. So, Danny was still zoned out when he got a text from Kim.

> why does ur mther hate me?

Feeling like cold water was just thrown in his face, he scrambled to de-fuzz his brain before answering.

> she doesn't

> yeah, then y did she ignore my family and me?

Danny could feel the steam seeping through the line.

> cn we talk ltr? gotta go to work. pick u up at 5, k?

> k

Now how am I going to handle this?

Mr. Hudson's son, Andy, came in at 4:30 to relieve Danny so he could meet Kim at 5. As much as he wanted to see her, he didn't know how he was going to explain his mother's actions.

At every stoplight, he had a new idea.
She was just so busy with everyone.
She was rattled seeing my dad.
She was making sure my sister Lauren was okay.
Everything sounded lame. The fact was his mother was just plain rude, and there was no way around it. He didn't know why—nobody knew. He had never been close to his mom, but he never remembered her being this bad. Was it just about Lauren?

None of this was going to help him explain her actions to Kim. The only thing he could do was apologize for his mother and hope Kim would accept.

She was waiting for him in front of the law office, where she worked for the summer.

She sure is hot, he thought. *Except for the scowl on her face.*

"Hey."

"Hey."

"Look. . ." they both began.

"You first," Danny said.

"I'm sorry for what I said. I don't know what I've done wrong to make your mother dislike me. I was just upset."

"I don't think she dislikes you, Kim. I think she's oblivious to her actions. It might be fear. She's so close to my sister, obsessively close, that she may feel threatened by you."

"Seriously. Me, a threat? That's just plain stupid."

"I don't know. I really don't. Let me talk to her and see if I can figure this out. Please don't write her off yet. Lauren does want to get to know you, and I think you should still come to visit. Maybe once my mom sees that you're just a good friend, she'll ease off."

"I hope it's okay with your mom that I see you."

"Not to worry. She's never been a helicopter mom where I was concerned."

Kim saw the shadow cross his face and then disappear.

"Can we get something to eat?" she said. "I'm starving."

✧ ✧ ✧ ✧

"Let me guess. Two iced teas," said Alice the minute they sat down in their favorite booth.

"Have you given any thought to that flyer I gave you, Kim asked?"

"How did you know that's just what I needed?"

"Oh, call it intuition. Are you interested?"

"I'm gonna' give it a shot. I even checked the play out of the library to start rehearsing."

"Would you like to rehearse your lines with me? I mean, I'm no actor, but I could cue you, or whatever it is they call it."

"I'd love that. Thanks. We make a good team."

✧ ✧ ✧ ✧

True to her word, Kim met with Danny to rehearse the script for the auditions.

He is SO good. I know he's gonna' get this. When I see him get into a part, his entire body changes. He becomes someone else.

Remembering their conversations about his childhood and his feelings of incompetence, she realized he was always playing a role—anything to cope.

That's how he got by. How could his family not see him for his awesome qualities—especially his mother? If we get involved, am I going to be judged too? Then again, I guess I already have, and I don't think I passed muster.

"Cue, please."

"Huh, oh, sorry."

"Where were you just then?"

"Just lost in my head. Here's your next line."

Sixty-Three

SITTING ON THE COUCH at the apartment, Kim watched Danny put an X through July 19th on his calendar at the end of the day. It bumped up against the big red circle of the next day, audition day, looking like the beginnings of a tic-tac-toe game.

Or the Xs and Os on a Valentine card.

He had read the script of *Our Town* ad nauseum, with her cuing him for different parts. She knew he had his heart set on the part of George, the teenage love of Emily. The role required transitioning from age eighteen to marriage and then fatherhood, stretching his acting abilities.

"Can I come with you?" Kim asked, "or will I make you nervous?" "That'd be great. If it weren't for you, I probably wouldn't be doing this."

"Don't sell yourself short. The acting bug would have caught up with you sooner or later. I'm glad it's sooner."

Her smile stirred his heart as a flush edged up his face like a sunburn.

"I want to be part of this so bad. I want to be up there under the heat of the lights, not able to see the audience, trading myself for my character. I can smell it, taste it. Do I sound crazy?"

"Maybe crazy in love—with acting, I mean," Kim replied, hurrying to explain herself.

It's too soon for me to feel this way about him. But he's like a magnet. I'm drawn to him more each day.

"Look, Kim. You know how much I want to be with you, to have you for my girlfriend. And you also know how much baggage I come with—the addiction, the failures, the screwed-up family. If you want out, now is the time. Now, before I won't be able to let you go."

The lines they had rehearsed resonated.

GEORGE: Emily, if I *do* improve and make a big change. . .would you be. . . I mean: *could* you be. . .

EMILY: I...I am now; I always have been.

Over the last few weeks, she had listened to the words come alive as he sunk deeper into the part of George, making it his own. The transformation was incredulous. He *was* George—at eighteen, then as a new husband, then as a father.

As the lines poured from his mouth, his posture changed. Gone was the insecure slump of the shoulders she often saw.

Gone was the tentativeness in his voice. Gone was the boy she knew. And before her stood a young man ready to take on the world.

✧ ✧ ✧ ✧

Kim was waiting for him outside the rehearsal hall where the auditions were taking place. The parking lot was rapidly filling up with cars—with hopeful actors inside.

"Holy shit," he exclaimed when he saw how many people were filing in. "Not sure I can do this. Maybe I'm not ready."

"Don't be ridiculous. You know this play inside and out. You're more George right now than you are Danny."

Reaching over to hug her, Danny smelled the sweet fragrance of her hair. He tamped down his desire for her knowing it would be a total distraction.

Maybe I shouldn't have agreed to have her here. What if I fail, mess up the lines, or forget them all together?

Get a grip, man. She's seen you before. Focus.

One after another, the aspiring actors read their lines.

The color receded from Danny's face.

He leaned over and whispered to Kim.

"I don't stand a chance in hell of competing with these guys. I may as well pack it in right now."

He stood up to leave and felt Kim's arm on his, gripping him, holding him back. She didn't say a word. Her look, the light in her eyes, was all he needed.

She believes in me. I need to believe in myself.

He squeezed her hand as they called his name. The sound of his mother's scathing comments reverberated in his head.

I won't let her win. I got this.

"We'll get back to you," was the next thing he remembered hearing from the director. The rest was a blur.

He climbed down the stairs and back to his seat.

"I really screwed that one up."

"You were great," she answered. Just wait and see."

Afraid to listen to the rest of the tryouts, he picked up his script. "Let's go. I need to get out of here."

"What's wrong with you," she said. "You need to have more confidence in yourself. Think about how good you were in high school."

She avoided mentioning the rehearsals she had seen down at school. It would bring up too many memories.

"Just chill. You'll hear soon."

"I'm glad you have such high hopes. Did you listen to those guys? They were amazing."

"And so were you, you idiot. You didn't see or hear yourself. Now just shut up and take me to lunch."

Sixty-Four

DAYS WENT BY, and Danny heard nothing. Discouraged, he returned the script to the library and turned his attention to the upcoming move. He had brought empty boxes home from the store, filling them with books, papers, clothes, and pictures of the family. He saw the lost look on his dad's face as he put a picture of Rose in the box. Despite the separation, Danny knew there were still feelings there.

"Do you think you and Mom will get back together?" he asked, careful not to bring Abby's name into the conversation.

"I don't know, Danny. I don't even know how we got to this point."

"Have you considered marriage counseling?"

"I don't think your mom would go for it. She's pretty rigid, and I don't think spewing out her feelings to a stranger would go over very well."

"Whenever I see Kim's family and how happy they seem, I wonder how we got so messed up."

"You never know what's under the surface. Speaking of Kim, are you still seeing her?"

"Yeah, she's terrific. I wish Mom would give her a chance. It's like she freezes up every time Kim comes around to see Lauren. Do you think she's afraid Kim will take her place with Lauren?"

"I don't know what your mom thinks anymore. But I thought Kim was lovely when I met her at the barbeque. I'm happy to see you happy."

"Thanks, Dad," Danny answered as his phone buzzed.

"I'd better get this."

Stepping away from the living room, he answered.

"Hello, this is Danny."

A gravelly voice he recognized began to speak.

"This is Jim from Reston Community Players. We'd like you for a call-back. One o'clock tomorrow."

"Uh, sure. You do have the right guy?"

"This is Danny Foster, correct?"

"Yes, it is."

"Then, we'd like to see you tomorrow."

"I'll be there. Thanks."

A grin spread from his lips over his entire face. He texted Kim immediately. He didn't want to share the news with his father just yet.

I still might not get the part.

BARBARA GALVIN

told u so. want me there?

ur my good luck charm. u bet.

✧ ✧ ✧ ✧

The skies broke open the next morning, flooding the roads with torrents of gushing water. Driving was treacherous as cars, caught mid-stream, began hydroplaning across the waterlogged streets. Rescue vehicles and Swift Water Rescue teams were called out to free stranded drivers and passengers. Flash flood watches were in effect for the entire D.C. area.

Mr. Hudson had closed the store knowing there would be few customers, so Danny had all day to rehearse his lines before his callback. He hadn't told Lauren or his dad just in case it came to nothing, but having Kim there was a no-brainer. She knew the lines about as well as he did, especially Emily's. Part of him wished she could get up on the stage and be Emily.

Carving his way between the boxes ready to be moved, Danny made his way to the kitchen but soon found that he had no appetite. Whatever was crawling inside his stomach made it impossible for him to eat.

I'll either have a celebration dinner or a consolation one tonight.

307

His callback was for one o'clock, so he left the apartment at eleven to pick up Kim, knowing the driving would be slow. The car's wipers raced to clear the streams of water snaking down his windshield. Sewers were overflowing, unable to keep up with the storm.

Kim was waiting for him on her porch, her bright yellow raincoat accentuating the new highlights in her hair. As much as he had fallen for her when she had her big oversized glasses, without them her green eyes glistened.

"Ready?" he said as he slammed the door of his car just a bit too hard.

"Whoa, what was that all about?"

"Just some rattled nerves escaping. Sorry."

"Chill, Danny. You got this. You never thought you'd get called back, and here you are. Just believe."

Danny leaned into her, slipping an arm around her lithe body, and kissed her, lingering on her sensual lips.

Gently pushing him away, she said, "Later. Now drive."

He would carry her response and the thoughts that went with them onto the stage.

The words, "we'll be in touch," once again cut across the auditorium as the director addressed the actors. The waiting game resumed.

"It's okay," Kim said, watching Danny pick at the threads on his shirt. "Let's go to dinner. You'll know soon enough."

"Easy for you to say," he snapped, shaking off her outstretched hand.

"Aw, shit, I'm sorry. I'm just fried. Could we maybe go back to my dad's and order a pizza? I'm not up for going out."

Kim saw the worry on his face and heard it in his voice.

This really is a make-it or break-it for him.

"I'd love that," she answered.

He's becoming paranoid. The last time his feelings were so screwed up, he fell hard. He's still so vulnerable.

Taking his arm and placing it around her waist, the warmth of his hand reached beneath her skin and into her bones.

Sixty-Five

STEAM ROSE FROM the pavement, the humidity rising with it.

"Another hazy, hot, and humid day here in the region," the TV meteorologist announced, confirming what everyone already knew.

Beads of sweat dripped from Danny's forehead even as he sat directly under the ceiling fan in his bedroom. Anticipating a response after his callback, he was glued to his phone, afraid of missing a call or text.

A familiar ping disrupted his thoughts.

> any news yet?

> nothing.

> keep the faith, see u ltr.

His phone rang. Not bothering to check the number, he said, "Thank God it's you. I really needed to hear your voice."

The voice on the other end answered, "Do I have the right number? Is this Danny Foster? This is Jim from the Reston Players."

Mortified, Danny said, "Oh, sorry, I thought it was someone else."

"Clearly. Sorry to disappoint, but I do have some good news. We've selected you for the part of George. The director was quite impressed with you. Rehearsals begin Friday night at six."

"Would you say that again?"

"You got the part, Danny. We'll see you Friday at six."

His mouth suddenly dry, he choked out a 'thank you' before hanging up. Releasing the breath he had been holding, he let the words sink in, words he needed to share.

> where r u? need to see u now.

> at work. meet for lunch?

> diner at 12?

> great. see u soon.

The morning crawled by, time seeming to stand still, while Danny waited to see Kim. Checking his phone every few minutes for the time, he replayed the director's words: "You got the part, Danny." This wasn't high school anymore. It wasn't Broadway either, but his exposure to the community would be widespread.

He was clean and sober, he was back to the theatre, and he had the girl. He had to believe this was meant to be. This was his path. Baby steps.

I guess this is our place now, Kim thought as she approached the diner. The noon sun glinted off the silver roof blinding her, so she didn't see Danny waiting out front until he approached her, his arms outstretched. His smile rivaled the sun saying everything.

"So!"

"So, what?"

"Stop it. Did you get it, or didn't you?"

"Just call me George, my dear."

Heedless of the customers surrounding them, Kim pulled his head towards her and kissed him.

A round of applause ensued while they settled into their favorite booth.

"Told 'ya."

"Thanks for having such faith in me."

"Oh, you're welcome. Someone has to have faith in you— you sure don't."

"Ouch, that stung. But you're right. I gotta believe in myself. How did you get so wise?"

"It must have been from all my parents."

"Huh?"

"Oh, forget I said anything. It's a story for another time. Right now, it's about you."

Alice came over to take their order, and Kim excused herself to go to the ladies' room.

Scratching his head, Danny wasn't sure what he had missed, but there needed to be another conversation. He couldn't just let her comment hang looking for a place to land.

Sixty-Six

GOOGLE SEARCH: DISABILITY DRIVING SERVICES IN NORTHERN VIRGINIA.

Lauren watched the search circle spin around, waiting for an answer to her question. Convinced that if she could find a certified driving specialist, she might be able to persuade her mom that there was life after paralysis.

Finally, the circle stopped turning, and a list of names popped up.

DRIVER REHABILITATION CENTER OF EXCELLENCE, commonly referred to as DRCE, was in Chantilly, Virginia, only about 45 minutes from Arlington.

Clicking on their website, she scanned the services available, from evaluation to driver training on specially equipped vehicles tailored for each individual. They dealt with a multitude of conditions, including paraplegia/quadriplegia. If a quad could learn to drive, so could she. The problem would be to convince her mother.

I understand her paranoia. The last time I was behind the wheel of a car, I ended up like this.

She couldn't think about Maddy. Maddy was gone—and she wasn't coming back no matter how much she 'talked' to her in her journal. Her sorrow was holding her back from moving on. Regret would always be part of her life now, but she had learned to trust other people with her feelings.

Lauren had to appeal to her mother's soft spot—her sense of wanting the best for her daughter. She was prepared with the website, the videos, and the services available. If she could at least be evaluated, she would have a professional voice to lend to her argument.

"I think I'll call Kim and run this by her," she murmured to herself.

"What's that?" Rose said, hearing her daughter's muted voice as she passed by her room.

"Um, nothing."

"What's that you're looking at?" Rose said, glancing at the cars on Lauren's screen.

Caught, Lauren decided to go for it.

"Don't get all panicky on me, Mother. It's just I found a fantastic place right in Chantilly that helps people with all kinds of disabilities learn to drive again."

"Oh, Lauren, not this again."

"Please, at least give me a chance to show you what I found."

Lauren plowed through the information, showing her mother the company's credentials, years of experience in the field, and the testimonials from their clients. Covering everything, she waited.

The silence was awkward as she watched the time on her computer advance. She could see her mother trying to process what she had just laid out, taking her glasses on and off as she did when she was nervous.

"Honey, I know this sounds like a good idea, and I appreciate all the research you've done, but I don't know how we can afford all of this. It means getting a specially equipped car. We don't mind taking you wherever you need to go."

"And I do appreciate that, but do you know how it makes me feel to have to rely on other people, ALL the time? I'm too young to be treated like I'm eighty and can't drive. You can't continue to keep me in a bubble. And besides, aren't you thinking about going back to work? If you do, you wouldn't have to worry about me so much. Could we talk to Dad about the expense?"

Once again, silence, except for the sound of the floorboards creaking under Rose's pacing.

"First of all, my going back to work was your idea, not mine. As far as driving, your dad has other expenses now with his own place. Let me think about it."

The statement hit Lauren hard. Forcing a smile, she said, "Thanks. This means the world to me."

Rose turned her face away, praying that Tom wouldn't be able to afford to buy a car for Lauren. She could continue to have her daughter to herself and put the blame on him.

Each time the cord holding them together began to fray, coming dangerously close to snapping, Rose loosened her grip, bottled up her fears and let Lauren have her way. Rather than try to reign her in, she played to her craving for independence. And once she had her hooked, she subtly began to tighten her grip again, her fears making her a master of manipulation.

Sixty-Seven

AUGUST 1ST ARRIVED, and with it came the U-Haul. Packing up what little they had, Tom and Danny were ready. There were no sad good-byes to the old apartment—it held too many uncomfortable memories: Tom's separation, Danny's plea for help, his rehab. Time to start over.

"What are we going to do for the rest of the furniture, Dad?"

"I'll scrape some money together, and we can go shopping."

"Is this it for you and Mom then? Are you really done?"

"I don't know. She doesn't want to talk about it. I don't know what else she's going through right now, but she seems very tense."

"I know. She completely closed up when she met Kim. I've never seen that kind of look on her face before. I keep thinking she might be afraid of losing Lauren to someone else, which is ridiculous. Lauren was always close to Maddy, and that didn't seem to bother her. Maybe it's just the accident that changed things."

"Your mother's always been a very complex human being. I think there are parts of her even I don't know—parts she's kept closed inside her where no one can see."

One of Danny's memory drawers opened.

He was sixteen and madly in love with a girl in his class. He couldn't stop talking about her. Out of the blue, his mom warned him about getting too attached to someone who might hurt him, break his heart.

Hell, he was only sixteen. Did she really think he was going to marry the girl?

It was the only time he remembered her caring enough to give him some advice. Strange advice. But she had been deadly serious.

Blinking, he brushed the memory aside and changed the subject.

"Um, has Lauren talked to you about this driving school she's looked into?"

"Yes, she has, and I say, 'it's about time.' It's time she came out from under your mother's oppressive hovering and stood on her own."

"Do you think she can do it? Can you afford the specially equipped car?"

"Not to worry. I'll make it happen. I don't know if your

mom's onboard yet, but we have to make her see that this is what Lauren needs."

"Good luck with that."

"I'll do my best to convince her. Things are rough between us, but at least we're still on speaking terms—her terms. In the meantime, get your back into these boxes, or we'll never get to our new place."

Our new place, Danny thought. *Starting over.*

His eyes clouded over momentarily, fearing the future. He noticed his dad's shoulders pushed back with the confidence he, himself, lacked.

I hope this play gives me some of those guts. I guess there's no time like the present to tell dad about my part.

"Dad, remember when you and Mom hated the idea of my going into theatre, and she finally said I could try out for Community Theatre as long as I didn't major in it in school?"

His cheeks burning, berating himself for his actions, Tom said, 'about that'. . ."

Danny held him off.

"It's okay, Dad. I just wanted you to know that I got the part of George in the production of *Our Town* by the Reston Community Players."

Grabbing him by both shoulders, Tom reached for his son, hugged him and whispered in his ear, 'I'm so happy for you.'

Not wanting to allow the tears to show, they held on to each other for a few extra minutes, each staring into the space behind the other. Finally, Danny broke the connection, looked into his dad's eyes, and said, 'Thanks, that means a lot.'

Tom slapped him on the back. "Now let's get this van loaded. We need a place to put our heads tonight."

A flashback to his dad's words the night of Lauren's accident when he said they needed to get a hotel room, came and went.

Maybe that was the beginning for us, and we didn't know it.

❖ ❖ ❖ ❖

"Need some help, guys?" Kim asked, showing up unannounced.

Danny's face erupted in a grin. She was just what he needed.

"What are you doing here?"

"I thought you might need some help."

"Seriously, Kim? These boxes are heavy."

"Watch me," she answered, as she reached down, bent her knees and hoisted a box up.

"Okaaay. Be our guest."

As they made their way back and forth to load the van, Danny mulled the words that had escaped her lips—words that completely confused him: 'from all my parents.'

I have no clue what that means, but she clearly didn't want me to pursue it. Do I dare mention it now?

Realizing the circumstances weren't ideal for a serious conversation, Danny vowed to bring it up at dinner later.

It's probably nothing—just strange.

His dad's voice broke in.

"Hey, you two, as soon as we get this over to the new place, we're going to a nice restaurant for dinner. My treat."

So much for alone time. I guess it will have to wait.

All through dinner, Tom watched the connection between his son and his new girlfriend.

Rose and I used to be like that. Before. . .everything. I pray they discuss everything with each other if it gets serious. Hopes, dreams, family. . .especially family. And no secrets.

"Dad. . .Dad." Danny's voice intruded on Tom's thoughts.

"Huh. What"

"I said Kim wants to go see Lauren, so we're gonna' take off. Thanks for dinner—and my new home."

"Say hello to your sister for me. Tell her I'll call or text soon to see how her new venture is coming along."

"Thanks, Mr. F. Dinner was great."

"We'll do it again sometime."

Sixty-Eight

A TWINGE OF NOSTALGIA swept through Danny as he approached the house—the house he had called home for so many years. Things he had never noticed while living there now seemed so obvious. The once spindly trees had turned into canopies shading the front yard. The shutters had gone from black to red and now to green. And there was a ramp to the back door for his sister.

The house that once held five now sheltered three. The site of laughter, tears, playful banter, and love—yes love—looked so peaceful from the curb. But Danny knew what had been inside: jealousy, competition, insecurities, arguments, and anger.

Jenny was outside roller skating in the driveway when first he, then Kim, pulled up, cramping her space. She rolled down to the sidewalk to greet them.

"Hey, kid, how's it goin'?"

Launching into all the typical eight-year-old drama which consumed her young life, she spilled the beans on all the latest neighborhood news until she glanced over to Kim, who had a gigantic smile on her face.

"Wow, it sure is different having a little sister. My brother hardly says two words. Hi, Jenny. Nice to see you again."

Feeling slightly chastised, Jenny answered, "Well, he asked."

"I'm sorry I was teasing you. It's nice to have someone who talks back."

"Hey, is Lauren here?" Danny asked.

"Yup. She's inside on her computer, researching something about driving."

"Great. That's what I wanted to talk to her about," answered Kim.

The front door opened, and Lauren yelled out, "Don't just stand out there, you two. Come in." She rolled away to make room for them.

Kim grinned. Lauren grinned back at her. Danny stared at the simpatico souls.

How quickly they've become best friends. Lauren so needed this.

"So, tell me about this driving gig," Kim said, her grin contagious.

The girls took off to Lauren's room, leaving Danny on his own.

Climbing up to his room at the top of the stairs, he glanced into the now impersonalized space where he grew up. The bed was stripped, the closet and dresser empty. All his personal touches—pictures, books, posters—were packed away, waiting to find a new home. An empty feeling settled in his chest.

He was out of his dad's apartment and not quite into the condo, leaving him in limbo. The old familiar feeling of not being grounded anywhere haunted him. The old insecurities tried to surface: the dorm, Chuck, the parties, the drugs and alcohol, followed by complete failure and humiliation. Then George and Emily/ Danny and Kim rushed in to take their place, centering him.

He heard the backdoor screen slam shut as his mother walked in. Closing the door to his room, to his old life, to his memories, he went downstairs.

"Whose car is that out there behind yours?" his mom asked without even a 'hello.'

"Oh, that's Kim's. She's in Lauren's room."

"Oh. And what are they up to?"

"Lauren's showing Kim the information she has on learning to drive again."

"Why would she show her? This is family business."

"Cut it out, Mom. Kim's just interested, that's all. She and Lauren have hit it off, and they're a couple of college girls bonding. It's good for Lauren to have someone—you know—since Maddy's gone."

Rose closed her mind, trying not to think about it.

"Help me with these groceries," she said, abruptly turning the conversation away from the reality staring her in the face.

Sitting out on the screened-in porch, Rose had her eyes closed, listening to the birds. The overhead fan was on full speed to compete with the August heat, ruffling the pages of the newspaper in her lap. She couldn't concentrate. Her world, what remained of it, was shifting. Tom was gone, Danny was gone, and Lauren seemed to be slipping away—with Kim. Only Jenny remained. Jenny, her baby. Her uncomplicated child. The one she'd neglected.

Voices broke her tormented silence.

"That's so awesome," Kim said, her voice floating down the hall. "You go for it, girl."

"Thanks for the support, Kim," Lauren answered, her eyes dancing in the sunlight.

I haven't heard her like this since Maddy, Rose thought. *If only it weren't this girl.*

"I gotta' get going. I'm going out to dinner with my family. Call me and let me know when you're free. I can pick you up, and we can go somewhere."

"I'm free *all* the time. Thanks."

"Bye, Mrs. Foster."

Rose gave a half-hearted wave.

Lauren started to leave the room, but her mother stopped her.

"Wait a minute, honey," Rose said, stopping her. "Do you think it's wise to involve that girl in your private business. You hardly know her."

"Mother, again, her name is Kim. She's been going out with your son, and she wants to be my friend. Let it go."

"If she's such a good friend, she didn't stay very long."

"She's going out with her parents for dinner. Anyway, what about my exploring that driving school? You've got to let me try."

Rose searched the space behind Lauren, not wanting to look her square in the eye.

"Did your dad say it was okay?"

"You heard him yourself, Mother. Yes, he supports my wanting to move on with my life."

"Fine. But get him to take you. I don't think I can watch."

Lauren saw her mother's hands clasp and unclasp in her lap. Realizing how hard this was hitting her, she softened her tone and spoke.

"I'm sorry if this is upsetting you, Mother. Thank you for letting me go."

Reaching over, she took her mother's hands in hers and held them fast. A moment passed between them—a moment of clarity and understanding. Lauren was moving on, and Rose knew it.

Regaining her composure, Rose pulled her hands away, turned, and left the room without looking back. Lauren heard her call out, 'Jenny, honey, where are you?'

Sixty-Nine

AT 2 AM, TWO WEEKS after moving into the new condo, Danny lay on his back in the dark, a sliver of the moon casting a finger of light through his bedroom window. In the eight months since he had been home, he had crashed and burned, gone into rehab, gotten sober, had the girl of his dreams in his life, and gotten a leading role in a community theatre production.

But he wasn't in school. His dreams of a degree in Theatre from William and Mary had blown up in his face. Kim had transferred to George Mason to study, but it was too late now for him to apply. The only option open to him was to begin a course of study at Northern Virginia Community College or NOVA as the locals called it. And there was still time to register before classes started.

Bits and pieces of a plan for his life gradually took shape in those wee hours that he lay awake.

"Cripes, I must have finally fallen asleep," he mumbled to himself, staring at the 9 o'clock hour flashing by his bedside. "And it must be Saturday because I smell breakfast."

How many times did I wake up not knowing what day it was or where I'd been?

Erasing the image, he pulled on his shorts, padded into the kitchen, and stood in the doorway watching his dad flip pancakes to the rhythm of some strange music coming from the Bose radio on the counter.

"Ahem," he coughed, trying not to startle the cook.

"Hey, kid, it's about time you got up. Want some pancakes?"

"If you're cookin', I'm eatin."

"How's the play coming? Do you have rehearsals today?"

"Yeah, it's crunch time. Opening night is next weekend. Do you think you'll come?"

"I wouldn't miss it," Tom answered, trying to hush the voices from his past chastising him for ignoring his son's dreams.

Between rehearsals, work, and going to AA meetings every day or night, Danny barely had time to get his application in to NOVA. Wasting the past year of his life haunted him. He was starting from scratch, and it hurt.

A few months ago, he blamed everyone.

Lauren was the perfect angel.

His mom never cared about him.

His dad thought he was a 'pansy' for wanting to go into theatre.

The fact was all these things were true. But, if he had more confidence in himself and his abilities, he would have been able to cope. He shouldn't have been so weak.

Shoulda, woulda, coulda. All lame. Get over it.

Texting Kim for a little confidence boost, he got the following reply:

> get a grip. it's old news.
> ur who u r now.

Ouch. She sure doesn't hold anything back. No wonder I'm falling for her. She doesn't put up with my shit; just accepts the me she first met, cracks and all.

Pity party over, he filled out his application online and picked some courses ready to begin again.

Seventy

PROMISING YOUNG ACTOR A BREAKOUT AS GEORGE IN "OUR TOWN," read the headline in the local paper.

"We remember this kid from high school, and he's back again in our local theatre. Danny Foster is a force to be reckoned with. He captured the role of George in all its complexity. We look forward to seeing more from him."

Tom tossed the paper over to Danny.

"Take a look. You're a star."

Danny's face turned upward, his smile filling the room. Two months of long rehearsals and late nights had produced a hit show. And he was part of it.

"I'm sorry I ever doubted you, Danny. This acting really is your schtick. I'm so glad you fought back and went for your dream."

"You can thank Kim for that, Dad. She was with me all the way."

Tom's eyes turned downward.

I should have been the one to be with you—your mother and me. We let you down.

"I'm glad she's in your life, Danny. She's a breath of fresh air, and she's brought more joy to Lauren than she's had in over two years. She's a keeper if you don't mind your old man's opinion."

Danny sighed deeply, his breaths coming slow and easy. Feelings of self-worth, so foreign to him, filled the empty spot in his soul. His relationship with his dad was healing, and he was finally able to bury the 'old' Danny, the damaged one. He was born again at age 20.

✧ ✧ ✧ ✧

That evening, when the reviews of the play came out, Kim headed straight over to the condo to see Danny. Reaching out to knock, she was caught short when the door opened.

"You're awesome. But, of course, I knew that all along," Kim said, her words singing into Danny's ears.

Squeezing the breath out of her, he stared into her gold-flecked green eyes, then slowly searched for her lips. She responded eagerly until they both heard, 'ahem' from the corner of the room. Pulling apart, Kim, faced flushed, said, "Oh, hi, Mr. Foster."

Not wanting to embarrass them further, Tom said, "What do you think of our boy, here?"

"He's everything I knew he could be. I saw him down at school, and this is *so* him. It's in his blood."

"Come on, you guys," said Danny. "You're embarrassing me."

"Fine, then, we'll shut up. But I'm still framing that review you got."

"If you don't, I will," added Tom. "This calls for a celebration. Let's call your mom, Lauren, and Jenny, and make some reservations for dinner for the six of us."

"Do you think your mom will mind my joining in the celebration?" Kim asked.

"It doesn't matter. You're coming. I'm sorry, I didn't mean to sound so harsh. But, you're my girlfriend and Lauren's best friend now, so, yes, you're coming."

I guess she is my best friend, Kim thought.

Danny slid his arm around Kim's waist and pulled her in to him. Her cheeks turned a pleasant shade of pink as she glanced over to Tom.

I'd better get used to this—especially in front of his family.

❖ ❖ ❖ ❖

As Danny and Kim pulled into the restaurant parking lot, Kim watched Lauren get herself out of the car without either her mother's or Jenny's help.

You go, girl. Prove yourself. You and your brother have more guts than either of you realizes.

Rose smiled when Danny got out of the car until she noticed Kim with him.

Couldn't this just be family?

Forcing a smile back from where it had disappeared, she reservedly greeted Kim and then congratulated Danny on his review.

"Thanks, Mom. That means a lot. Now let's get inside out of this heat."

The cold, almost frigid air blew across their bodies, mingling with the sweat from outside, causing Rose to shiver. The staccato sounds of chatter filled the lobby as the family sat on the benches waiting to be seated.

Jenny started telling Kim about her latest swim meet and how she shaved a few seconds off her butterfly stroke.

"Can you come see me swim sometime?"

"Oh, Jenny, I'm sure Danny's friend has lots more important things to do."

"No, Mrs. Foster. I'd love to come to a swim meet. I used to swim when I was Jenny's age, and I know how much it means to have family there to support you."

You're not family.

"Just let Danny know when and where, and we'll come to your next one."

Jenny was all smiles as the waitress came over to seat them.

Rose, her back going rigid, followed the waitress to the table, not waiting for anyone else.

The chill at the table during dinner felt like someone had left a freezer door open. Lauren attempted to focus the conversation on Danny's success in the play while Kim stole glances at Rose, still in the dark about what she had done to warrant such dislike from her.

As the waitress began clearing the table, asking if anyone wanted dessert, Kim cleared her throat, daring to speak.

"You've all been so nice to include me in your family celebration, and now I would like to invite you to mine. My parents are throwing me a birthday party next weekend, and I'd like all of you to come. And no presents."

"I thought your birthday was a few months ago," Danny said.

"Well, I celebrate two birthdays."

Jenny's head whipped around.

"Whoa, that's so cool. Do you like celebrate your half-birthday too?"

"Something like that."

"Anyway, I'd like for all of you to be there."

"Like hell, we will," Rose mumbled under her breath, shoving her chair back so hard it toppled over. Diners at the next table winced at the sound of the chair legs scraping across the concrete floor.

"What was that, Rose?" Tom said, getting up to right the chair.

"Nothing. I need to go. I'm not feeling well. Come on, girls. Get your things."

"Are you okay to drive," Tom asked. "I can drive you home."

"Leave me alone, Tom. Girls, I said, get your things. We're going."

"Let them stay for dessert. I'll take them home later."

"Fine."

She turned on her heels and left.

"Maybe I should just go," said Kim. I think I upset your mother."

"No, please stay. I'm sure she just has a bit of an upset stomach," pleaded Tom. "I'll check on her later. Now, what does anyone want for dessert?"

Danny reached over and squeezed Kim's hand reassuringly. All thoughts she had of leaving disappeared into his bright blue eyes.

Seventy-One

Hi,

I know I haven't written for a while. Sometimes I'm not sure you can even hear me. I think I'm starting to lose you. Are you still there?

Anyway, tonight we all went to dinner to celebrate Danny's great review in the newspaper for his role as George in Our Town. My mother was her usual rude self again when she saw that Kim had been invited. I don't know what her problem is, but if she doesn't cut it out soon, I'm going to confront her. This crap has to stop. Danny really likes her. And she's become a good friend to me too. I mean, not like you, but a good person to talk to.

Kim thanked us for including her in the celebration and then invited us to her birthday party. Once she said she celebrates two birthdays, like some people celebrate their half-birthday, my mother stood up, knocking over her chair and said she had to leave. She was so obnoxious, the people at the next table stopped with their forks mid-air to listen. She looked like a ghost had just entered the room.

I'm so done with this.

Bye for now.

Seventy-Two

ROSE LAY ON HER BED in the dark, a cold compress on her forehead, her eyes shut tight. Her migraines had always been bad, but tonight's was brutal.

Kim's presence at the family celebration spun around and around in her head, intensifying the nausea she was fighting. As she fell into a drug-like sleep, threads of memories from the past wove themselves together until she was unable to separate them.

We should never have taken you. You're nothing but trouble.
You are so precious to me. I'll never let you go.
Keep acting like that, and we'll send you back.
I can't imagine life without you.

Around and around the words floated as distorted, disconnected faces loomed over her. An image of a little girl, tears streaming down her delicate cheeks, was suddenly replaced by another little girl, laughing as she smeared birth-day cake all over her face. Who were they? Why were they vying for her memories?

Rose thrashed around on the bed until she mercifully slipped into a deep sleep, the visions tucking themselves back where she had stored them so many years ago.

Morning arrived like a balm, the light of day bringing with it a new perspective.

I'm over-reacting. She was trying to be nice.

The annoying sound of the doorbell roused Rose from her bed. She always hated its greeting, claiming it sounded like church bells—ironic since no one in the family went to church.

Peering out the sidelight of the front door, she saw it was Tom. She opened the door noticing the troubled look on his face.

"Rose, we need to talk."

"About what?"

"Your behavior last night. Your behavior in general. What is this thing you have about Kim? She's a nice kid. Give her a break. You're hurting Lauren with your attitude. I'm telling you, Rose, you're going to lose her if you don't stop trying to control her life."

"Leave me alone, Tom. You're all ganging up on me lately. Doesn't this girl get under your skin? Doesn't she make you uncomfortable?"

"Frankly, I'm very comfortable around her. She's fit in very nicely with our family."

"Well, she's *not* our family. She should go back to her own."

"I give up. You're so over the top. Give it a rest."

"How dare you talk to me like that. Is this the way you talked to your girlfriend?"

"Don't go there, Rose. Abby's gone. She resigned and moved on. And just so you know, there was never any real affair. It was a bit of flirtation. I certainly wasn't getting much attention from you."

"So, it's my fault now. Have you ever taken any responsibility for your actions? You screwed up big time years ago."

"That again? I thought we ironed that out a long time ago. You still resent me for being honest with my feelings—something you've never even tried to do."

"I can't do this now, Tom. Please leave. I'm getting another migraine. Just show yourself out."

"Someday we're going to have to deal with this. Mark my words, you're on thin ice with your daughter. This isn't over yet."

Tom, anger fighting with guilt inside him, turned and left.

Seventy-Three

THE EARLY SUNRISE cast pink and gray shadows into the clouds. Lauren stared outside, mulling over her discovery—the hidden box in the bottom of the closet. Why did it contain only her birth certificate and a lock of hair and none of her siblings'? Asking her mother would only roil the already unstable atmosphere between them.

I'll bounce it off Kim first. See what she thinks.

Her throat closed, threatening to suffocate her. She had always turned to Maddy for advice, even after. . .writing in the secret pages of the journal. She had kept her close, pouring out her heart, her anguish, her fears. Until recently.

She dug out the slightly tattered book, glancing over to the "secret box" and turned to her last entry, zeroing-in on the date.

Has it been that long? It's when Kim came into my life. How could I let this happen?

Grief tried to re-surface. But try as she may, her heartache had receded, and she couldn't connect with it anymore.

Had she accepted Maddy's death? Was she finally ready to move on?

Opening the tear-stained pages, she made a new entry—her last.

> Hello dear friend,
>
> I don't know how to begin. It hurts so much to do this, but I need to let you go. You've helped me so much, but it's time.
>
> I wish I had been able to go to your funeral. I know I would have stood up and spoken. The words have swirled through my head so many times—best friend ever, soulmate, confidante. I would have talked about our silly times, our sad times, our joyous times together. I would have cried and laughed and cried again. And then at the cemetery, I would have put a rose on your grave and said good-bye.
>
> Well, I'm doing all these things now, dear friend. This will be my last entry to you. I know we will meet again someday and pick right up where we left off. I will remember you forever.
>
> Good-bye,
> Lauren

Closing the journal, she kissed it gently and put it in the secret box with her lock of hair, laying Maddy to rest.

Seventy-Four

WHEN SHE ARRIVED on the George Mason Campus in Fairfax, Virginia, for her Transfer Student Orientation, Kim's thoughts returned to her first days down at William and Mary—to the first time she spotted Danny hiding inconspicuously in the back of the lecture hall.

His curly, dark hair and bright blue eyes had her dumbstruck. Then he tripped over her backpack, and when he looked straight at her, the words in her head refused to come to her lips until he started to apologize, and she saw how embarrassed he was. The pull between them was instant, magnetic. But what complexities lay behind his eyes. And he still surprised her.

Gathering all the information about the campus and her schedule, she glanced at her phone to see missed calls from both Lauren and Danny.

I hope everything's okay. Why would they both be calling at the same time?

She answered Danny's first.

"Hey, I saw that you called. So did your sister. Is everything alright?"

"Oh, yeah. She just wanted to get together with you, somewhere out of the house. Do you have any time? I could bring her over to your house or any other place you'd like to meet."

"I'm just finishing up with orientation, and I should be home by 3. Why don't you bring her over?"

"Done. Now, how was orientation?"

Kim imagined the sadness and frustration in his eyes over not getting his application in on time. He had yet another disappointment to digest.

"Oh, it was fine. When do your classes at NOVA begin?"

Her attempt at bolstering his mood was not lost on him.

"Kim, you don't have to underplay moving on with your education. I know I screwed up big time, and now I'm paying the price. But I'll catch up, and maybe I'll be able to transfer in January. Now, enough of this. I'll call Lauren and set things up for later."

◇ ◇ ◇ ◇

Kim's brother, Todd, was shooting baskets in the driveway when Danny pulled up with Lauren. Conscious of his sweat-soaked T-shirt and grimy hands, he avoided shaking hands with Danny but offered a wide grin to Lauren.

"Wow," she said to Danny before Todd reached the car. "He doesn't look anything like Kim. You'd hardly know they were brother and sister. I didn't pay much attention at the barbeque. I was so focused on Mother's behavior."

"Well, you and I don't look alike either. Nobody'd peg us for siblings."

"Hey, Todd, how's it goin'?"

"Nice to see you again, Lauren."

"Is Kim inside?"

"Yeah, go on in," Todd replied, then realized that Lauren might need help getting out of the car—but she was out of the car on her own and into her wheelchair.

"Hey, give me a call, and I'll pick you up whenever. Oh, you forgot this," Danny said, handing her the box she had been clutching in her lap.

Danny clapped Todd on the shoulder, realizing how little he did look like Kim.

The inside of Kim's house was a breath of fresh air. Instead of neatly manicured rooms, it looked lived in—happily lived in. Mail sat on the counter—unheard of in the Foster house—newspapers were haphazardly tossed on the side tables in the living room, and signs of recent snacking lay on the kitchen table. Not exactly disorder. More signs of comfortable living. Lauren felt a sense of calm—of belonging.

The one-level house made it easy for her to get to Kim's room. Following her down the hall, she saw family portraits covering almost all the wall space. Kim's mom and dad, then mom and dad with Kim, and then mom and dad with Kim and Todd. A growing, loving family.

Lauren was acutely aware that in her house, there was an overabundance of pictures of her alone. Yes, there were family pictures, but hers far surpassed the norm. A curiosity? An anomaly? First child syndrome? Troublesome at the very least.

"What's that you've got?" asked Kim noticing the box Lauren was holding.

"I was looking for someplace to hide my journal, and I discovered this."

Lauren opened her newly discovered treasure to show Kim her lock of hair neatly tied with a pink ribbon.

"Oh, how sweet. My mom has locks of hair of Todd and me."

"You see, that's the thing," Lauren said. "I can't find any of my brother or sister."

"Maybe they're somewhere else."

"Why wouldn't they be all together?"

"Good question. What's in the envelope?"

"My birth certificate. I never knew I was born in New Jersey."

"No kidding. So was I. At St. Francis."

Lauren startled. "Seriously? Me, too."

"Was your family from up there?"

"I didn't think so, but they must have lived there before we moved here."

"We always lived in Arlington."

"Then why were you born in New Jersey?"

Kim hesitated. She hadn't even told Danny her full story yet.

"I'm sorry," Lauren said, picking up a vibe of uncertainty. "I don't mean to pry into your family's business."

"No, it's fine. I just thought I'd tell your brother first, and it just hasn't been the right time. It's not that significant. But, since you're asking, I'll tell you."

Taking a deep breath, Kim began.

"My mom and dad couldn't have children, so they adopted me when I was a baby. My birth mother was in New Jersey and gave me up when I was born. She was very young and didn't feel she could raise me the way I deserved."

Lauren stared into Kim's eyes, trying to process what she had just heard.

"Did you hear what I just said?" Kim asked.

"Um, oh yeah. It just took me by surprise. You're so. . .normal."

Laughing, Kim said, "I have a great life. What's not to be normal about? But can you do me a favor and not tell your brother about my being adopted until I tell him? It's no big deal. I mean, these are my real parents as far as I'm concerned, and I love them to death. It's just that I want him to hear it from me."

"No problem. It's your story to tell. Maybe when we have more time, you could tell me how it feels to be adopted. But I've got to get home now," Lauren said, picking up her phone. "My mother will get irritated when she knows where I am. Oh, I'm sorry. I didn't mean that. She just gets her nose out of joint when I go anywhere."

"How is she going to deal with you driving?"

"She knows I'm gonna do it, so she'll have to get used to it. Whether she likes it or not, she's gotta let me go. Anyway, let me call Danny."

"I'll take you. It'll give me a chance to see him."

"You guys are really a thing now, aren't you?"

"Yeah, pretty much. He's very special."

"I'm happy he found someone like you. He had a rough time growing up, especially with my mother, and you've given him a sense of belonging he never had. Maybe someday we can talk about it. Just not now."

"Before you go, do you mind if I ask you about the journal you wanted to hide?"

"Oh, yeah. I'm sure you know about my best friend, Maddy, who died in the accident that left me this way. Well, she gave me a journal a long time ago, and I wrote her a lot about my feelings. I talked to her a lot, sometimes even waiting for an answer. But I realized the other day that I wasn't writing to her much anymore—that maybe it was time to let her go. So, I needed to find a place to hide the journal from my mother's constant snooping. That's when I found the box. I just want you to know that getting to know you has allowed me to accept Maddy's death and move on."

Trying to conceal her moisture-filled eyes, Kim reached out to hug Lauren. Sniffling, she said, "You've become very special to me, too. I feel like we've known each other forever. Now, let's get out to the car before I lose it altogether. Ooh, let's get a selfie first."

Lauren felt a sense of connection she had never felt before and put her arm around her friend. She flashed a smile worthy of framing to put on her nightstand. . . next to the picture of her and Maddy.

Seventy-Five

"WHAT A LOVELY GIRL," Kim's mom said when she returned. "She seems to have adjusted amazingly well, although I'm sure she must have scars. What a testament to how she was raised to have such strength and courage."

Kim bit her lip and didn't say that Lauren had survived so well *despite* her upbringing.

"Danny's been a rock for her, emotionally and physically, but it wasn't always that way. All I know is that I am so blessed to be in this family. I couldn't love you guys more."

Sarah was overwhelmed by the emotions coming from her daughter. She hugged her tight and signed, 'I Love You.' It was a bond they had developed when Kim was just a toddler; whenever words were difficult, they just signed, saying it all.

✧ ✧ ✧ ✧

Back at the condo, Danny received a text from Kim—no words—just a picture of the selfie with Lauren and the initials BFFs.

> u guys sure look great together. kindred spirits. want to come over?

> on my way.

Danny's heart flipped inside his chest.

How did I get so lucky?

When Kim arrived, Danny brought up the subject of the box he had seen Lauren carrying.

"I know I should wait for her to tell me, but what was such a big secret?"

"First, I need to tell you something I should have shared with you a long time ago."

"I'm listening."

"Don't look so worried. It's all good. Did you know Lauren was born in New Jersey?"

"Nope. I guess that's where my parents lived before we moved here. I never thought to ask. Why?"

"We discovered that we were both born in the same hospital in New Jersey. I told her I was born in New Jersey because that's where my mom lived—my birth mother, I mean. Danny, I was adopted at birth. My mother was very young and couldn't raise me. And I was so incredibly lucky that my parents entered her life and gave me a home."

Unable to process what he heard, Danny's brain began firing on all cylinders, pieces starting to come together. She didn't look like her brother, she got her smarts from "all of her parents," she had two birthdays. It all suddenly made sense.

"Say something," Kim said, her eyes clouding over.

"Why did you wait so long to tell me? It doesn't change anything. I would like to have known."

"I'm sorry. I didn't know where we were going for a while, and it's not something I just blurt out when I first meet someone. I'm just glad you know now."

"Do you know where your birth mother is?"

"No, but when I turned eighteen, my mom said she was okay with me searching for her. I do know her name, but so far, that's all."

"This is huge."

"Are you okay with it?"

"Why wouldn't I be? You're who you are because of how you were raised, just as much as the genetics. But now I know why you and Todd don't look much alike."

"Well, actually, he was adopted too. But that's another story for another time. Anyway, Lauren knows now, too. And I don't mind if your mom finds out. It's all part of who I am."

"You're amazing, you know. No wonder I fell for you."

"Now, tell me about your NOVA classes."

Seventy-Six

"WHERE HAVE you been, Lauren? I tried calling you, but it went to voice mail. Did you go out with Danny?"

Lauren debated whether to tell her mother she went to see Kim. Maybe it would be safer just to say she went out with her brother.

"Yeah, we just went for a ride. I need to get out of this house sometimes. I can't wait until I can drive myself."

Rose flinched.

"Mother, did we ever live in New Jersey?"

Rose looked uncomfortable.

"Yes. Before we moved here. Why?"

"I found a box at the bottom of my closet, and when I opened it, I found a lock of my hair and my birth certificate. I was surprised to see it was New Jersey. I guess I just never thought to ask where you and dad lived when I was born."

Rose seemed to recover. A little.

"That little lock of hair is such a wonderful reminder of how tiny you were," she said quickly. "I think all moms save them."

"The thing is, where are Danny's and Jenny's? Why aren't they all together?"

Rose's face went pale.

"Oh, I guess I have them somewhere else. You know how confusing things get sometimes. What would you like for lunch?"

"Why do you always deflect my questions when you get uncomfortable?"

"I'm not uncomfortable. I just don't think it's a big deal. I'll look for them and show you someday."

Lauren realized she was fighting a losing battle. "I'll get my own lunch."

✧ ✧ ✧ ✧

The temptation to take out the journal again and talk to Maddy pulled at her.

I can't. I've already said good-bye. I have so many more questions. Maybe I should go to Dad.

Before she changed her mind, she punched in his number.

"Hi, sweetheart. How nice to hear from you? What's up? You want to get some more driving practice?"

"No. This is something else. I want to talk to you without

Mom around. Could we maybe go out for dinner—just the two of us?"

❖ ❖ ❖ ❖

Call me. We need to talk. Now.

Tom was busy changing his clothes and didn't hear the text come in.

CALL ME. RIGHT NOW.

He ignored the buzz; it was probably someone at work. Lauren's voice had a note of urgency when she'd called, and nothing was going to interfere with his time alone with her.

❖ ❖ ❖ ❖

Scrambling to get her purse and keys, Rose yelled to Lauren and Jenny, "I have to go out. I'll be back before your father gets here." "What if you're not?" said Lauren. "What do I do about Jenny?"

"Send her over to Lisa's. But I'm sure I'll be back."

If she could catch Tom, she could waylay him.

"Geez, mother, you might as well let Jenny live with the Franconi's."

She'd have more fun there anyway.

Lauren heard the door slam, the garage door go up, and her mother race down the street.

What the hell is her problem?

❖ ❖ ❖ ❖

Tom looked in the rearview mirror in time to see Rose's vehicle blocking his driveway.

"Didn't you get my messages?" she confronted him when he stepped out.

"I haven't checked. Can this wait? I have a dinner date with my daughter."

"I know what she wants to talk to you about, and you have to keep your mouth shut. Tom—she was asking about New Jersey."

"So?"

"*New Jersey*, Tom. She's getting curious. She found her lock of hair and birth certificate and was asking why she couldn't find Danny's or Jenny's. I lied to her. She can't know why hers were separate."

"Look, Rose. We lived there, that's all. As far as the birth certificate, tell her I forgot it when I cleared out my office for Lauren's bedroom. It doesn't have to go any further than that. I told you a long time ago that we were making a mistake. But you had to have it your way, as always."

"Don't go there, Tom. You forced my hand when you dug in your heels."

"This is old news, Rose. But it's still not too late. We can come clean about all of it."

"You know my reasons for that. Don't defy me. Everything's comfortable now. Just leave it. Be evasive. Lie. I don't care what you do if she gets too curious. Just keep your mouth shut."

"I have to go. Lauren's waiting. This doesn't have to be the mess you created. I'll cover your ass again, but we need to have a serious sit-down about all of this. It's gone on long enough. Now leave. I'll give you a few minutes, and then I'll come over."

A twinge of nostalgia pulled at Tom as he pulled up to the house. Whenever he thought he was settled and adjusted to his new surroundings, a visit to his home of twenty-plus years re-ignited the memories within. Although they had roller-coasted throughout their marriage, the highs were the ones that first came to mind. But once those memories dissipated, the troubles pushed their way to the forefront. Then the accident, Rose's out-of-control moods, then Abby, and then Danny's problems settled in. He wondered if Rose hadn't thrown him out whether he would have left on his own anyway.

The front door was open, Lauren sitting just inside, waiting for him.

"What a nice surprise it was to hear from you. I'm looking forward to our dinner."

Feigning ignorance, he asked, "Is there something in particular on your mind?"

Turning to make sure Rose was not in earshot, Lauren answered.

"Yes, but can we discuss it at dinner. I need some privacy—which I never get here."

At the restaurant, Tom was still having an internal battle between what he wanted to say to Lauren and Rose's warning. He decided that until he had a chance to talk to Rose seriously, he would play it her way.

Seventy-Seven

ROSE SCRAMBLED to unearth Danny and Jenny's birth certificates and locks of hair to show Lauren as she spiraled into chaos. What if Tom caved under Lauren's questions? She and he had never agreed on what had happened so long ago.

It's that girl Kim. Why did she have to come into our lives? Every time she smiles, my stomach lurches, and I feel like I'm going to faint. Why? And so, what if she and Lauren were born at the same hospital. They're a year apart. It's just a coincidence. I don't want Lauren asking too many questions about the past.

Jenny bounced into her mother's office just as she was examining the locks of hair she had finally found.

"What's that?"

"It's a lock of your beautiful hair from when you were a baby," Rose said.

"Do you have Danny's and Lauren's, too?"

"Here's Danny's. Lauren already has hers. I. . . let her keep it. Every parent wants to remember the precious fine locks of their baby's hair before their first haircut. It's just like you wanting to keep something special that Lisa's given you. It's just a nice memory. Now, you best get ready for bed. You have school in the morning."

Pulling her in close, Rose kissed the top of her head and whispered, "My precious girl. I've missed so much of your growing up."

"Mom let me go. You're squeezing me."

Rose loosened her grip and watched wistfully as her daughter sauntered down the hall to her bedroom, head-phones on while checking for texts from her friends. Just like Lauren used to do.

Rose heard the scraping squeal of the garage door open-ing when Tom brought Lauren back from dinner. She flew down the stairs to catch him before he left.

Too late, she turned to Lauren to gauge her mood, hoping she wouldn't start in again with questions.

"How was dinner with your father?"

"It was good. The food was great."

"What did you two talk about?"

"Really, Mother? Can't I have some alone time with Dad without you prying?"

Rose looked hurt or anxious; Lauren could not tell which.

"He just told me a little about what it was like to live in

New Jersey and how it compared to here. He said you moved because of his job."

"That's right. And I think it was a wise move," said Rose, hiding the real reason she didn't want to stay in New Jersey.

"I've got research to do for my classes, so I'm going to my room now."

"Glad you had fun," Rose answered, the quivering in her hands calming a little.

When Lauren was gone, Rose's phone rang. It was Tom.

"Relax, Rose. The situation's under control. But we need to meet somewhere. Immediately. I won't do this anymore. I'll be at the corner café in a few minutes."

"I'm scared."

"Of what exactly?"

"Of it all coming out, of losing Lauren, maybe having her hate me."

"I'm sorry, too, Rose. I'm sorry for my feelings twenty-five years ago when I said I'd be fine with not having any children. I had gotten used to being just us after five years and started concentrating on building up the business. The truth is, I was bitterly disappointed, but I know that hurt you a lot. Who knew, then, that we'd end up being a family of five. And I couldn't love them more, especially Lauren. When she came along, I realized how much I wanted to be a father."

"Things snowballed, Tom after we had Danny. Time passed, and I buried things to avoid confronting them. And you know damn well why."

"Just because your childhood was miserable didn't give you the right to control everything about theirs," he said, his voice escalating with the irritation that always ensued in his encounter with her since their separation.

"What do we do now?"

"There's always the truth, Rose—all of it."

"I can't. It's too painful. Please don't do this to me. We can get past her curiosity."

Once again, Tom being the pacifist he was, conceded to Rose.

"I'll try. But it still may all implode."

"It can't. I've worked too hard."

"That's the point, Rose. You've hyper-focused on Lauren and just made her resent you."

"This can't be happening. I'll ease up, I promise. Just promise me you'll not say anything to her."

"Let her go. Encourage her independence, and you'll win her back."

Tom watched Rose soften around the edges, the old Rose resurfacing. He remembered why he had fallen in love with her. It was still all there, just buried under years of lies and deceit.

Seventy-Eight

MORNING BROKE with a crash of thunder, rain pelting the window outside Lauren's bedroom, the last remnants of the summer heat washing in through the slightly open sash.

Another day stuck in this damn house, she thought.

Snatching her phone from her nightstand, she called Kim.

"Want to come over? I need a friend."

"You got it. Be there in a few."

Just like old days with. . .

"I don't want to pry, but I've just never known anyone who was adopted, and I'm curious," Lauren said as she and Kim settled in on her bed.

"Oh, no problem," Kim answered.

"I told you my birth mother, Brittany, was too young to care for me, so she gave me to my parents. They told me as soon as they thought I would understand. But I do remember them reading me stories when I was young about children being "chosen" and being "special." So, I always knew that it was something to be proud of."

"So, your birth mother's name is Brittany. Do you know her last name?"

"It's Sullivan. Or at least it was when I was born. I don't know if she's married now or not. I've done a bit of searching when I could but haven't located her yet."

"What will you do if you do find her?"

"I'll send her a message and let her take it from there."

"Are you nervous?"

"Kind of. But my mom says she was sweet, and heartbroken that she had to give me up. She was in pretty bad shape."

"That poor girl. I don't know how she could get over something like that. I hope she straightened out."

"Me too. But enough about me. What was it like for you growing up?"

"Interesting."

"And. . ."

"Well, as far as I can remember, my mother was always overprotective, to the point of being obsessed even when I was born and especially after Danny and Jenny came along. I don't think I realized it at the time, but after talking to Danny about it last year, I found out that he resented me— even hated me for getting all the attention. I felt so bad for him because it wasn't anything I wanted. My mother is a complete mystery to me."

"So, it looks like you and Danny are okay now, right?"

"Oh, yeah, we're great. He's been a real rock for me since the accident."

"He's like that," Kim answered, a smile inching up 'til her face hurt.

"I see that look. You love him, don't you?"

"I hope you're okay with that."

"Hey, if you two ever get married, you'll be my sister. How cool would that be?"

"The best," Kim answered.

"Look," Lauren said. "It's really late. I think you should stay over. I've got a pull-out in my room."

"I'll text my mom now. Thanks, 'sis,' she said with a wink as she pulled out her phone.

❖ ❖ ❖ ❖

Settling into Lauren's room for the night, Kim zeroed-in on the framed selfie Lauren had taken the last time they were together. Something struck her.

"Hey, look at us together. Look at our smiles. Honestly, we really could be sisters."

Lauren studied the photo.

"You're right, especially since you got rid of the glasses and colored your hair. Maybe that's why my mother has such a strange reaction to you. She doesn't want me to have any competition. It sounds crazy, but then she's a bit on the crazy side herself."

"I'm determined to win her over," said Kim, putting on a borrowed pair of shorts and a T-shirt.

"Good luck with that. Sometimes I worry about my little sister. I feel like she gets lost in the mix. Good thing she has Lisa and her mom. They've been great to her, especially after my accident."

"If you ever want to talk about it, I'll listen," Kim said, her eyes dropping briefly to the wheelchair.

"I will—someday. I'm good now, at peace with Maddy and my condition. I'd rather not resurrect it just now. Hope you understand."

"I think you're courageous. I don't know if I could have handled all you've been through."

"I'm not sure how I would have handled being adopted. I guess we all have our demons."

Struggling to keep her eyes open, Lauren looked over to see Kim already asleep.

Seventy-Nine

ROSE WAS A BIT CALMER after Tom's reassurances. She raised the garage door and pulled in but not before noticing Kim's car in the street. Pulse racing and her heart beginning to pound with rage at the intrusion, she found the house unusually quiet. Then she realized how late she and Tom had been out and realized the girls must be in bed.

Oh, God, why now. Why can't she go away?

Taking a sedative to help her sleep, Rose steeled herself for the morning when she would have to see Kim again.

But before it kicked in, her brain fired on overload. If her suspicions were right, things were about to collapse. The last thought she had before drifting off was losing her oldest daughter.

✧ ✧ ✧ ✧

She could smell breakfast cooking as she descended the stairs, still groggy, and found Kim in her kitchen, spatula in hand, flipping eggs in the frying pan.

"Good morning, Mrs. Foster. I hope you don't mind, but Lauren and I were up really late last night, and she didn't want me to drive home, so I stayed over."

Rose, forcing a weak smile, merely said that it was okay, on her way over to give her daughter a morning kiss on the head.

Lauren, unused to the strange display of affection right in front of Kim, stared into her mother's cold eyes.

Here we go again. Why can't she just let it go?

Changing her mood and the subject, she asked, "Did you and Dad have a good time last night?"

"It was fine. We just had a few things to talk about. What were you up to?"

"Oh, just some girl talk."

Kim brought the full plates over to the table. "Would you like any breakfast," she asked Rose.

"Sorry, I'm not hungry," came the curt answer as she exited the kitchen.

Once again, Lauren felt the need to apologize for her mother's behavior and did when Rose left the room.

"No worries," Kim shrugged it off. "You know, if you ever

transfer to George Mason, I'd love to be roomies. It would be fun to live on our own."

"I'll get to work on it right away."

Lauren watched Kim go down the back ramp and wished they could live together. Turning, she went back to her laptop to research what courses she would need to go to George Mason, realizing how awesome it would be if she, Danny and Kim were all at the same school.

"Out with it, Mother," Lauren ranted when Rose appeared on the heels of Kim leaving. "I'm so sick of this. What is your problem?"

"Oh, nothing, sweetheart. I'm just stressed out about a few things."

"That's bull, and you know it."

"Lauren. Watch your tone with me."

"Seriously, Mother. Kim is the best thing that's happened to me since Maddy died, and you continue to treat her like dirt. We had a great time together until you walked in this morning."

"I'm sorry. I don't know what's come over me. What did you girls talk about last night, if you don't mind my asking."

Intrigued by her mother's sudden curiosity about a girl she seemed to despise, Lauren answered.

"We talked about her adoption. Oh, that's right, you didn't know, did you, seeing as you've never been interested in anything about her."

The sudden pallor of Rose's face alarmed Lauren. "Are you okay?"

Recovering, Rose insisted, "I'm fine."

"Anyway, we found it interesting that we were both born in New Jersey. I know you and Dad lived there for a while, but her parents went up there to get her right after she was born. She said her mother was very young and couldn't care for her. And she even had to give up another child before Kim. That is so sad."

Lauren watched as Rose gulped for breath, looking like she was about to faint.

"What is it, Mother. Oh, God, I'd better call Dad."

"No, I'm fine."

"You're not fine."

She was turning to find her phone when, in a moment of clarity, memories and observations suddenly made sense.

She didn't look anything like Danny or Jenny.

She had green eyes, and the rest of the family had blue. Kim had green eyes, too.

She had always been the favored child, loved more, fawned over more.

Wheeling around to face Rose, the words just came out.

"Was I adopted, too? I was, wasn't I?"

Rose's face was steely. "What a crazy idea."

"You didn't answer the question. Was I adopted?"

Rose was fumbling for a reply.

"This can't all just be a coincidence. You've hated Kim since Danny brought her home. You suspected, didn't you?"

"You're not making any sense."

"You've been terrified that we might be sisters."

"No, no, I'm not." Rose's eyes were wild, pleading. "You have to believe me."

"Right now, I don't believe anything you say."

Lauren felt herself going numb. The unthinkable had just dawned on her—and yet, now everything suddenly made sense.

"Go ahead, Mother. Admit it."

Rose broke.

Trembling, her voice raw and shaky, she shouted, "Yes. It's true. We didn't think we could have any children, so we adopted you from foster care when you were one. You were so wanted and loved. There, now are you happy?"

"If I was so loved, why have you lied to me?" Lauren retorted. A fury like nothing she had felt before overwhelmed her.

"It's so complicated."

"Then try me."

"Your father and I tried for years to have a baby, but nothing happened. He was adjusted to the situation, but I wasn't. I wanted a child to love."

"Why from foster care? And why when I was a year old?

What was wrong with me that I wasn't adopted as a baby? What aren't you telling me?"

"Nothing. I just wanted to give you a chance. Your mother was so young but wasn't ready to give you up for adoption, so she placed you in foster care with the hopes that she could get you back when she was ready. But it just didn't work out for her. She ended up pregnant again and knew she wasn't ready to be a mother."

"What was my mother's name, and don't tell me you don't know."

Defeated, Rose uttered, "Brittany."

Lauren's head was swimming. "You do realize that the other child must be Kim. We were born in the same hospital in New Jersey, a year apart. And look at us, Mother. You see the resemblance, don't you? Is that why you hated her so much? Did you suspect, too? How could you? How could you not tell me all these years? Did you not think I would want to know? Did you not think that I would love you and Dad as my own parents? I need to be by myself."

"Wait, I need to be with you."

"And that's another thing. Why have you always been so obsessed with me? What about your 'real' children? Didn't they matter at all to you, Mother? Or shall I just call you Rose, now." Realizing she just disowned her mother, Lauren cringed. But her torrent of rage continued.

"This can't be explained away. My whole life with this family has been a lie. You can tell me a million times how much you wanted me, but if that were true, you would have been honest with me as soon as I was old enough to understand. Kim's always known about her adoption, and she loves her parents dearly. I don't know how you and Dad could have done this to me. Now, leave me alone."

Leaving her mother beaten and crushed, she escaped back to her room. First, came the tears. Then the shaking. Her life had just imploded, and she wasn't sure how much more she could handle.

Eighty

JENNY SAUNTERED in from her sleepover at Lisa's and found her mother sobbing uncontrollably.

"What's wrong?" she asked, terrified. "Is somebody else hurt?"

Rose wiped the tears with the back of her hand and looked at her youngest child, with no idea how she was going to explain the situation to her. She drew Jenny in, snuggling her close, and lied—again.

"It's nothing, honey. Lauren and I just had a disagreement, that's all. We'll be fine."

She noticed how tall Jenny had gotten, how much her face was changing from a little girl to a blossoming pre-teen. How much of this child's life had she missed? And Danny's?

I've gotten so much wrong. I've alienated everyone, and I don't know why. I've lied to Lauren, pushed Danny away, and all but ignored Jenny. I'm not fit to be anyone's mother.

"Just make up. That's what you always tell me when I have a fight with Lisa."

Surprised at the maturity in her youngest child's voice, she answered, "I'm sure we can, honey."

We have to. Maybe if she knew what went on in my life and what happened between her father and me—and everything else, she'd forgive me.

Even as she thought this, Rose knew she'd never dig up the past. There were no excuses. Nothing could make up for what she had done to her two younger children.

I just always thought that since they were really my own, they would know that I loved them. I needed to try harder with Lauren.

She felt as if her heart had stopped beating.

✧ ✧ ✧ ✧

pls call me. I need help

The words flashed in the little red bubble on Danny's screen.

He knew this wasn't just the same old drama with Rose. This was desperation. He called Lauren's cell instantly.

"Are you okay? Are you hurt?"

Through broken sobs, Lauren haltingly blurted out the story.

"Danny, do you know what this means?"

Danny's mind reeled, trying to take it in. "Yeah, it sucks that nobody knew."

"What it means is that we're not really brother and sister. You and Jenny are family. I'm not."

The line went silent as Danny absorbed her words.

"Don't you get what this means for you and Kim?"

"What does this have to do with us?"

"Danny—*duh*—think about it. I'm almost sure we have the same birth mother. We're *sisters*."

"Ah, shit. That's right."

Holy crap. As soon as Kim finds out, I'm shit out of luck. She'll bolt on me. No way will she want even to be associated with this family.

Lauren was rambling on. "Look at us. We have the same smile, we both have green eyes, we both twirl our hair when we're nervous. The signs were all there. I don't know how any of us missed them. Except for Mother. I think that's why she always disliked Kim. She suspected and was afraid it would all come out. Now she's in deep shit. And Dad's just as guilty. I don't know what to do. Right now, I hate them both."

"Yeah, well they may have just caused me to lose the only girl I ever loved."

"I don't think so. Nothing seems to faze her. She loves you and that's all that will matter to her."

"We need to talk to Dad. Maybe he could explain things better."

"What could be any better, Danny? They've lied to me, to us, about something sacred. I have another mother somewhere that I should have known about. No excuses. They're both selfish people. And it still doesn't explain her obsession with me."

The silent sound of hatred roared like a hurricane in Danny's ears.

"Let me come get you. We have to get you out of the house."

"For good," Lauren barked.

Raindrops prickled off his windshield as Danny approached the house. Lauren was already on the back porch waiting for him, looking devastated.

Without even waiting for him to get out of the car, he watched her roll down the ramp, rain dampening her hair.

Boy, this is really bad. She can't wait to get out of the house.

This time he helped her into the car, noticing how exhausted she looked. A flashback of seeing her in the hospital after her accident with the hollow, dark circles under her eyes re-emerged. The only thing missing was the bandages that he knew were still hidden inside.

I can't imagine how she must feel right now, considering how pissed off I am.

Just when he thought the tangled mess of their lives

couldn't get any worse, a bomb had gone off, shattering what was left of their family like shards of a kaleidoscope breaking apart.

"I think we need to talk to Dad. I know you hate him right now, but maybe he can give us a better idea of how this got all out of control. I need to get some answers, too."

"I don't think I can face him. He's just as guilty as Rose."

"Then what do you want to do about it?"

"I want to leave home, but I don't have anywhere to go. I can't go live with you because of Dad, and I can't stay home. I'm shit out of luck. Maybe I could go live with Kim. I need to tell her, anyway."

"Let me do that. At least give her a heads up before you unload on her. You're angry right now—and you have every right to be—but you want to get it under control before you talk to anyone else."

Danny saw the flecks of gold in her eyes disappear. He wasn't sure she would ever recover from the damage their parents had done.

✧ ✧ ✧ ✧

Driving around for hours, Danny observed his sister. He feared the return of the depression she had muddled through. He saw it in the blank expression on her face. She had been beaten down so many times and now this. And he could so relate to the feeling of not being wanted. He had never felt wanted—until Kim. He didn't care that he and Lauren weren't blood. He loved her to death. She was, and would always be, his sister.

In the vacuum of the silence in the car, he finally realized the implications this would have with him and Kim. He was in love with his sister's sister. If it weren't so ludicrous, it would be funny.

This could complicate things. Or maybe not. It all depends on Kim. At least she's not my *sister.*

"Come on, Lauren. We have to go somewhere. Won't you give Dad a try? Just see what he says.

"Fine. But it's not going to change the way I feel. I still don't even know where to go to get away from this hell I'm living."

"We'll figure it out—together. I promise. I'll text Dad and prepare him. He needs to come clean with us."

Eighty-One

THE FLICKERING LIGHT of the TV aggravated Tom's already monstrous headache. Danny's text had told him that the dam had burst, and Lauren was consumed with anger—even hatred—for her mother and him. His heart hurt for his child, who was already so severely wounded.

Hearing the rattle of the key in the lock, he braced himself for his encounter with Lauren. The fact was, he and Rose had no excuse for keeping such a secret from her. Well, maybe Rose did, and he cow-towed to her. He only hoped he could offer her some reasons to help her accept and understand. But even he didn't know what they were going to be.

Danny appeared first, keeping himself between Tom and Lauren like a shield protecting his sister.

He said nothing.

Looking past him, Tom caught Lauren's stricken gaze.

I've never seen such hurt in those eyes. Not even when she lost Maddy. How am I ever going to repair the damage Rose and I have caused?

She spoke first.

"Just so you know, there isn't anything you can say to make this any better. I only came because Danny wanted me to."

"I understand," Tom answered, his voice barely above a whisper.

"I need to hear this, too, Dad," said Danny. "I need to understand how you and Mom could be such liars. And why Lauren was the only one who mattered to Mom. Did Jenny and I even count just because we were your natural-born children? Or, were you just in denial that none of it would ever come out and we could live 'happily ever after.'"

Running his hand across the stubble on his chin, Tom stalled for time, hoping the right words would come.

"Would you be willing to listen if I tried to explain all of it?"

Tom watched Danny defer to his sister for an answer. When he saw her soften a bit and nod, he scrambled to organize his thoughts before speaking, not wanting to misspeak and make things worse.

"I need to go way back to the beginning of our marriage. Your Mom and I were so very much in love in and couldn't wait to start a family."

Tom watched his daughter's tense jaw and cold eyes, but he continued.

"Five long years went by, and we weren't able to get pregnant. Your mother began talking about adoption. She desperately wanted to love a child. But, by then, I had gotten used to being just the two of us, I was building up the business, and I balked. It caused your mother a great deal of pain, and she has never forgiven me for it."

Tom saw Lauren's face contort with rage. But he wasn't going to lay all the blame on Rose. It was time to own up to his part in the nightmare.

"Wait, so you never wanted kids after that?" Danny stared at him, his face grim. "Explains a lot—*Tom*."

This was getting worse, but Tom pressed on.

"Your mother persisted and won me over." And. . ."

Lauren lashed out.

"Oh, so I was just a compromise. *You* never really wanted me—or any of us. And Rose only wanted one child to dote on and suffocate with her so-called love. What a nice thought. It still doesn't explain why she hovered over me and ignored her REAL children."

She turned around to leave, and Tom made a desperate bid.

"No, it wasn't like that at all. Yes, I fought with your mother, and I was a selfish bastard. I pushed her away because of the way she pushed me away."

"And Jenny and I have suffered because of it our whole lives," Danny said.

"No—well, I didn't mean it to be that way."

"But it was that way."

Tom's head was throbbing, and his voice was choked.

"Lauren, adopting you was the best decision we ever made. You became the light of our lives. And after that, Danny, you and Jenny were like gifts from God."

"Ah, bullshit, Dad. I was the disappointing kid who didn't like sports. Admit it."

"No. I just didn't know how to relate to a son who liked reading and theater. It was my flaw, not yours."

"It sure as hell felt like I was the kid you wanted to scrape off the bottom of your shoe."

"I was lost in my head."

"I'm supposed to care?"

Lauren had been listening, seething. "I was the light of your life—and Danny and Jenny were gifts? Don't make us laugh."

Hatred, shock, and disappointment choked the air.

Lauren had calmed just enough, though, to assault Tom with more questions.

"Why did you let all this go on so long? Did you ever think how much it would hurt us if we ever found out—like we just did—on our own?"

Tom cleared his throat. "I guess—I guess we just hoped it would never come out. Things settled into a pattern, and

I guess we didn't think we should upset the proverbial apple cart."

"Stop it now. It's just going to be more excuses. I need to go."

"Please. I said, I know it was wrong. Your mother knows it was wrong. But when secrets are kept for too long, it's difficult to reveal them. It's no excuse. It was unforgivable."

Tom glanced over to the perplexed look on Danny's face.

"What is it, Danny?"

"I'm just trying to figure out why I became the black sheep when this was all about Lauren?"

"There were circumstances in your mother's life that propelled her to over-spoil and protect Lauren. I don't think I should go into that now. Maybe someday she'll tell you. And you were the fallout. I'm so sorry, Danny. We hurt you badly."

"So, you're telling us that there are more secrets buried in our family? When are you ever going to be honest with us? Our family is a shit-mess. And what about Jenny? Is there something about her we should know?" Lauren asked, a coldness almost shutting her down.

"No, honey. Jenny was just a wonderful surprise."

Drained, Tom sat silently, waiting for his children to react.

It was Danny who spoke next.

"You do realize that we've all figured out that Kim and Lauren are sisters. How am I supposed to deal with that?"

"I don't know, son. It's all a scrambled mess."

"Damn straight it is. This family needs some freakin' therapy. We're all screwed up."

"If that will help, I'll do it. I'm not sure about your mother, though. I can't see her talking to a counselor."

Lauren felt a surge of rage. "I'm so tired of her being in control. She doesn't have a choice. It might be the only thing that I'll accept from her to try to make this right. Now, I need to go. Danny, take me home. I'll go back, but don't expect me to talk to Rose. Right now, I want to be there for Jenny."

Tom watched his children turn their backs on him to leave.

In a moment, all that remained was the silence of being alone.

Eighty-Two

THE BACK RAMP to the house loomed in the shadows of the giant maple tree in the Foster's back yard. Once a symbol of Lauren's path to freedom, she now saw it as the downhill slope that it was. She was kidding herself that she could accept all that had befallen her because her life had always been a lie. Her dad—in her mind, he was just *Tom* now—had not even wanted her. She just was an outsider to this so-called family.

Rose appeared at the screen door, and Lauren, rolling herself uphill, looked right past her. Rebuffing her mother's attempts to reach out to her, to apologize and explain, she pretended she wasn't even there.

Calling after her, Rose asked, "Can I get you anything?"

"Just another life," came the caustic retort.

"Please, can't we talk?" Rose begged, almost gagging on her choked-up tears.

Lauren didn't afford her an answer. She was done, finished with the woman she called mother for twenty years. Rose and Tom's sins had wounded her beyond rehabilitation.

I need to re-invent myself. I could have been a Foster if they had told me. But I'm not. I'll never be. I can change my last name. Divorce myself from them. But what would that do to Danny and Jenny? They'll always be my 'brother' and 'sister.' And Kim, too. Unless she doesn't want anything to do with me either. First, I lose Maddy, and now I may lose Kim, also.

Unimaginable pain snaked its way through her heart.

His car was like a tomb. Danny sat in front of Kim's house, scraping his brain to find the right words to tell her what he had just learned. His sorrow for Lauren was only matched by his selfish sorrow for himself, fearing that he would now lose Kim.

He watched the curtain pull aside, and seconds later, Kim opened the door and waved him in. He struggled to find the right character to play to get through the lines he was about to utter.

"Hey, handsome. Whatcha doin' out there all by yourself?"

Focusing on the flushed cheeks and terrified, darting eyes, she knew he was in trouble.

"Danny, you're scaring me. What's wrong?"

Climbing into the passenger seat, Kim reached for his hands.

"Talk to me."

"My life just turned to shit."

Kim moved closer, touching his face, staring into his eyes.

"Lauren just found out she's adopted. My parents have been lying to her and the whole family. And that's not the worst of it. My dad didn't even want kids, at least not at first. So, Mom smothered Lauren because she was 'special', and Jenny and I just brought up the rear. It's all crap now."

"That's awful. I'm mean, not about the adoption, but about the lying."

"Oh, there's more."

He pulled a loose thread at the bottom of his shirt and drew his other hand away from Kim's.

"Go on."

"Her birth mother is the same as yours. You're sisters."

Watching as the words sank in, Danny sat frozen waiting for her reaction.

"It all makes sense, Danny. The connection we've always felt. This is fantastic. I mean, I'm sorry that you've both been hurt so much, but I love Lauren and now I know why. What can I do to help?"

Danny leaned his head against the seat rest, feeling drained.

"It's Lauren who needs the help. I think she's in shock right now and she won't talk to either one of our parents."

Terrified of speaking his next words, Danny said, "I'm in love with my sister's sister."

Kim paused, then answered calmly.

"But you're not my brother. We can still love each other."

"How can you be so understanding? My family's a lunatic mess. You don't need to be part of any of it."

"I want you, Danny. I want Lauren and Jenny. My whole family just grew, and my heart is full right now. We will get through all this, you'll see."

"Right now, Lauren could really use you, but I think she's afraid to call."

Kim pulled out her phone and sent Lauren a text.

> *im here for u girl. always*

Eighty-Three

THREE WEEKS of angry silence passed in the house while the family waited for their appointment with Dr. Goldman for family counseling. Backed into a corner, Rose acquiesced to Lauren's demand that if she didn't agree to therapy, she would cut her out of her life permanently. Jenny had been told the secret and was to be part of the sessions to help her digest the dynamics of a shattered family.

In the midst of the drama, Lauren got her driver's license and newly equipped van which had been ordered before her world fell apart. Insisting on driving herself, not wanting to be with either of her parents, she drove the all too familiar route to the therapist's office.

I never thought I'd be coming here again. But I need answers, concrete explanations about how this could have evolved. I don't want to hate my parents, but I'm so bitter right now it stings.

Dr. Goldman had extra chairs set out in his office to accommodate the whole family. Their uniform grim facial expressions spoke of the tension they were all under.

Cutting through the stilted air in the room, he began.

"It is very courageous of all of you to agree to counseling."

"We didn't have much choice," Rose blurted out. Then seeing the daggers coming from Lauren, she retreated.

"I know it's hard to be in a room with your entire family, but that's the only way we will get to the bottom of your issues."

Tom shifted nervously in his chair before he spoke.

"It's long overdue," he said, glancing in Lauren's direction.

"Who'd like to begin? Why are we all here today?"

Lauren, hurt the most by the lies and deceit, plunged in.

"I just found out that I was adopted. My life as a Foster never really existed. I've never really been part of the family."

"That's not fair, Lauren," Rose interjected. "We've always loved you."

"Well you had a funny way of showing it."

"I can explain," Rose uttered in self-defense mode.

Dr. Goldman let the angry exchange play out.

"I let my upbringing shadow everything I did with all of you, especially you, Lauren—because of the fact that you were adopted."

In the pause that ensued, four sets of eyes focused on Rose.

"Continue," said Dr. Goldman, quietly taking notes at his desk.

Tears smearing her mascara, Rose spoke very quietly, almost in a whisper.

"This is so hard for me to say."

She hesitated.

"You have to tell them, Rose," said Tom.

"I—I can't."

"Rose. It has to come out. Go ahead. We're all listening."

"I was raised in foster care most of my life," Rose whispered.

Tom, aware of Rose's past, focused on his three children. Lauren gasped, Danny's eyes glazed over, and Jenny's mouth hung open.

Finally surrendering to all the rage and resentment she had harbored for so many years, Rose began pouring out the rest of the story.

"I was discarded by my mother when I was five." Her head fell into her hands, unable to look at anyone.

"I bounced from house to house. Some were good, some not. The last couple I ended up with from thirteen until I aged out at eighteen were cruel. Whenever I did something they didn't like they threatened to return me. Sometimes I wished they would. I would have been better off in an orphanage"

Her face blanching then flushing, Lauren kept her eyes focused on her mother.

Rose, focusing back, continued.

"I was so terrified that you would hate me if I told you. I know I smothered you, but I desperately needed you to know how much I—we—loved you. I never wanted you to feel the pain and dread I had all my childhood. And I ended up screwing it all up."

Hardening again, Lauren shouted at her.

"Not only did you alienate me by your actions, you ignored Danny and Jenny. Do you know how much that hurt them, too? This is just a bunch of excuses and you know it. You had an unhappy childhood, so made it weird for *us*?"

Sitting forward in his chair, Dr. Goldman interrupted.

"There is a lot of emotion in this room right now. But it's good. Feelings need to be expressed in a safe environment."

"Can you help us work through this?" Tom asked quietly.

"Only if you are completely honest with each other."

"Honesty. Now there's a concept," sniped Lauren.

"I know you've been hurt by this, Lauren. Maybe take out your journal again and blast your thoughts into it instead of your mother," suggested the doctor.

Lauren thought of the journal she had laid to rest. She couldn't resurrect it now. She couldn't go back to Maddy. She was on her own.

Dr. Goldman focused on Danny.

"Would you like to contribute?"

"Yeah, but I think we've had enough drama for now. Maybe next time, if there is a next time."

Drained, each of them slid back their chairs. The atmosphere in the room was heady but they all agreed to come back. Dr. Goldman shook everyone's hands and escorted them back to the receptionist's desk to schedule another meeting.

Out in the parking lot, Tom and Danny hopped in one car, Jenny climbed in with Lauren, leaving Rose by herself. Lines of separation were drawn, leaving Rose alone to cope with the fallout.

Eighty-Four

SEPTEMBER'S COOLING AIR added to the chill that engulfed the family. Through several sessions with the psychotherapist, feelings were laid bare, stinging like arrows in an already scarred family. Tempers flared and calmed while the family aired their emotions.

As the children returned to school, Jenny to fifth grade, Danny to NOVA and Lauren to her goal of transferring to George Mason, life occasionally seemed normal.

And in a surprising moment of clarity, Lauren recognized the hurt that had festered in Rose for years. Compassion replaced anger, although forgiveness was still not there. Healing was still a distant dream.

Jenny broke the ice.

"Mom, were you really sad when you were growing up?"

"A little, honey."

"I'm sorry. Nobody should be sad when they're a kid."

"When did you get so smart?" Rose chuckled, the first time her mood had lightened in. . . years.

"I guess it was from you and Dad."

Rose reached out to hug her youngest child, realizing how much she had missed it.

Seeing them in an embrace, Lauren's self-protective shield began to crack.

Maybe there is healing happening. Just not yet with me. I pray I can get where Jenny is.

Rose caught the expression on Lauren's face and gave her a weak smile—a smile of hopefulness.

◇ ◇ ◇ ◇

Continuing to see Kim, the awkwardness now fading, Danny saw a future with her for himself.

Their favorite diner, with its comfort food and fond memories, continued to be their safe haven.

"Hey, Alice, how's it goin'?" he greeted their favorite waitress after he and Kim finished up classes for the day.

"Nice to see you both," she answered, nodding to Kim. "The pancakes are particularly good this morning."

"Sounds good to me. How about you?" he said, his eyes focused on Kim.

"I'm in."

"What's on your mind? You're different today," she asked

noticing a spark in his eyes that hadn't been there since their family crumbled.

"I need to ask you something."

"Go on."

"Um, first I have a nice surprise."

"Well, don't just sit there, spill it."

"I got into Mason for the January semester."

"That's –"

He held up his hand. "Let me finish before I lose my nerve. I know how badly Lauren wants to be on her own. There is some healing going on between her and my parents, but the only thing that's going to help her now is to be on her own. So, I was wondering. . .how would it be if the three of us got an apartment together? I need to be with you, and it would help Lauren a lot. And we could share the expenses and arrange our schedules so that we could go to classes together, and –"

"Are you finished?"

Aware that he had been rambling, Danny mumbled. "Yeah. I guess."

"You make me very happy, Danny Foster. And yes, I would love to share an apartment with you and *our* sister."

Danny's heart missed a beat.

"I'm glad that's over. I was afraid you wouldn't like the idea."

"What's not to like. I get to live with the love of my life AND my best friend and sister."

"Let's go tell her," Danny said knocking over his glass while reaching for his jacket.

After sopping up the spill, he grabbed the check, leaving Alice a generous tip.

This is better than any play I've ever been in. And it's my life now.

Eighty-Five

AS THE FAMILY COUNSELING continued into the fall, the walls isolating the members of the Foster family began to crumble—slowly. Rose, giving her family a glimpse behind the veil of her childhood, began to realize that what she had endured and how she felt growing up was not her fault. What she did with that, though, was. And Lauren's lack of forgiveness haunted her. The only option left to her was so private she was terrified of sharing.

Knowing it was her last recourse to regain her daughter's trust and understanding, she unearthed a long-buried diary containing her raw feelings growing up. The painful words she had committed to it pierced her own soul. She carried it downstairs, the weight of it pulling on her shoulders, and knocked on Lauren's door.

"I'm busy."

"Please just give me a few minutes, sweetheart. I'd like to share something with you."

Trying her best to overcome her twisted feelings toward Rose, she gave in.

"Fine. But I only have a few minutes."

Quietly opening the door to a room she had not been allowed to enter for months, Rose padded in.

"Thank you," she began. "How are you?"

"I thought you had something to show me."

Rose handed her a once bright red, now a dirty brown locked diary with a key.

"What is this I'm looking at?" Lauren answered, fully aware of what it looked like.

"It's my diary from when I was growing up. I'd like for you to read it. Not now. Just when you're ready. What's in it is not an excuse for my lies, but a mirror to reflect why I am the person I am."

Placing it on Lauren's desk, she turned and left the room, closing the door quietly behind her.

❖ ❖ ❖ ❖

For days, the diary lay on Lauren's desk, untouched, unopened until, in a moment of weakness and curiosity she slid it onto her lap, took the key and cracked the leather binding brittle with age. Instantly, words flew off the page.

Sorry they took me in. . .

"You're just a nuisance" . . .

please help me, God. . . .

"Be careful or we'll send you back" . . .

I'm trying so hard. . . .

Riveted, Lauren slowed her pace to concentrate on her mother's pleas. Teardrops joined those on the already stained pages.

How awful. How could anyone treat a child like that? How could a child endure such a lack of love and warmth and not be destroyed? Yes, destroyed. But doesn't she realize that her overprotective love for me almost destroyed me, too?

She couldn't finish. Closing the book and locking it, she sought out her mother in the kitchen and handed it back to her. With a softness in her demeaner slipping through, she whispered, "I'm sorry."

She now understood. But forgiveness was still not within her reach. Not yet. What if she softened toward Rose and was smothered again?

Eighty-Six

AS OCTOBER TURNED to shades of the holidays, Rose's grand Thanksgiving celebration was not on the agenda. Remembering how she always insisted on everyone saying what they were thankful for, Rose was almost glad they weren't going to be together. There would be dead silence this year at the table.

Lauren and Danny had both been invited to Kim's for turkey dinner, leaving Jenny alone home with her mother.

"Mom, why can't we just have a small turkey for ourselves?"

Hugging her last child, Rose answered that it just wasn't the same without the entire family around the table.

"We could invite Dad," she said hoping to cheer her mother up.

"I'm not sure he'd come, honey. He's got his own life now."

"I miss everybody."

"Well, we'll just have to do something special, just the two of us. Let's go out to dinner."

"Okay," Jenny answered, masking her disappointment with a weak smile. "But I'm going to call Dad and wish him a Happy Thanksgiving."

"That would be nice," Rose answered.

That would be really nice. I wish I could do it, too. But too much hurt has wrecked our life together.

Rose went online and booked a reservation at a favorite restaurant she and Tom often went to. This time it was for mother and daughter.

Her phone vibrated.

"Hello, Rose. It's Tom. Would you like to have Thanksgiving together?"

✧ ✧ ✧ ✧

Tom's eyes shot over to his wife as she cleared the table at the end of their holiday meal.

"This is nice," he said. "It's been a long time."

Jenny had already left the table to text Lisa, leaving Tom and Rose alone.

"I'm not sure what it means," Rose uttered, reluctant to broach the subject of the two of them.

"I don't either, Rose. I know how devastated you are—we both are—but this has been the hardest on you. I just wanted you to know that I'm still here."

A flush raced through Rose's veins.

"Thank you," was all she could say before she heard keys rattle in the back door.

Ambling into the kitchen, she found Danny, Lauren—and Kim standing there. Struggling to contain her emotions, she said, "What a lovely surprise." Her eyes rested on Kim with a gentleness she had never displayed before.

"We saw Dad's car. Is he here?" Danny asked.

"We had a nice dinner together with Jenny. But it wasn't the same without all of you."

Kim focused on the word *all*, hoping this was a breakthrough.

"We want to talk to you about something," Lauren said.

Hearing the voices, Tom came into the kitchen, thrilled to see his children again.

"Tom, they want to talk to us about something."

"Fire away."

Tom and Rose took the two armchairs they were accustomed to sitting in, while Danny and Kim sat on the edge of the sofa with Lauren nearby. A blank silence ensued while each waited for another one to start.

Finally, Lauren took the lead.

"You know that both Danny and I are going to be able to start at George Mason in January. See, the thing is, we thought it would be a great idea if we all got an apartment to share. We could split the costs and drive into classes together whenever they jived.

Another blank silence filled the room as Rose and Tom digested the news. Rose's natural instinct was to put the skids on the whole idea, especially for Lauren, but one sideways glance from Tom told her differently.

Choking out an answer, Rose said, "I think that's a grand idea. Can you afford it?"

"Kim and I both have jobs and Lauren has her disability check to help with the rent. I know we can make this work," said Danny.

Feeling her life's foundation crumbling, Rose knew she had no choice. If she wanted Lauren to forgive her and have her back in her life, she had to approve.

Attempting to break the ice she felt forming around her she turned to Kim.

"Are you sure you can handle these two?"

Realizing that this was the first time Rose had spoken to her without scathing words, Kim flashed a radiant smile, echoes of Lauren, and said, "you bet."

"Thanks, Mom, for understanding. You too, Dad. I guess this means you're finally getting rid of me," said Danny.

"It's all good, son. It's time for all of you to make your way in this world."

As Danny and Kim rose to leave, Lauren stayed behind to talk to her mother.

"This doesn't mean that all is forgiven yet. I'm still working on it. But I'm happy you're letting go of me without a scene. This is what I need—what I've always needed, and I hope you get it. You need to start living *your* life now. You need to come to terms with *your* issues, too."

Hearing her dad come back into the room, Lauren halted the conversation.

"I'm going to start searching for available apartments," she said, changing gears.

Turning around she looked back over her shoulder and yelled out, "Nice to see you two in the same room again."

Not knowing what to do with that comment, Tom said he had some things to take care of, thanked Rose for a lovely dinner and shouted his 'good-bye' up the stairs to Jenny.

"Bye, Tom."

"Bye for now."

If there was anything Danny had learned in his AA program, it was the importance of seeking forgiveness by making amends.

Memories of trashing Jenny's room continued to haunt him. He had bought her a new Barbie dollhouse, but it occurred to him that he had forgotten about the kaleidoscope. He knew Jenny had swept up the broken glass and put the pieces in a bag in her dresser drawer, too sad to just throw them away.

Maybe I can put it back together. It's the least I can do for her.

He wondered, too, if his family could ever be put back together. . .if anything could be made of the broken pieces of their lives.

Epilogue

ROSE OPENED HER desk drawer and pulled out a bright green diary. Heeding Dr. Goldman's advice, she had taken to writing in it every day. Some entries were sad, but many more were hopeful.

On the day the kids moved out and into their own place, Rose, casting a fleeting glance at her journal from her traumatic childhood, tossed it into the fireplace, and watched the record of her past life go up in ashes.

Some measure of healing had begun, but there was much yet to be resolved. She and Tom, but mostly she, had hurt her children badly in an effort to erase her past and assuage her guilt. For twenty-five years she had lived a lie and now the truth bore scars.

Looking at the jagged line left on her arm, the line that had drawn blood and painted her whole world an angry red, she closed the journal.

Lauren was gone. Danny was gone. But Jenny was still there. She could still save her. Show her the love she had withheld all her life.

Calling up the stairs to her youngest child, she summoned the last one left to her. "Jenny, honey, why don't we...."

BARBARA GALVIN grew up on Long Island, New York and went to the University at Albany where she received her BA in English and MA in Education. She has spent the past several years writing short pieces and poetry for submission and personal gratification. She attends weekly writing workshops and frequent writing retreats to hone her craft.

When not writing, she enjoys traveling, especially to Europe, playing the piano, reading and listening to classical music.

She lives in Leesburg, Virginia, with her husband of fifty years, surrounded by her three children and seven grandchildren.

Made in the USA
Middletown, DE
08 September 2022

72628800R00235